Readers Love ANDREW GREY

Steal My Heart

"This was everything I could want in a mystery: romance, sex, great characters, and a miscarriage of justice."

—Paranormal Romance Guild

Paint by Number

"I loved all the sights and sounds and scents Andrew Grey brought to life, it enhanced the story and made me want to go there to see it for myself."

—Rainbow Book Reviews

The Northern Lights in His Eyes

"It's rare that a setting is so well done that it comes across almost as a character in and of itself. This story is one of those rare occurrences."

—Sparkling Book Reviews

Heartward

"Each aspect of this story gives great insight and depth to the characters, which just added to the chemistry…overall, a really enjoyable book."

—MM Good Book Reviews

Homeward

"Getting to figure out how to make a real relationship is not an easy path, but one they are willing to work at. Recommended for fans of couples reunited after many years and finally figuring out their lives."

—Love Bytes Reviews

By ANDREW GREY (cont'd)

CARLISLE DEPUTIES
Fire and Flint • Fire and Granite
Fire and Agate • Fire and Obsidian
Fire and Onyx • Fire and Diamond

CARLISLE FIRE
Through the Flames • Up in Flames

CARLISLE TROOPERS
Fire and Sand • Fire and Glass
Fire and Ermine • Fire and Iron

CHEMISTRY
Organic Chemistry • Biochemistry
Electrochemistry
Chemistry Anthology

COWBOY NOBILITY
The Duke's Cowboy
The Viscount's Rancher

DREAMSPUN DESIRES
The Lone Rancher
Poppy's Secret
The Best Worst Honeymoon Ever

EYES OF LOVE
Eyes Only for Me • Eyes Only for You

FOREVER YOURS
Can't Live Without You
Never Let You Go

GOOD FIGHT
The Good Fight • The Fight Within
The Fight for Identity
Takoda and Horse

HEARTS ENTWINED
Heart Unseen • Heart Unheard
Heart Untouched • Heart Unbroken

HOLIDAY STORIES
Copping a Sweetest Day Feel
Cruise for Christmas
Frosty the Schnauzer • A Lion in Tails
Mariah the Christmas Moose
A Present in Swaddling Clothes
Rudolph the Rescue Jack Russell
Secret Guncle • Simple Gifts
Snowbound in Nowhere
Stardust • Sweet Anticipation
With Amy Lane: Holiday Cheer
Anthology

LAS VEGAS ESCORTS
The Price • The Gift

LOVE MEANS…
Love Means… No Shame
Love Means… Courage
Love Means… No Boundaries
Love Means… Freedom
Love Means … No Fear
Love Means… Healing
Love Means… Family
Love Means… Renewal
Love Means… No Limits
Love Means… Patience
Love Means… Endurance

LOVE'S CHARTER
Setting the Hook • Ebb and Flow

Published by DREAMSPINNER PRESS
www.dreamspinnerpress.com

HUNKS OF THE MONTH

ANDREW GREY

Published by
DREAMSPINNER PRESS

8219 Woodville Hwy #1245
Woodville, FL 32362 USA
www.dreamspinnerpress.com

Hunks of the Month
© 2025 Andrew Grey

Cover Art
© L.C. Chase
http://www.lcchase.com
Cover content is for illustrative purposes only and any person depicted on the cover is a model.

Trade Paperback ISBN: 9781641087889
Digital ISBN: 9781641087872
Trade Paperback published May 2025
v. 1.0

*To Dominic, for all his support,
and to the real Lucille, who is just as feisty as the character.*

Chapter 1

"OH, JUST kill me now," Sterling Vaughn told himself as the blazing-red minivan pulled into his driveway. *Out of the frying pan and into the fire.* He sighed as he set his mug of coffee on the counter and flipped on the studio lights. His camera, backdrops, and settings were ready, and after a half knock, half demanding pound on the door, it opened and what could only be Mrs. Wilson stepped inside, followed by two younger carbon copies of herself. The twins—at least that was how Mrs. Wilson referred to them, as though they had no identity outside of each other. Sterling couldn't help wondering how much that was going to cost the girls in therapist bills once they left home. "Good afternoon."

"Yes, it is. I'm Gladys Wilson, and these are my twins, Mandy and Tawny." She half pushed the girls forward and went right on, even when Sterling extended his hand.

"It's good to meet you." Sterling had no idea what else to say. Mrs. Wilson hadn't bothered to indicate which girl was which, and they didn't say a word. Probably out of self-preservation. "Which of you is first?" He went into business mode, trying to get his head where it belonged.

Mrs. Wilson drew herself up. "I thought you could take them together." She wrinkled her nose in an unflattering manner, like she had smelled something bad. "As I said on the phone, we want just one appointment for the two girls."

Sterling didn't roll his eyes and cleared his throat and his mind. He needed to be sharp with this cobra of a mother. "And as I explained, that isn't how I work. If you want senior portraits for the two girls, then they need two appointments, which is what I made, with the pricing I quoted you over the phone." He had already explained this to her at least twice. "Now which of you would like to go first?" He wasn't arguing, and this wasn't a bargaining session.

"I still don't think—"

"It's either that or I'll cancel the session, you'll forfeit your deposit, and I'll call someone on my waiting list to take their place." Sterling crossed his arms and stood firm, staring her down. He only had so many appointment slots available, and there were people who could fill in the later appointment, at least. Sterling knew this type of stage mother. She wanted the best, always, but didn't want to pay for it—like everyone's talent and time were at her beck and call.

Mrs. Wilson sighed deeply as though it was worth a try.

Sterling knew when he'd won. "Who's first?"

The girl on the left stepped forward without saying a word. Sterling was starting to wonder if either of them actually spoke at all or if they had simply given up trying to get a word in on their mother. "Where do we wait?" Mrs. Wilson asked, looking around the small reception area where Sterling kept a single upholstered chair. It was as uncomfortable as it looked. He hated when people hung around while he was working. It made him feel like they were looking over his shoulders, which were already crowded enough with the history he carried.

Sterling smiled with professional warmth. "There's a coffee shop two places over. They have great muffins and drinks. You're welcome to wait here, though. I can get another chair." He made no move to retrieve it.

"No need. Tawny, you wait here for your appointment, and I'll get something to drink."

"Then, Mandy, let's go get started. There's a changing and restroom right there. Take your time and put on your first outfit. Most people start with more formal dress and go from there. Once you're done, exit by the second door right into the studio and we'll get started."

Sterling left the reception area and entered the studio by a separate door.

He had set up a number of scenes throughout the space and had a large number of backdrops. He made some adjustments based on Mandy's coloring, and when she stepped out in a royal blue cocktail-length dress, he smiled and got to work, reminding himself that this was his life now, even if it wasn't the one he had envisioned for himself. He knew it could be worse: he could be photographing squirming young children who screamed and never looked at the camera.

"BUT I WAS thinking of having some pictures taken in my lacrosse uniform," Tawny said when they were about halfway through her session. It had taken each of the girls a little time to warm up, but Sterling did his best to put them at ease with him and the camera, and they came to life through his lens. Sterling knew that was his talent—making models comfortable with the camera so he got the best shots and they looked as good as possible.

"That's a little expected." He always liked to do something different. "How about we take some pictures of you with the lacrosse stick, using it as a prop, but in these clothes?" Where Mandy had been happy with two outfits, Tawny seemed to want to change every five minutes. "They take team pictures and things in the uniforms, don't they?"

She nodded. "I'll get the stick. It's with my stuff." Tawny seemed happy, and thankfully the remainder of the session went smoothly, and he ran Mrs. Wilson's payment and got her and the girls on their way with a surprising minimum of additional fuss.

As soon as the door closed behind them, Sterling sighed, and his shoulders slumped. What the hell was he doing? He wandered into the studio he had developed in what had once been his parents' home in Carlisle, Pennsylvania.

His father had been in the process of moving into a senior living community just as Sterling's life had taken a turn south and then shattered into little pieces. Sterling had been trying to put them back together for a while now, but the picture they presented wasn't anything like what he had envisioned for himself. Sterling hated that his mind had decided to go down these paths again and again. His old life was over, and he was making one here, back where he grew up. Still, it wasn't the same. He needed something different, something to take his mind off his troubles and maybe give him a second chance. But opportunities like that didn't just walk in the door.

The vibration of his phone on the wood of the desktop pulled his attention. He checked the caller and stifled a cringe. That was the third time today someone from that number had called him without leaving a message. Sterling was sure it was a telemarketer and was about to let it go to voicemail once more, but he pressed the green button to take the call, if for no reason other than to try to stop them.

"I HAVE COFFEE, tea, or some soda," Lucille Hillyard said the following afternoon as Sterling sat at her kitchen table along with another woman he had yet to be introduced to, wondering why she had wanted to speak to him so urgently. When the old friend of his mother's had called the previous afternoon, she had been evasive, but when one of the grandes dames of Carlisle telephoned, you apparently didn't argue. Lucille also had a bit of a reputation as a steamroller, which she had apparently earned, judging by how quickly she'd gotten him over. Sterling's head still spun over that, but he had a couple hours before his next appointment, so he'd figured he'd drink some tea, hear what she wanted, then politely decline and go back to his work.

"Tea will be fine, thank you." He offered to help and received a momentary withering look.

"I may be old, young man, but I'm not helpless. I've served tea to university presidents and even one actual president, but that was before Georgie got elected to that particular office." Apparently Lucille had worked as an administrator at a number of universities and had crossed paths with a certain president while he was still a student. "I can do this in my sleep, so sit down and relax. I'm not a shark and I don't bite. When I was younger, I might have nibbled a little, but sadly even those days are over." She brought two mugs and set them down exactly in the center of the placemats before sitting herself. "I have some questions and I'm an old lady, so I don't have the time to beat around the bush." She seemed to remember her manners. "Do you know Judy Weidmeyer?" Lucille asked and completed the introduction before getting up. "She and I have been in the garden club for, what…?"

Judy smiled a little nervously. "About fifteen years, I guess." She leaned forward. "Lucille and I agreed to be president and vice president in order to try to save the club. It's on its last legs, and both of us would hate to see it die." She accepted the glass of water Lucille handed her.

Sterling lifted the mug and took a sip of Earl Grey. He swallowed and wondered for the hundredth time what she could want. "Shoot."

"Do you like taking high school pictures?" She raised her eyebrows. "All those mothers and their precious sons and daughters, every one of them thinking they know how to do your job because they have a camera on their phone." She cracked a smile. "Believe me, I know. I'm one of those people. I always know better than everyone else, and if I'm wrong, I don't admit it." He got another wink. If she were younger, he would have thought she was flirting with him. Hell, maybe she was. There was no age limit on that sort of thing.

Sterling chuckled. "I bet you do." He took another sip as Judy sat quietly. It seemed Lucille was going to be driving the conversation.

"You didn't answer my question," Lucille pressed. "Is that something you like doing?"

Sterling set down the mug. "I'm good at it, and my clients are happy with the pictures I produce for them." He wondered what she was getting at.

She leaned slightly forward. "That's not an answer." Man, she had a steely gaze worthy of either a seasoned poker player or a serial killer. Sterling wasn't sure yet which one. "I know you were a fashion photographer up until last year, and then you returned to town and opened the studio in the family home. That had to be a real comedown from the travel and excitement of the fashion world. Now you take graduation and baby pictures for people in town." Lucille sighed softly. "It seems like a lot of change and a real step down the ladder."

Judy stiffened, and her gaze shifted to Lucille and then back to Sterling.

Sterling pushed his mug away and stood. "If you asked me here to insult me, I…." He checked his watch and did his best to hold his temper. "Things didn't work out, and I have a different life now than I did then. But this is the one I'm building, and it's mine to control and live." He hadn't realized he was that sensitive to his change in station until that moment. Sterling felt himself color, but he wasn't going to back down. "I don't appreciate you or anyone else casting aspersions on it." It was his job now, and Sterling was still trying to make peace with it. Sure, he had trepidation and a certain amount of dissatisfaction, but he was good at what he did, and the business allowed him a decent living.

"That wasn't my intention. Please sit." She waited, and he slowly lowered himself back into the chair. Once he did, she patted his hand gently. "Please forgive me. Sometimes I can be too brusque for my own good, always have been. It just seems to me…." She paused and rolled her eyes. For a second she looked much younger. "I should shut up now." Lucille now seemed like a naughty teenager.

Sterling breathed with relief that that line of questioning was over. "What is it you wanted?"

She shared a look with Judy before turning back to him. "In my own bumbling way, I was asking about your situation to feel you out and see if you might want something different." She cleared her throat, then stood up and left the room. As Sterling sipped more of his tea and wondered what Lucille was up to, he heard drawers open and close in the next room and then a door. He was about to ask if he could help when she returned and placed a calendar on the table. "I want to do one of these."

Sterling paged through a few images and lifted his gaze, sliding the calendar back toward Lucille. "You're kidding, right?" The calendar was of ladies of Lucille's age, all doing various activities, seemingly naked, but with the delicate parts covered. They could be a bit shocking, but then that was the purpose, he supposed. "Why?" Of all the questions he could ask, that seemed to be the one that threw her.

"No, I'm serious. The Garden Club of Carlisle and Cumberland County celebrated its ninetieth birthday last year, but now it may be breathing its last. The membership is aging rapidly, and due to some unforeseen circumstances…." Anger flashed in her eyes, and Sterling wondered what had happened but didn't dare ask. "The treasury is nearly empty. I was hoping that something like this would allow us to make some money and could generate interest to build membership." The anger dissipated, and along with it some of her enthusiasm.

Judy set down her glass, leaning forward. "Someone decided that their retirement needed a little offsetting, so when they moved to Florida, they took the kitty with them." It was the first time Sterling saw fire in her eyes. He liked that. It would help them no matter what they decided to do.

"I'm serious too. This has been done before." He lifted the calendar and turned it over. "Here in town, as a matter of fact. This naked little old lady calendar was produced two years ago by the Civic Society. How many did they sell? And do you really think doing it again is going to raise the money and interest that you're looking for?" He cocked his eyebrows, and she shrugged. Sterling knew he had a point. "It needs to be fresh. People use their computers now, so calendars are less important unless the images really catch the eye."

"I have to do something or I'll be the last president of the club and an institution here in town will die out. We do a lot of good, or have in the past: scholarships, greening the community, planting trees, the flower baskets downtown, gardens in the parks, as well as education." She was obviously passionate about the club, but Sterling wasn't sure what he could do about it. He had a black thumb. The only reason his backyard wasn't brown and dead was because he had a service that maintained it so he could use it as backdrop for photographs.

"Okay. Then we need to come up with something different and unique, something eye-catching and interest-grabbing. Doing the same thing over again isn't going to get you what you want." He hated to be the bearer of bad news, but that was the truth. "I suspect they sold a decent number of calendars." He looked it over. The calendar was good quality, the pictures satisfactory, though there were flaws in the image composition and the photos seemed more passive and lacked movement. But it was clever and kind of cute. "There are tons of calendars out there, everything from cats and dogs to cartoons to origami. What we have to do is make one that will catch people's attention."

Lucille took the calendar and set it on the telephone table behind her. "We're a garden club—we could do flowers," Lucille offered. "But I bet there are plenty of those too." She sighed and drank the last of her tea. "I suppose I'm going to need to look somewhere else. One of our members, Bette Wood, is in that calendar, and she said that they did really well with it. I thought we could try, but I think you're right. We need something fresh, and this isn't it." She seemed to have deflated considerably, and Sterling hated that he had been part of that, but letting her go forward with a project that wouldn't have much chance of doing what she hoped would only delay the disappointment and could run the risk of taking away some of the club's limited resources rather than making them money.

"Think. What sort of thing would attract attention and make folks take notice? There has to be something." Images flashed through Sterling's mind, but they were of hot men cavorting on beaches in Saint-Tropez, not ladies in a garden club meeting. Okay, so maybe he needed to figure a way to get out and take some of the pressure off. Being around hyped-up teenagers all day was really starting to get to him.

She shrugged. "I guess this was my big idea and I kind of shot the wad on it." Lucille got up and took the now-empty tea mugs to the sink. "I want to thank you for coming to see me, and I really appreciate your time. Maybe I'm just the old fool my nephew seems to think I am." Clearly there were some interesting family dynamics going on behind the scenes.

"I wouldn't say that. The idea is sound. We just have to come up with...." His voice died away when the back door thunked closed behind him.

"Aunt Lucy," a rich voice rumbled, and Sterling couldn't help turning toward it. That sound resonated deep inside him, and Sterling felt his toes curl in his shoes. That was a wonderful voice. Heavy boots thumped on the tile floor, and as Sterling's eyes widened, a god of a man came around the corner, skin glistening with sweat… and there was a lot of that skin on display. Even Judy seemed to fumble with her glass, not that Sterling could blame her.

Holy cow, what the hell had just happened? Sterling blinked a few times just to make sure he hadn't somehow stepped into the pages of a Highlander novel. Hair the color of spun gold flowed to wide, bare shoulders. Sterling swallowed hard, his eyes sliding down a chiseled chest and narrow waist. But it was the kilt that caught his attention most of all. The man looked amazing in it, and few people looked decent in olive green. Of course, a million questions raced through his head; most of them he didn't dare ask. Who gardened in a kilt? Did he wear them all the time? Most naughtily, what did he wear under it? That question held quite a bit of fascination as his gaze traveled down the beefy legs that protruded from below. Damn, that was an upward trail he'd love to be able to follow.

"Sterling, this is my great-nephew Connor Hillyard, my brother's grandson." She smiled, and Sterling held out his hand. Connor shook it firmly, and when they let go, Sterling had to stifle a whine, because damn it all, this was the most attractive man he had ever seen. Sterling had spent five years around some of the world's most beautiful people: men, women, it didn't matter. Beauty had been a never-ending parade in front of his lens. But in all that time, he had never seen someone who exuded masculinity and even grace the way Connor did.

"It's good to meet you," Sterling managed to say, his throat bone-dry.

"You too." Connor turned to his great-aunt.

"Sterling is the photographer I was telling you about. The one I was going to ask about the garden club project." Her earlier enthusiasm seemed to have dissipated, and Sterling was disappointed that he had been the wet blanket, but he'd told her the truth about how he felt.

Connor glanced at him and nodded, then returned his attention to his great-aunt, which gave Sterling a chance to appreciate his wide back and cannonball shoulders. This was someone active and full of life. As gorgeous as he was, Connor wasn't one of those guys who got his body in a gym. His was the result of hard work, which made him all the more attractive and got Sterling wondering what the kilted god did for a living. "I finished weeding the beds around the side and that section of the backyard." He pointed. "The roses are tied up and should stay on their trellis for now." Sterling noticed that a few red lines crisscrossed one pec, and damned if he didn't want to take Connor into the bathroom and play doctor for a while. He cleared his throat and pushed away those particular thoughts. "I also cut some flowers for you to put on the table." He held out a bouquet, and it was like a light went on in Sterling's head.

"That's it!" Sterling exclaimed as he jumped to his feet.

"What?" Lucille and Connor said in unison, looking at him like he'd just sprouted a second head.

Sterling grinned, an idea racing through his mind at a million miles an hour. "This…. You…." Sterling couldn't take his gaze off Connor. "Think about it. This is your calendar. Who in their right mind would turn down him… giving you flowers?" He grabbed the calendar. "If you really want to do one of these, then let's do it with guys like Connor here—sexy, hot, tender—all with flowers in hand. It fits the garden club, it's something that will make people stand up and take notice, and we can use local men." And frankly, the idea was as hot as Connor standing right in front of him. "Connor here could be Mr. April." He waited to see how the others would react.

Connor set the flowers on the table, speechless at Sterling's obviously fantastic idea. Lucille blinked at him a few times and crossed her hands on the placemat. "You know, you may be onto something."

"I'm going to get a vase," Connor said and half stomped out of the room.

"You can't be serious about this," Judy gasped, spilling her water across the glass table, soaking the area in front of her. Lucille quickly took away the sopped floral placemat, then wiped up the table and refilled Judy's glass.

"Well, what Sterling suggested, no. But he's right—we have to think bold." She sat back down. "Late last year, I was in the mall, and they had one of those calendar stores with everything from cars to cartoons. There were shirtless guy and skimpy bikini calendars." She shrugged. "I think we need to be bigger. I like the idea of shirtless guys bringing flowers, because hey, I'm old, but I'm not dead. But we need to shock folks. Make them take notice, like you said."

"But Lucille…," Judy breathed. "It's the garden club. We do flowers, not beefcake."

"Piffle. We need to bring interest, and we need money. We have scholarships to fund and commitments to the town." She turned away from Judy.

"What were you thinking?" Sterling was almost scared to ask.

Lucille must have spent her entire life perfecting the innocent look she flashed them. It was priceless, even as Sterling saw the mischief in her eyes. "Well, if one guy giving you flowers is good, then two are better." She grinned. "Connor is gay, and so is Sterling here." She showed her brightest smile. "So why not have a gay old time with it?" She sat back.

Sterling was shocked into near brain death, and Judy seemed scandalized.

"If a garden club in Central Pennsylvania wants to make a splash and be noticed, let's go hog-wild. Let's put images of two shirtless guys on each month. Can you imagine it?" She crossed her arms over her chest.

No one said a word until the crash of breaking glass shattered the silence.

Chapter 2

THEY WERE all crazy—that was the only possible explanation.

"What?" Connor demanded more loudly than he intended. The thought of being the model for some page in a gay calendar was about as ridiculous as he could possibly imagine. "You have to be joking." Even Sterling seemed shocked, which was a relief.

He lifted his huge blue eyes, and Connor forgot what he was going to say for a second. "Why not?" Sterling said.

There had to be something in the water. That was the only explanation. "No way in hell." He couldn't stop his great-aunt from doing what she wanted, but he wasn't having any part of it. No matter how those incredible blue eyes gazed at him.

"The calendar is a great idea, but instead of the *Calendar Girls* thing, we do a sort of Hunks of the Month." Sterling grinned, and his eyes shone with an excitement that Connor found intoxicating. "You would be great for one of the months. I picked April because of spring and the kilt. It would be perfect. Especially if we can get a second kilt guy."

Connor could almost picture Sterling behind his camera, taking his picture. He shook his head. "No way." He expected that to be the end of it. He had used his best authoritative tone. That usually worked; it certainly did with his students.

But Sterling only cocked his eyebrows and met his gaze. "Really?" It was almost unnerving, the way Sterling didn't look away. The attention didn't give Connor the creeps, but it was evident that Sterling liked what he saw. And the more Connor looked back, the more he realized how interesting Sterling was. The guy wasn't what you'd call gorgeous. He had these little lines around his eyes that grew more pronounced when he added a slight squint. What surprised him was how exposed he felt under that gaze. Or maybe not exposed so much as worried that somehow Sterling could see inside him.

He grew warm in the air conditioning of the house and figured that rather than argue, he should simply extricate himself from the situation. "I should go back outside and finish up the beds."

Connor turned and strode out of the house. He needed to get away from Sterling's intense gaze. It made him feel… naked.

Once outside, he went into the garage. He snatched a shovel off the hook on the wall and strode outside into the sun. This entire idea was too outrageous for words, and hopefully his great-aunt would realize that. Either way, she wasn't going to drag him into her beefcake-fest.

Connor inhaled deeply, taking in clean, fresh air, hoping it would cleanse away the thoughts he knew he shouldn't be having. If he was honest, the idea of a calendar of hot guys didn't sound bad at all, and the whole flower angle was brilliant for the garden club. What he objected to was being part of it. Not that there wouldn't be pressure now that the idea seemed to have sprouted legs—as his great-aunt said when an idea had merit.

Aunt Lucille was the most persuasive person he had ever met. She usually got what she wanted, and Connor had no illusion that if she decided that this was what she wanted to do, she'd take his no for an answer. Still, he had to be strong and stick to his guns. It was the only way. Any show of weakness and she'd pounce like a tiger and it would all be over.

Connor shook his head to try to get this whole notion to fly the hell out of it and stalked around the side of the house. His great-aunt wanted him to transplant some daylilies for her, and he figured attacking them and the dirt would be a good way to do just that.

DAMN IT all. He finished moving the last plant and had cleared the bed of all weeds, but he still couldn't get that damned calendar idea out of his head. He was also aware that Sterling and his great-aunt were still talking, and that was even worse. A few times while he was working, he thought he could feel Sterling watching him. Connor disregarded the notion and continued with his work. Maybe if he ignored him and pretended he wasn't interested, Sterling and his great-aunt would finish up their idea and planning session, or whatever it was they were doing now. Sterling would go back to whatever it was he did all day, and Connor could stop worrying about him.

"You know, you have to do more than lean on the shovel to get it to do something," Sterling said from close by, startling him. "Hey, I'm sorry. I didn't mean to scare you or seem creepy or anything. I'm leaving, and I wanted to say goodbye before I left." He smiled, and sweat broke out on Connor's forehead. When Sterling smiled, his face transformed, and more lines appeared around his mouth and eyes, giving him a truly joyful air. Damn, Connor needed to be careful or that smile was going to get under his defenses.

"Did you and my great-aunt figure out what you're going to do?" He picked up the shovel and scooped up some loose dirt. Not that he had a reason to, other than needing something to occupy his hands.

"She really wants to move forward with the calendar." Sterling placed his hand on Connor's shoulder, and Connor stilled because that simple touch felt good. It had been a long time… too long. "I'm sorry I blurted out that you should be one of the months. I got a little excited." Sterling's hand slipped away, and Connor turned to look at him. "I should have asked and not tried to pressure you. I just got the initial idea because of you, and then your great-aunt took it to a whole new level."

"I see." Connor stiffened warily, wondering what Sterling was up to. "You know, you're all crazy to even think of doing this. Here?" He motioned around him. "There's a church on every corner."

Sterling shrugged. "Your great-aunt is amazing, and this will get noticed. Think about it. Madonna, Lady Gaga—they made careers of being outrageous. Why not the garden club?" He took a step closer. Damn, that wicked glint was back in a big away. "I think I understand."

Why did Connor get the idea once more that Sterling could read his mind? It was frightening, but he'd be damned if he was going to let him think he got the best of him. "Pretty sure of yourself, aren't you?" Connor retorted. "You have no clue about me or what I know or want." He let the shovel fall to the ground, crossing his arms over his chest. He was growing more and more curious about and yet annoyed with Sterling. He had thought this was a guy who just took pictures, but there could be more to him than that, and it intrigued him. But he didn't intend to let Sterling—or his great-aunt—pull him into this craziness.

Sterling smiled again. "You're right, I don't know what you want. But I do know some things about you."

"Like what?" Connor asked. This was getting interesting. Maybe Sterling fancied himself as some modern-day Sherlock Holmes. "Come on, tell me what you think you know." This could be fun, and the intensity in Sterling's deep blue azure-flecked eyes intrigued him.

Sterling took a step back. "You aren't as put off by the idea of posing for the calendar as you'd like us to think." His gaze raked over him, and Connor did his best not to shiver under its intensity. Instead, he stared and refused to back down. Damn, this man was forward and made no pretense to hide his attraction. No straight man would ever look at another guy that way. That was interesting, and his body thought so too. That was one of the beauties of wearing a kilt. Certain conditions could remain hidden, at least most of the time, and at the moment, he didn't want Sterling to know just how attractive he found him. Not that Connor intended to do anything about it. He'd had enough with men to last him a lifetime. A little amusement was okay, a bit of fun, but nothing more. And Sterling had more… a lot more… *tons* more… written all over him.

"I'll bite." Connor bared his teeth a little, and Sterling shivered. That was interesting. "Why do you think so?"

Sterling grinned. "Let me see. You're out at your great-aunt's doing yardwork in a kilt and boots, nothing else. And looking the way you do, I'd say you want to be noticed and that maybe there's a little bit of exhibitionist in you." He stepped back. "That's not a bad thing. I made my living with models and exhibitionists. If you were shy and retiring in the modeling game, you got eaten for lunch. I'm just saying that there's nothing wrong with showing off a little. Especially when you've got plenty to show off." Sterling actually blushed at that point, and Connor was grateful that Sterling had at least *some* shame. Not that he intended to fall for Sterling's hotness. He'd met plenty of guys like him, and they were all flash and no substance.

"For your information, it's hot out here *and* I wear a kilt almost all the time—except in the dead of winter, because I like my nuts where they are, thank you very much." If Sterling could be forward, then Connor had no intention of playing the shrinking violet. "I'm a history lecturer at Dickinson College, and I'm proud of my Scottish heritage. My mother was related to the Laird of Clan MacIntosh, so I have plenty to be proud of. And as for working outside without a shirt, it's sweltering and I promised Aunt Lucille that I would help her." He glared at Sterling. Let him try to get around that.

Sterling put his hands in the air, and Connor half grinned, knowing he had won that round. "Okay. But still…." He waved his hands up and down. "I think the idea gives you a thrill. Your breathing certainly says so."

Connor cleared his throat and controlled his breathing, earning a smile. "Fine. I'm not shy. Is that a crime? And I'm a teacher. Granted, at the college level, but I don't need my freshman European history students bringing in a calendar with me as one of your Mr. Aprils and asking for autographs." He cocked his eyebrows.

"I understand. We could give you and whoever we find to pose with you the cover, if you'd rather," Sterling quipped and then laughed. "I'm kidding. You don't have to look like your kilt just Marilyn Monroed."

"Okay, fine." Connor picked up the shovel. "I need to finish up here and then go home so I can work in my own yard. I wish you and Aunt Lucille all the luck in the world with this insane calendar idea." He was about to turn away, but he stopped. "The garden club may sound really little old lady… and it largely is. But those women do a lot for this town, and they don't ask for any credit. I only hope that I have the chance to give back to the community the way they do. It's important to me, and maybe I can even run for office. So whatever you do, you give it your best. My great-aunt throws her heart into everything she does, so don't you think of taking advantage of her or leading her down some garden path—no pun intended." He'd take on anyone who hurt his Aunt Lucille. She was about all the family he had left—well, family he was speaking to, or were speaking to him.

"I want to help," Sterling said. "Your great-aunt has passion, and she wants to make a difference."

Connor nodded. "She always has." He went back to work and did his best not to turn to watch Sterling walk away, even though he wanted to. Instead he focused his attention on his great-aunt's flower bed.

"Aunt Lucille, I'm done," Connor called an hour later. His back ached a little, and he was covered in dirt. He washed his hands and wiped his face, using some paper towel to dry off. He needed to go home, shower, and get truly clean. His own garden would have to wait for another day.

His great-aunt responded from deeper in the house, and Connor took off his boots and strode, in sock feet, farther into the house. He expected to find her in the kitchen or her family room, but he followed her voice back to the master bedroom. "Connor, thank you," she said from where she was lying down.

"Are you okay?"

"Yes. I usually take a nap in the afternoon, but today it isn't working." She slowly sat up and got off the bed. "Getting old sucks. You have pain in places you never knew you had and feel tired a lot of the time, but the worst part is that you can't do shit." She stood up.

Connor knew what she meant. His great-aunt had designed and lovingly tended her garden for decades. She nurtured and cared for it, putting some of herself into the soil. He was more than willing to help, but he knew it wasn't the same for her. She didn't move the way she used to and was sometimes unsteady on her feet. But she was still just as determined; at least that hadn't dimmed. "I don't think any of us can stop that."

"True," she said with a sigh as she passed him in the doorway, heading out toward the kitchen. "I want to ask a favor." She didn't pause for a second. "I know you don't want to be part of the calendar… and that's fine, I understand. And no one should be forced into anything, but would you be willing to work with Sterling on this project? I really want it to be a success, and I can only do so much."

Connor was sure she was up to something. Aunt Lucille never backed away from anything, and she didn't admit defeat under any circumstances. He picked up his shirt from the chair where he'd placed it earlier and pulled it on. "Are you really going to do this? A gay calendar?" She grinned like she was a teenager, and Connor couldn't rain on her happiness parade. She was more excited than Connor had seen her in a long time. "What are you up to?"

"Nothing. I'm going to need some help, and there are going to be a lot of moving parts on this." She handed him a business card. "Just work with him and help me out. I knew his mother before she passed away. She was in the garden club for about a year, and she and I were friends." His great-aunt seemed defeated, and Connor hated that. It seemed so out of character. "I just need help with a proposal and some mock-ups so I can take the idea to the club and get their approval. She rolled her eyes. Connor figured that was going to be a really hard sell… no pun intended. "Besides, you spend way too much time at home alone and you need to get out and meet people."

So that was it. "Are you matchmaking? Again?"

"Definitely not. I learned my lesson with… what's-his-name." She had the grace to look appalled. "I'm sorry I had anything to do with you meeting… *him.*"

"Trevor," Connor supplied flatly, trying not to think about him. He had his work and his great-aunt, and he kept himself busy.

His great-aunt rolled her eyes. "He who shall not be named," she quipped, and Connor had to agree with her on that. Trevor had started out as excitingly good but had ended in an epic crash and burn that he didn't want to speak or think about. His heart still had the burn marks around the edges. "I'm sorry I even introduced the two of you." Her eyes blazed for a few seconds, and Connor leaned over and hugged her gently.

"There was no way you could have known just how rotten and despicable he was on the inside." Connor closed his eyes and took comfort when she held him in return. Everyone had made a mistake or two in their love life, but Trevor had been more than a mistake. "I'm doing better now, and I'm moving on. It's a one-day-at-a-time situation, but you know that."

Aunt Lucille was one of the toughest, most determined people he knew, and he knew of her battle with alcohol, which she never claimed to have truly won. She didn't talk about it much any longer, but he remembered her sitting down with him when he was in high school. She had shared her story that drinking had nearly cost her her life and that she had nearly lost everything she had and everyone important to her. She told him her story as a cautionary tale, but it had cemented his absolute love for her. So when Trevor absolutely shattered his life and he'd thought about trying to escape, it was Aunt Lucille who kept him from going down that path. And Connor loved her for it.

"Will you help me?" she whispered, and Connor nodded as he still hugged her. "Thank you." She tightened her hold for a few seconds and then released him.

Connor straightened up and grabbed his keys and wallet off the table. "I need to go. Is there anything else you need help with?"

"No, I'm fine." She put the kettle on the stove, probably to make herself some tea. Connor swore she lived on the stuff. He went for the back door. "You will call Sterling and help me figure out this calendar business?"

"I will. I have his number." Connor held up his wallet to emphasize his point.

She plunked a mug down on the granite counter. "You know, you two should go to dinner. It's easier to talk business over a good meal." She turned away, and Connor groaned as he pulled open the door and got out of the house before his great-aunt made them reservations and decided what he should wear. She was never going to change, no matter what she said: a matchmaker was a matchmaker was a matchmaker. God help him.

Chapter 3

"THAT'S WONDERFUL," Sterling told Dean, a shy boy who seemed to want to disappear into the backdrops. He wore tan slacks and a blue sweater that his mother had probably bought just for the pictures. Dean immediately chose a blue background, and Sterling had felt him receding by the second. It took nearly half the session, but Sterling was able to pull Dean out of his shell, and now he was smiling and even talking to him. Fortunately, he had an extra half hour after this session, so he let it run over to see if he could get a few more outstanding images. "Do you ever wear contacts?"

"A few times, but I don't really like them." Dean's nerves spiked once again.

"It's no problem. Let's just take off your glasses so we can see your eyes." He had great big blue eyes, and as soon as the thick glasses were gone, Sterling got to work once again, taking some of the best images of the session. "There you go." Once he was done, he flipped through the images and showed a few to Dean.

Dean's lips curled up into a smile. "Dang," he drew out, and his smile turned to a grin. "Is that all? Maybe I should think about contacts."

"Go ahead and change and join your mom." He waited until Dean returned to the changing area before rejoining Dean's mother in reception.

"How did he do?" she asked, concerned. Sterling pulled up a few of the later images on his computer and turned the screen. She gasped at the first image, putting her hand in front of her mouth, unable to look away. "He's… that's my son, but not my son."

That was one of the things Sterling loved about his job. Sometimes the stars aligned and he and the sitter really connected. These pictures weren't him doing some photographer magic; it was him and Dean working together. "I love the pictures without his glasses." Dean joined them, and his mom put her arms around him, hugging tightly. "We'll go to the eye doctor and see about new contacts and some help for you to put them in."

Dean nodded. "Okay." They thanked him and left the studio, happily just as Sterling's phone vibrated. He answered the call with a smile still on his lips.

"Vaughn Photography, this is Sterling." He pulled up his schedule on the computer in preparation.

"Sterling, hi…. This is Connor." The last person Sterling had ever expected to hear from again. "Look, I know I may have come off as a bit… harsh."

Sterling found himself nodding. "I don't think either of us was shown in our best light." What else was he going to say? If hot Connor was willing to backpedal a little, then so was he. "What can I do for you?"

"Aunt Lucille asked if I'd work with you. Actually, she pulled out her rack and thumbscrews." He chuckled. "I think she's really sold on this calendar idea, and she asked if I'd help. I was wondering if maybe you might want to get some dinner or something to talk it over. I still don't think I want to be one of the calendar guys, but I'll try to help put this together." This was about the last thing Sterling expected. "Don't get me wrong, I still think the idea is off the wall, but Aunt Lucille is convinced it will work, and I don't want to disappoint her."

Sterling smiled to himself just as his next appointment arrived. "That would be great. Is seven okay? I'll make arrangements, if you like." He gave Connor his address. "Come around to the back, and once I'm done with my last appointment, we can go."

"I'll see you then," Connor told him, and Sterling set down his phone, a little surprised and kind of pleased. He still had hopes that he could convince Connor to do the calendar. He would be a huge hit. But if nothing else, some help organizing something like this was always appreciated.

EVERYTHING THE rest of the day seemed to go completely to hell. Clients showed up either early or late, and Sterling's schedule was all out of whack. Instead of a photographer, he seemed more like a circus performer as he tried to keep them all happy. At least fashion photography didn't have nearly as many stage mothers. Finally he got the last person out the door and the follow-up appointment set up to view the final images and choose their portraits.

"Connor," Sterling said when he closed the studio door. "I'm sorry for keeping you waiting."

Connor stood dressed in a white shirt and red plaid kilt. Sterling assumed it was the MacIntosh tartan, or at least one of them.

"I just need to lock up."

"Will you show me your studio?" Connor asked, and Sterling opened the door and let him inside. Out of habit, he grabbed his camera and followed him.

"I do a lot of portraiture, but I also love floral and purely artistic images." He led the way over to one corner. "I'm doing a series of artistic pieces right now. It's classic still-life paintings, then brought to life in a single image. The Smithsonian is interested in it, and I'm hoping that once I'm done, they'll jump on it."

Connor nodded as he looked at the intense still-life tableau in front of him with glasses and fruit practically overflowing the table. "Where did you get the rabbit and the deer hides?"

"I found both of the hides in an antique store, so no animals were hurt specifically for my art." He sighed. "I know it's a little over-the-top, but the more normal still-lifes were easier to compose. This one took a lot of time, but I think it's pretty intense. Both classic and modern at once." He moved the screen back into place. "I don't let my clients see that, as a rule." It was his own personal project.

Connor stared at the screen that hid the still-life setup. "Why do you do it? I know you love photography. That's evident by the images I saw online. Some of the images are stunning. I know they were fashion and meant to be commercial, to sell clothes and things, but yours had a style, an artistic flair that added something." He finally looked at him. "So why do you do it?"

"Why take pictures? I always have. I snitched my father's camera when I was seven. He was so mad that I shot four rolls of his film. I begged him to develop them, and he said he would but would take the cost out of my allowance. When they came back, he sat at the table, leafing through the pictures. He handed me the camera and said it was mine. I adore my father for that." He hadn't thought about that in years.

Connor nodded. "No… well, yes, I suppose I was asking that, but why the art? Fashion has a commercial purpose, but the still-lifes and things…." He seemed perplexed.

"You mean, why art for art's sake?" Sterling supplied. It was a question he'd asked himself on a number of occasions. "I can't give you an answer in words because I don't have one. It's something inside that wants to come out. So I do it for me."

"Is this where you do portraits?" Connor asked, looking at the rest of the space.

Sterling nodded as Connor wandered out onto the large white backdrop that continued down the wall and onto the floor.

"Yeah." He motioned to Connor, who hesitated before stepping in front of the background. Sterling flipped on the lights and then picked up his camera and snapped off a few shots. He didn't have Connor pose or even look at him. He just took a few pictures of the man, then brought the camera over and showed them to Connor. "You take great pictures." Sterling had known that he would as soon as Connor stepped into his line of sight at Lucille's.

Connor narrowed his eyes. "Is this some ploy to get me to agree to do this calendar thing? Because I can't. I have my students at school, you know that. I know Aunt Lucille is keen on this calendar and that she is trying to do something good, and so am I."

Sterling stepped back and took a few more pictures. Yeah, he was trying to convince Connor to do the calendar, but just playing with the camera like this was fun, and Connor seemed so at home. Sterling hadn't experienced that since he left the fashion world. "Did your great-aunt put the screws to you to try to get you to do it?"

Connor chuckled. "In her own way. She said that I was to do what my heart told me to do." He turned to the camera, and Sterling shot some more images. Damn, he wanted to ask Connor to take off his shirt. Well… if he was honest, he wanted Connor to take off everything, leave that shirt and kilt in a pile on the floor, and…. Sterling dragged his rampant imagination back to where it belonged.

"That doesn't sound bad to me," Sterling commented as he set the camera aside.

Connor chuckled. "That was Aunt Lucille being passive-aggressive. She wants me to follow my heart and feels that it should lead me back to her and the project she has in mind. She would never actually plead with me to do it, but she will try to plant the seeds of guilt in order to get me to agree." He glanced up at the ceiling. "The crappy thing is that it usually works."

"Really?" Sterling snickered. "I'll have to keep that in mind: 'Connor can be guilted into things.'" He pretended to make a note of it.

"Only by Aunt Lucille. She has magic powers, I swear. Didn't your mother do that?" Connor asked. "Guilt was a regular part of my life growing up. Mama used to tell me that when I was bad, I was making baby Jesus cry or that the angels were sad." He sighed.

"Thank goodness my mother didn't do guilt. She had other ways," Sterling observed as Connor stepped off the photo mat and Sterling turned out the lights. "My mom was big into taking away my allowance or trying to use logic. She loved to explain the consequences of things."

"That doesn't sound so bad," Connor said.

Sterling groaned. "Yeah, except her logic was always on these grand scales, like if I broke the neighbor kid's bike, that was somehow going to lead to the zombie apocalypse. Looking back on it, she was a real hoot." He sighed at the old loss.

"Sounds like it," Connor said.

"She would have loved you. Mom was part Scottish, though I don't know which clan or anything. It was quite a ways back, but at any festival, she could sniff out the bagpipes before anyone played a note." He smiled as Connor got a faraway, sort of melty look. "Mostly she'd have loved the kilt." Sterling couldn't resist. "I miss her sometimes." He pulled himself out of the funk he knew would spread like spilled paint on carpet. "Let's get out of here. I got us a table at the new brew pub in town. I'm told that their beer is really good, and their food is supposed to be awesome."

"I'm game if you are." Connor followed him out of the studio, and Sterling closed the door and locked up.

They decided to walk. It was only a few blocks, and that way they didn't have to worry about the amount of beer they had. Which turned out to be a godsend. Sterling ordered the stout and Connor the Redcoat, an extra special bitter. Even before they ordered their food, one beer turned into two. By the time they ordered and their food arrived, they were well into a third beer before they dug into the best chicken sandwiches Sterling had ever tasted—crispy and juicy—and he was about to reach across the table to smack Connor at any moment.

"If you preen any more, they're going to write a song about you." It was too good not to tease a little.

Connor scowled. "I don't preen."

Sterling snorted and then took another sip of his beer. "Yes, you do. Every time someone looks at you twice or their gaze doesn't stray away, you sit up straighter and act like you're the center of everyone's attention. Are you always like this?" It was another curious thing about Connor, and somehow it got under his skin. It shouldn't. He had just met the guy, and they were going to be working on a project together, nothing more. Besides, hunks like Connor didn't look twice at a guy like him. Sterling had no illusions that he was ever going to win any Sexiest Man Alive contests. "Not that I blame you. If I looked like you, I'd probably preen a little too." He finished the last of his sandwich, suddenly wishing he had simply kept his damned mouth shut.

"And you say what you mean, don't you?" Connor retorted. "For the record, I'm not preening, even if it looks that way. After working in Lucille's garden for hours, my back is a little sore, so I keep moving it to try to loosen it up." He shifted in the chair to make his point.

"Oh." Sterling wanted to slap his hand over his mouth, but instead he smiled and then laughed at himself. Thankfully, Connor joined him. "I guess I'm a little overreactive tonight." He wasn't sure if Connor was interested in him. Maybe he was barking up the wrong tree.

"Ya think?" Connor teased and then winked. Sterling's mind raced at that, wondering what Connor meant by it for a few seconds before tossing the notion aside. He was allowing himself to get drawn into Connor's orbit. That would be so easy to let happen, but it would only end in heartache and pain, just like the last time. "I like that you're straightforward." Connor lightly scratched his head. "I think."

"Okay…." Sterling flagged their server, who brought another round. He had a slight buzz and was a little warm. It felt pleasant, and he was enjoying Connor's company. It was nice to be out with someone and just have a few beers, some good food, and…. Shit, had this somehow turned into a date? Sterling's belly clenched for a second, but thankfully Connor didn't seem to notice the sudden sense of impending doom that overtook him for a minute.

"We should talk about the calendar before I can't think straight," Connor said once their beers arrived.

"Heck, I can never think straight. Never could." He snorted and lifted his glass, setting it down again as his clouded mind processed what he'd said. "Sorry, I think my brain is reaching its beer limit." He pushed the glass away. "We should talk about this." He took a deep breath and got a strong whiff of Connor's scent. He closed his eyes, letting it wash over his dulled senses, his brain willing to follow the deep richness anywhere. God, that was even more intoxicating than what he was drinking, and he leaned forward slightly, just to get close. "I should have brought something to write with." Though he hadn't had so much to drink that he was going to have to worry about a memory blackout or anything.

"We'll be fine," Connor told him. "Have you done something like this before?"

Sterling nodded, and for a second, his head spun. He reached for his glass of water and drank half of it, then felt a little better. "Yeah, a few years ago. We have to find a printer and someone to design the calendar itself, but the biggest thing is to dig up the local guys who are willing to pose for it." At least that was the first hurdle. "The next part is that I need to photograph them."

"So, two dozen guys...." Connor grew quiet.

"Fewer, if I can convince you to do it," Sterling's mouth was starting to run away with itself. Connor hit him with a glare, but he didn't say he wouldn't do it. Maybe Sterling was starting to wear him down.

"Nobody wants to see—" Connor began, and Sterling leaned over the small table and got right into his space.

"Every woman in town would snatch up that calendar to get a look at you in your kilt, handing them flowers. You're gorgeous, and I'd...." Sterling managed to stop his lips before they got him in more trouble. Connor might not appreciate him blatantly coming on to him when they were both a few sheets to the wind. Sterling needed to sober up a bit and think clearly.

"You'll take the pictures?" Connor lightly tugged at his shirt collar.

"Of course. That's the really hard part: getting professional-quality images and looks from amateurs." He sat back and groaned. "It can be hard enough getting the best image possible from professional models. I once worked with Mara Thundston. She's gorgeous and incredibly talented, but the session was a complete bust. I couldn't get any of the images we needed out of her. Sometimes things need to flow from within, and I can't tell a model what I need. It just has to come, and that day it wasn't coming, no matter what. It was hot, and we were outside in the natural light. The damned wind blew shit around the entire time, and not a thing was the way it should have been."

"What did you do?" Connor asked, leaning in.

Sterling shrugged and realized that the conversation at the next table had ceased and that the four guys there were all listening to him. "I scrapped what we were doing and told her to jump in the pool. She looked at me like I was crazy, but she did what I asked, and when she came out, I got the cover of *Vogue*." He grinned. "But the point is that it isn't easy, and with amateurs, it's going to be more difficult, especially if we want the images to have movement." He drank the rest of his water.

"Dude, you worked with Mara?" the guy from behind him asked. "Did you work with other models?"

Sterling turned, pasting on a smile. "Yes. Lots of them. For the most part, they're nice people." He nodded and turned back to Connor. "I'm going to do this and spend the time and effort, using my spare time, to try to make this work because your great-aunt, a friend of my mother's, asked me to." He raised his eyebrows in a silent challenge.

"Fine, I'll do the calendar." Connor drained his beer and thunked the glass on the table. "Are you happy?" He crossed his arms petulantly over his chest.

"More than." Sterling finished his beer as well and wondered for a second if Connor was as buzzed as him.

Chapter 4

GOD, HIS head hurt. Connor got out of bed and wondered why he had drunk so much. And what the hell had he done, agreeing to be in that damned calendar? He must have been out of his mind.

Well, in a way, he had been. *Note to self: stop at one beer when you want to stick to your guns.* Because clearly he could be talked into anything after a few more.

His phone dinged with a text, and Connor cringed at the sound. *When did I turn into such a lightweight?* He glanced at the screen and groaned, clamping his eyes shut so he didn't have to think about any of this.

Yes. I'm fine, he replied in answer to Sterling's message.

You were a pretty sloppy, but lovey-dovey drunk, and I wanted to make sure you were okay and not too hungover. Connor groaned. Last night's details were fuzzy. He seemed to remember Sterling smiling a lot and them discussing what he had on under his kilt, and then an urge to show Sterling what it was.

"Oh God." He held his head, hoping like hell he hadn't mooned everyone in the tap room. He tried to remember and couldn't. *Thanks for that picture.* He did remember their server being friendly and a string of double entendres that had him cringing once again. *Did I do something really embarrassing?* Yeah, no more than one beer. Period… no matter what.

Other than sitting in my lap and asking if I'd ever been inside a kilt? Sterling answered.

Connor climbed back into bed, pulled the covers over his head, groaned, and wished the world would go away.

I'm kidding, came the next message, followed by a smiley face. *You had just enough beer to loosen you up. You were a little entertaining, but I kept you from doing anything permanently embarrassing.*

Connor was both relieved and pissed at the same time. *Thanks for that, I think.* He rolled his eyes, wishing Sterling was here so he could smack him. Well, not exactly here, since he was in bed, naked, and well.… The idea got certain nether parts going, but Connor didn't have the energy to do anything about it and willed his dick to go back to sleep. The damned thing had a mind of its own, and the more he thought about Sterling, the more insistent it became.

I'll see you tonight. Come to the studio at six and we can talk about plans for what Lucille wants us to do and figure out a way forward.

Connor tried to remember if he'd agreed to that. He must have, and he didn't have anything else planned as far as he could remember. This entire idea was crazy, but he had agreed to help, and he couldn't back out without hurting his great-aunt, and he wasn't about to do that. Lucille had been there when the rest of his family had decided to be real idiots about a number of things in his life, both the fact that he went into history rather than something "not stupid" and the fact that he preferred guys to girls. That announcement had gone over like a lead balloon. Aunt Lucille had apparently called his father when she heard, reamed him out from one end to the other, and then informed him that she was changing her will and Connor's father was going to get "squat," as she put it. He owed Aunt Lucille a lot, and he wasn't going to disappoint her, even if he thought that she was starting to lose it a little.

I'll see you then, Connor sent because he felt like crap and didn't want to argue. Maybe once they made their plans, this whole thing would be over and he could get back to normal.

"OKAY, SO I thought that if this is going to work, we should have each month be something special. Maybe firemen, policemen, things like that," Sterling said as they sat at his kitchen table with notes and some images strewn everywhere. "I got a few things from the internet to get the ideas going. We won't use any of these pictures because all of the images should be original. These are stock photos."

"Okay. So…." Connor drank some Diet Coke. Sterling had offered him a beer, but he declined. "Why don't you call some of your model friends and get them to pose for the pictures? We could put them in something to denote the profession we want and that can be the end of it." Easy-peasy and they were done.

Sterling shook his head. "First thing, models are paid. They like to eat, even if it's like a bird, and we don't have the budget for that. Besides, if this is going to be interesting, it has to be real guys, so the firemen would be real local firemen. Same with the cops… and so on. Part of the appeal is going to be that it's people that everyone in town might meet."

"Are there that many gay people in town?" Connor asked.

Sterling got that look again. "They don't have to be gay, just willing to do the photoshoot. We aren't going to discriminate here." He looked serious for a second and then smiled. "God, you're so easy to tease. Connor, lighten up a little. This is going to be fine." He pushed a sheet of paper across the table. "I made a list of some of the kinds of guys we could go for. This isn't all of them by far, and we'll have to adjust depending on who we can get to participate."

Connor took the list. "Do you know all these people?" He looked up from the page. "I don't know any chefs well enough to ask them to pose for this kind of thing." He shivered and wondered how that conversation would go. "How do we ask them? Like, 'Dude, would you be interested in supporting a garden club project? All you have to do is strip down so we can take your picture nearly naked while you hold flowers… oh, and with another guy'? That's going to go over huge… not." He slid the page back to Sterling. This was hopeless.

"Yeah, right. Look, we talk to friends and friends of friends. This is for the garden club, service, and helping people do good in the community. That's what you start with, not the stripping off part." Sterling leaned over the table. "And before you protest too much, I know you get a thrill out of the idea of showing off your assets just a little bit." Damn Sterling and that knowing glint in his eye, and that slightly cockeyed way he tilted his smile that made it seem extra dirty. Connor was determined not to react to the games Sterling was playing, but he couldn't help smiling, and his cheeks heated just a little. "See, I knew I was right all along." He leaned back, grinning smugly. "So knock off the shocked virgin routine and let's see if we can get anywhere. I know a couple of guys, Carter and Donald. One of them is a police officer. His partner works for child services, and they have a son, so I doubt they would do it, but they might know some other guys who would be interested." Sterling was already making notes.

Connor thought about the guys he knew, and unfortunately none of them would work. Most of the college professors he knew wouldn't know sex appeal if it appeared in their course syllabus.

The oven timer rang, and Sterling got up, took a dish out, and placed it on a hot pad in the center of the table. "I made some dip with sausage, spicy tomatoes, and cream cheese. The stuff is amazing but lethally hot right now."

Connor had to admit the aroma was incredible. He waited a few minutes and used a tortilla chip to scoop out some of the concoction, blew on it to cool it further, and took a small bite. It packed big flavor, and Connor hummed before finishing the chip and going back for more. "That's incredible. I love the punch of spice without it being too hot."

"I don't make it too often because it's so bad for you, but it is addicting." Sterling took his own bite. "Where do we start?" he asked, tapping the tabletop. "I'll talk to Carter and Donald and see if they can get me anywhere. Do you have any ideas?"

Connor nodded as he chewed and then swallowed. "I'll talk to Aunt Lucille—she might be able to help." Lord knows he had no idea where he was going to find people who were interested, but if he didn't try, then nothing was going to happen. This whole project seemed like a stretch, but maybe if they didn't find anyone, then that would be the end of it.

"Okay, but we need to get beyond her. Lucille may know people, but we need young guys if the calendar is to be a success." Sterling grabbed another chip, took a dollop of dip, and popped the whole thing into his mouth. Dang, his lips were red, and Connor found himself staring at them. "Connor… I…."

Connor realized Sterling was talking and he hadn't heard a word he'd said. "Sorry." He needed to pay attention to the conversation, not imagining the magic things those lips could be doing to him.

"I was saying that one of the restaurants in town is run by a couple. They might be willing to help us out. They own a few of them, including the Belgian place and the Greek place. I've eaten at both restaurants, and they're really good."

"Then all we can do is ask. But firemen, really? How are we going to approach those guys?" Connor asked, afraid that one of them was going to get their nose adjusted. "I mean, we don't need to make a huge deal of this, do we? Just get some good pictures and put together a calendar to make Aunt Lucille happy. That's all this was supposed to be. Not some huge production where we're going all over town to recruit guys to take off their clothes." This was a hell of a lot more than he had bargained for, and Connor had things to do. Just because he wasn't teaching classes at the moment didn't mean that he didn't have work to finish. He had been working on a paper to document his research into the Scottish Independence movement of the eighteenth century and how that still influenced the culture today. He was finally making progress, and now he had this to contend with.

"Fine. I'll approach the restaurant guys and see if there's any interest. You work the cop angle and see if you get anywhere. Maybe if we get a few guys lined up, we can get others and they can pass the word." Honestly, Connor thought this a fool's errand, but he had promised he would try, and he always did his best.

"That's true," Sterling agreed and stood up, pulling a couple of large bowls out of the refrigerator. "Since it was hot out and I already spiced you up with the dip, I made a couple of large salads for dinner. I thought they would be fresh and crisp." He put some containers on the table, including a mayonnaise jar without the label. "That one is my homemade ranch dressing." He refilled their glasses before taking his seat once more. "Help yourself to whatever you like."

Connor took some of the ranch for his salad, and danged if it wasn't fresh and a little tangy. The stuff was really good. So it seemed that Sterling could cook. "Don't you have evening appointments?"

"I have them three days a week. It helps keep me sane, and I like having some time to myself. Otherwise I swear I could work seven days a week and I'd never have time for anything else." Sterling smiled brightly. "I've gotten a real reputation in the area, so I have people coming in from Camp Hill and Shippensburg to have their pictures taken. I even have people who will offer to pay extra if I can fit them into the schedule. Sometimes I do it because… well… the money is too good to turn down. But mostly I need some time away." Sterling ate slowly and deliberately.

"What about your family?" Connor was curious.

"Dad moved to a senior community about the time that I needed a place to live, so I moved in here, and he went to a place with a lot less maintenance. He has a cottage out at Briar Ridge, and he loves it there. Mom passed away some years ago, and Dad stayed here alone. He's really social." Sterling rolled his eyes and smiled a second.

"What's so funny?" The quirk to Sterling's lips had him curious.

"Well, Dad moved out there, and apparently now he's the local stud. Dad dates a lot, and he spends his afternoons talking to the ladies and his nights romancing them." Sterling tried to keep a straight face and then broke into laughter. "I really wish I was kidding. But I'm not. My dad is a retirement-age Lothario. The last time I went out there was in the morning, and he was saying goodbye to his company from the night before as I drove up. I tried not to pay attention to it, but they were both giggling like schoolkids, and my father—the quiet guy I remembered who stayed home and doted on my mother—waving goodbye to his night's company was almost too much."

"You weren't upset?" Connor tried to imagine his father acting like that and came up with a total blank. His father was more the grumpy old man type and would only get worse, he was pretty sure, if his mother passed away first.

Sterling shrugged. "About what? My dad is an adult. He's old enough to make his own decisions and young enough to enjoy life. He's talking about taking a safari to Zambia next year. He wants to see wild animals. Dad's earned the right to act how he wants, and if that means reverting back to a teenager in some ways, I say go for it. He worked hard his entire life, so he may as well enjoy what's left of it. He won't always be able to be as active as he is. What about your parents?"

"They live outside Lancaster. Dad's a roofer and spent much of his life up in the air on top of other people's houses. He still does it part-time. He wanted me to go to business school, come home, and take over for him. I fell in love with history, but not just the past. I think the power of history is in what studying the past can teach us today about ourselves and our society."

Sterling chuckled. "You sound like a history professor—you really do. Not that I mind at all. History is full of stories, especially racy ones, and I'm all about the story. Mom read me stories at bedtime for years, but when I was young, she used to make up her own too. Those were my favorite. Amelia Aardvark, Ronny Racoon, and Harvey Hippo were friends I knew and loved. They were products of my mom's imagination. Then, as I got older, she used to tell me stories about how she grew up. Mom had a younger sister, and her mother used to braid her hair and then fasten the braids on top of her head. When the braids would come loose, they used to call her Horns Heddy, and she'd chase them all around the yard. Aunt Heddy is gone now. She died a year before Mom of the same thing—heart disease."

"Well, I could tell you stories. Maybe someday I'll tell you the story of Catherine the Great. She reportedly had a prodigious libido and even commissioned an X-rated set of parlor furniture. Only pictures of it survive, but it's explicit." Connor blushed when Sterling did the same. God, how did he let himself get pulled into telling stories about penis furniture?

"See? What sort of things could be more interesting? If they taught stuff like that in my high school history class, I might have become a professor too." Sterling finished his salad and sat back in the chair, drinking his soda. "You know, maybe that's what they should offer in college. Everyone would take it. History as told through sex."

Connor threw back his head. "I do teach that. It's called the human condition through history, but yeah. It's the history of sex and how it shaped who we are. But yeah, like they say, sex sells."

"And that's why, if we do this calendar right, we can help your great-aunt save the garden club." Sterling grinned, and somehow Connor knew he'd been led down the primrose path and there was no turning back.

Chapter 5

"THE GARDEN club is really going to do something like that?" Donald Ickle asked when Sterling called him. "I love the idea. I never thought the ladies actually had it in them, but I think it's pretty awesome. Tell them to let me know when they go on sale. I think I'll buy them for Christmas gifts." His excitement was almost palpable.

"We're trying. The thing is, I'm trying to find people who'll pose for it. I would love a couple of police officers, and I was given your name as a contact. I'm hoping that you could talk it over with your husband."

Donald's voice became more cautious. "Not us, definitely. My job is to work with children, and that would raise plenty of eyebrows." He paused for a few seconds. "I don't know if I can recommend anyone offhand, but I'll talk with Carter. He might know one of the guys who would be game to do it." He might have been enthusiastic about the overall idea, but finding models seemed like another story. Not that Sterling could fault him. He had been contacting other people to feel them out and had gotten polite "I'll think about it" responses that Sterling knew just meant they didn't want to tell him no right away.

"I'd appreciate it. It's harder than I thought to get guys to agree. I had sort of figured that they would love it. They'll be photographed professionally, and they'll be part of a project that will help the community." Sterling tried thinking on his feet. "Can you imagine telling your grandchildren about this and even showing them the pictures? Suddenly you'd be the cool grandpa for sure."

Donald actually laughed. "Yup, posing in a calendar photo half naked will definitely make you the cool grandpa." He seemed to get it. "Carter and I will see what we can do."

"Thanks," Sterling said, knowing he couldn't ask for more, even though he was disappointed. He ended the call and sat staring at his phone, wishing he had some other ideas.

Have you had any luck? he sent Connor as a text.

Nope. Aunt Lucille gave me a few names. I called and they were nice enough and said they'd think about it. So nothing yet. I have one more lead, and I left a message. They haven't called me back yet.

Okay. Thanks for trying. Maybe this wasn't going to work out after all. *Do you want to get together tomorrow for dinner? We can commiserate and try to figure out our next steps.* He wasn't sure if Connor would agree. Since their meeting at his house, they had mostly texted and tried following up on their leads. Sterling was pretty sure Connor was avoiding him. Maybe it was just how he was, or it was also possible that Sterling had come on too strong. He needed to remember that most people weren't models and weren't used to being told about all the little cues they gave off all the time. Sterling saw all of them. That had been his job. High fashion was more than just taking pictures of clothes—it was telling a story with the clothes, the set, and the stance, expression, and attitude of the model. All of it had to come together in sometimes very subtle ways to tell a story that the viewer would see, become intrigued by, and want to see again. Or better yet, want to be a part of and would therefore buy whatever was being featured in the photograph. A single image could sell thousands, even millions of dollars of merchandise if it ticked all the boxes. And that required an eye that saw more than the normal person.

Sure, Connor answered. *See you at six?*

One of the things Sterling hated about text messaging was the lack of personal reference. So much communication was nonverbal, and Sterling was very good at picking up on those cues, but with text messaging that was cut off, so he had to imagine what was behind the words. That often got him in trouble, because naturally, he was usually wrong. This time he decided to take the words at face value.

It should be nice. We can cook out. He sent a smiley face and tried to think of his next steps with the project… and with Connor.

Sterling would be lying to himself if he didn't admit that Connor not only attracted him but intrigued him. He was different, driven, but in his own way. And there was something sexy about his single-minded focus. It made Sterling want to broaden Connor's horizons. Sterling sighed and forced his thoughts back to the task at hand. He wasn't going to think of Connor and the way he'd looked in nothing but that kilt….

Like hell he wasn't.

THE BELL at the front door sounded. "Dad, that would be Connor. Could you let him in, please?" The timing was perfect—like the perfect train wreck. His father had shown up half an hour ago, and it didn't seem like he was leaving. Thankfully Sterling had enough food, but he had planned on a nice dinner for two with some talking about the project and maybe a little flirting. Instead, he'd been cockblocked by his own father.

He heard his dad and Connor greeting each other as he finished prepping the steaks. Everything else was ready, so he washed his hands and dried them quickly before going to see what the two of them were up to. "Hey, Sterling," Connor said, handing him a bottle of red wine and offering a smile. They shook hands, and then Sterling took the bottle.

"I see you met my father, Grant," Sterling said. "And thank you for the wine." He felt a little like a fumbling teenager stumbling over his words as Connor turned his intense gaze and smile in his direction. "Dad popped in a little while ago."

"No problem. Maybe he'll have some ideas." Connor stepped inside, wearing a white shirt and a different red tartan kilt.

"MacIntosh," Dad said. "I always loved that tartan." Sterling had no idea his father was familiar with that sort of thing. "Mildred—one of the ladies in the community—her family is Scottish, and she had a wall art piece made of the clan tartans." Dad grinned, and Sterling did his best not to roll his eyes.

"Is Mildred your girlfriend?" Connor asked innocently.

Sterling stifled a snicker.

"No. Mildred is just one of the ladies."

That did it. "More like one of your conquests." Sterling couldn't hold it in any longer.

His dad turned, scowled, and smacked him on the arm. "Every one of the women in the community is a lady, and I treat them all that way. Just because they like a little male companionship every once in a while doesn't mean anything different." His dad's smile was back now that Sterling had been properly admonished. "So how do you know my son?"

Connor hesitated, so Sterling answered. "He and I are working on a project to help the garden club. They want to do a calendar, and we're trying to find local guys to pose for it."

Sterling's father was okay with him being gay, but it wasn't something he understood particularly well. Sterling had always been grateful for his dad's support, but he hadn't waved his lifestyle in front of his dad's face like some giant rainbow flag either.

"I see." Grant half hummed and motioned toward the living room like it was his house. Well, it had been, so old habits probably died hard. "Tell me about it."

Sterling met Connor's gaze to try to get him to steer the conversation in a different direction. "My great-aunt, Lucille Hillyard, is president of the club, and she wants to raise money and the profile of the organization." It seemed Connor was going to plow forward. "She decided to make a calendar to sell, and she wants to do couples giving flowers."

"That sounds…." Sterling knew that tone. "Kind of dull, if you ask me. Cutesy, but dull."

Sterling figured he might as well rip off the Band-Aid. "Dad, the couples will all be shirtless guys like cops, firemen, stuff like that. She wants to do a gay calendar."

Grant nodded, thinking. "Good idea. All the ladies in the community will buy one. They love a hot-looking man." He might have seen his father pump himself up a little. He certainly acted like a stud, gray hair or not. It was priceless. "What's the problem?"

"We can't get anyone to do it," Sterling answered. "It has to be local guys—that's part of the appeal—but no one seems willing to step up and do it, so we were going to meet to figure out what our options were."

"Hmmm, Lucille Hillyard. I remember her." Dad got the same look he did when he watched one of those Miss Universe pageants on television. "Your great-aunt was quite a beauty." He sighed. "Anyway… I'm sorry, boys, but I don't know anyone who can help you. That sort of thing isn't my cup of tea. But I'll keep my ears open. Some of the ladies have gay grandsons and stuff, so I'll put the word out." He sat back, and the conversation stalled. "So, Connor, what do you do for a living?"

"He's a history professor," Sterling explained, and Connor went into a short elaboration of the types of things he taught as Sterling excused himself to start the grill. He also had some things to do in the kitchen. He had hoped that he might have had a few hours alone with Connor. Yeah, he wanted to talk about the calendar and maybe come up with a few more ideas about where they might find some guys who were interested. But it seemed that their little project was doomed from the start, and as much as he liked Connor, he wasn't going to have a reason to keep on seeing him. Sterling doubted Connor was all that interested in him in the first place.

Not that Sterling was hugely interested in having a boyfriend or anything. Lord knows he had the worst luck in that department, especially if you counted the selfish backstabbers. And if Sterling didn't count them, he'd still be a virgin.

He got the last of dinner ready and went out back to put the steaks on the grill.

He'd just closed the lid as the screen door banged behind him. "Can I help you?" Connor asked softly.

"Where's Dad?"

Connor approached until he stood close enough that Sterling could smell his citrusy cologne. It tickled the edges of his senses, and he closed his eyes, inhaling deeply just for a hint of more of it. "He's watching the game."

"And you aren't interested?" Sterling turned, facing Connor's intense gaze.

"Not in baseball, no." There was heat behind Connor's eyes, and it lit a fire hotter than the grill behind him.

Sterling swallowed hard and leaned slightly forward, drawn to the attraction. When he blinked, it was gone, doused. Sterling took a second to wonder if what he'd seen was real or just a trick of his imagination.

"What does grab your interest?" He met Connor's gaze, challenging him, making sure his own was obvious.

"Reading. I don't watch a lot of sports. I find it kind of slow and boring, though maybe I'll turn on a big game. Mostly I've worked and spent years studying so I could earn my doctorate. Then I taught and published like crazy so I'd be of value and could be awarded tenure." He seemed so innocent and unaware of how adorable and beautiful that was. His eyes were so soft and kind, and when he talked about his work, his expression lit up with excitement. "I think you might want to check the steaks."

Sterling whirled around and lifted the lid of the grill. He turned them over, grateful he hadn't burned them while his attention sank into thoughts of what Connor looked like without that white shirt.

"I'll watch those for you, if you like," Connor offered, and Sterling nodded blankly, his mind having skipped a beat.

"I'll get a plate." Sterling went inside and returned with the large plate for the steaks, which he handed to Connor. Then he went back inside, where he took a few deep breaths to cool himself down and settle his mind. What the hell was he doing? Ever since he'd met Connor, the guy had some sort of grip on his attention, and Sterling needed to clear his head and get that idea out of it. He and Connor were supposed to be working on a project together, nothing more. And it looked like that project was going to fizzle and burn. So, it seemed, was the time that they would have to spend together. Connor had his life, one of students, papers, and high expectations. Sterling hadn't even been smart enough to see what his ex had been doing to him until it was too late and his entire career, everything he had built, had come crashing down around him.

Sterling got the rest of dinner on the table just as Connor brought in the steaks. "I keep thinking of people who might be interested in the project, but I've got nothing. I talked with Aunt Lucille, and she said she was going to try to help, but she didn't seem to have anything concrete either." He set the platter on the table, and Sterling grabbed some napkins and called his dad in.

"I honestly didn't expect it would be this difficult to find the guys. I mean, in my experience, guys aren't shy. Granted, I worked with models, but it was usually the women who tended to be a little reticent. I remember a fashion shoot where I had four guys and four girls. The guys just changed clothes and were on set in an instant with all the crew milling around. The girls took turns behind a screen in the corner rather than just changing together." Sterling smiled as he watched Connor set out the last of the silverware. It seemed just putting the cutlery on the table wasn't enough. Sterling liked that Connor wanted things to be nice. It made him feel kind of special that he cared. "Not that there's anything wrong with a little modesty. It's just that a lot of guys don't really have it. And you'd think being in a calendar would be a lot of fun."

"You know, speaking of that, we could try one of the gyms to see if some of the guys there would be willing to take part." Connor put the last fork in place as Sterling's dad came in and sat down.

"I tried that and got a complete cold shoulder. I would have thought that guys who preened and watched themselves in mirrors for hours would go for it, but no such luck. All I got were sideways looks, so I got out before someone punched me in the face." That hadn't been the most affirming experience. Sterling had actually felt a little dirty after that, and he hated that the testosterone-juiced guys had brought out an old sense of shame he hadn't felt in years. "As much as I hate to say it, maybe this just isn't meant to be." He took a helping of his pea-and-bacon salad before passing the bowl to Connor. They filled their plates largely in silence, and Sterling wondered how he might keep the project alive, if for no other reason than as a chance to be able to see Connor again.

"I tend to agree with you, but I hate to go back to Aunt Lucille and tell her we struck out." Connor took a steak and some of the potatoes before passing them on. "She's done a lot for me, and I'd hate to have to tell her that we failed."

"Then give yourselves a break," Grant interjected. "And for God's sake, end this pity party. You two sound like someone just killed your puppy. If you want this to be a success"—Grant alternately steeled his gaze on each of them—"and I'm not sure you do, find a way to make it happen and stop whining about it. You can't expect people to just agree to what you want. If this is truly something you think you want to do, then go out and talk to people, put the word out. Do something other than make a few phone calls. If this isn't something you care about, then be honest with Lucille and move on." He rolled his eyes and crinkled his forehead in exactly the same expression he'd worn when Sterling had dented the car at seventeen.

Sterling leaned over the table. "Do you have any ideas, then?"

Grant scoffed. "What, me? I'm not the gay one in the family. If you were doing a calendar of two women giving me flowers, I'd jump at that, but this is your area of expertise, boys, not mine." He cut a piece of steak, and Sterling shook his head.

Connor glared across the table for two seconds and then began laughing. Sterling followed seconds later. It was a ridiculous notion. Asking his father, the stud of the retirement home, where to find hunky men was like asking a whale for directions to Las Vegas. "Good point, Dad." Sterling continued smiling. "So, Connor, any ideas where we can find hot, willing men?" He grinned. "Maybe we could put up a sign and turn the house into a gay club?"

"You know, you could turn it into a bathhouse. That would get plenty of gay men in here. Tile the living room, turn it into a steam room, the dining room into a sauna. The upstairs could be turned into private rooms. You'd be beating them off with a stick."

"Now you guys are being absurd," Grant muttered. He might try to put on a good face, but Sterling knew all this gay talk was making him uncomfortable. "I know you're kidding and all, but you have to think outside the box, and you need to be honest with Lucille." His voice held a scolding tone.

"He's right. I'll call Aunt Lucille tomorrow and let her know that things aren't working out. Grant is right. It's only fair that we're honest and up-front with her. Disappointment or not, maybe she can develop another idea."

Sterling didn't have any other alternative, and he reluctantly agreed. "I mean, we couldn't get even one couple for one of the months. How can we expect to round up enough for twelve?" It was disappointing, but sometimes you had to cut your losses and move on to something else. He'd had to do that with his career in fashion. It was over. He could have tried to stick around and pick up the crumbs, jobs no one else wanted to do. He might have been able to make a living, but Sterling had his pride, and being looked down on by everyone, the object of pity, wasn't what he wanted. No, it was better to back away and leave. He had managed to start over, and he was sure that Lucille would be able to come up with something else.

Connor shrugged, and Sterling pulled his attention away for his trip down the dark lane that was his past.

"If that's what you think is best," Grant said, and Sterling took a second to scowl at his father. He hated that tone. He and Connor weren't giving up. They had done what they could. But the project couldn't happen if there was no one else interested.

"What are we supposed to do? Take out an ad in the paper?" Sterling snickered. "What exactly would we say? 'Wanted: hunky guys to pose with other guys for a sexy garden club calendar. Must be built, handsome, and secure in your sexuality.'"

"Maybe we could add that being gay is not a requirement but might be helpful. Touching of other guys is required." Connor's eyes danced. "Or we could just say 'must be prepared for man-on-man photographic action with flowers.'"

"You two are hilarious." Grant scowled. "I'm trying to be encouraging, and you're acting like a pain in the ass." That was directed squarely at Sterling.

"Don't say 'pain in the ass' to gay men. It takes on a whole new meaning," Connor retorted.

Grant sputtered as some beer went down wrong. Worried about how his dad would react, Sterling did his best not to laugh but failed completely.

"You two…." Grant scowled more darkly before wiping his mouth.

"Lighten up, Dad. We were joking with you. It's a sign of affection." He grinned, and Grant rolled his eyes.

"Affection my ass. Shit. I need to lay off asses. It only gets me in trouble with you two." He actually smiled, and Sterling lightly clapped his dad on the shoulder, grateful that his father's sense of humor had kicked in. It had been a while since he and his dad had laughed together, and it felt good.

The rest of the meal was nice, with plenty of conversation, and his dad even told a few jokes. They were off-color and funny as hell. Connor had a deep, infectious, sexy laugh that Sterling wanted to hear over and over. Fortunately, Sterling's dad was in rare form. Now, with the calendar project going nowhere, Sterling moved on to how he was going to be able to get to see Connor again.

Chapter 6

CONNOR HAD been dreading this call ever since he'd left Sterling's the night before. He hadn't been sure about Grant at first, but as the evening wore on, he'd warmed up and actually laughed with them. That had been great, but what had been best was the change in Sterling. When he'd first arrived, the tension in the air had been thick enough to cut. Those two had plenty of shit to work out between them—though maybe laughing together would help break down some of the barriers. What Connor found most amazing was how the tiny lines around Sterling's eyes smoothed out as the evening went on. Connor knew that Sterling probably liked to think of himself as someone who noticed things about other people, but Connor didn't think he had that same vision about himself. When Sterling relaxed, he became more open, and sometimes the naughty teenager still inside him came peeking out, especially in the way he teased his dad. That had been priceless, especially when Grant had teased right back. But right now, Connor had his own family issues to contend with.

He dialed Aunt Lucille and half hoped she didn't answer. He kept hoping that they would come up with some idea that would change things and allow them to go forward. "Hi, Connor darling," Aunt Lucille said brightly when she answered the phone. "What have you got for me?"

Connor hesitated. "I wish I had good news, but we haven't been able to find anyone willing to do the calendar. Everyone we approach has either turned us down or said they'd think about it. But Sterling and I aren't encouraged. People we thought would do it have hesitated, and we're running out of people to ask." There, he'd said what he needed to say. "I'm afraid this idea isn't going to work."

"I see," Aunt Lucille answered in that way she had that always made Connor feel like an errant child who had disappointed someone important. And the thing was, he'd done just that and he felt like crap about it. "It's a good idea, but if we can't get anyone, then we'll have to try to think of some other way to raise money. I mean, we can try to get together a perennial sale like we've done in the past, but we don't have a place to sell the plants. The venue we had has changed hands, so it isn't open to us any longer." She seemed tired and lacking her usual energy, which worried him. Aunt Lucille was getting older, and it pained him that he wasn't going to have her around forever.

"We've both tried and made quite a few calls, but we can't do the calendar if no one is willing to be a part of it." Connor hated to give her this kind of news, but he and Sterling couldn't conjure up willing people out of thin air. "I was thinking that you might want to rethink the kind of fundraiser you wanted to have. There is still time to come up with something else, and no money has been spent." At least that was the good news. The only expenditure had been his and Sterling's time to try to find models.

"I understand," Aunt Lucille said, even more defeated. Connor wanted to say something to help her feel better, but he had no words. "I'm sorry" seemed stupid and unnecessary. "Let me think about what we can try to do."

"Okay." He should be relieved. Connor hadn't wanted to do the calendar in the first place, but he'd let Sterling talk him into it. But now that it seemed like it wasn't possible, he was disappointed. "I'll be over next week to see to the roses and help get them tied up."

She said goodbye, and Connor found himself staring at his phone. He wanted to make it better for her. He knew his great-aunt put a lot of herself into the garden club and her civic projects. It was something she started doing when she retired, and civic pride and service were something she had instilled in him from an early age. Connor remembered going to council meetings with his great-aunt, watching her stand and speak in front of the council against a proposed casino or in favor of an ordinance to strengthen the historic district. She made sure that Connor was part of that and understood how important it was to have a voice and to use it. Aunt Lucille was listened to and respected for many reasons, in part because she always gave back. She worked with the library and the parks department. Through her garden club, she and the ladies paid for hanging baskets downtown, helped send local kids to college, and more that Connor probably wasn't even aware of, so disappointing her hurt.

He phoned Sterling and left him a message to let him know that he'd spoken to his great-aunt. Sterling was probably with a client. Connor figured he'd try to get some work done. He sat at his computer and pulled up the paper he'd been working on along with his notes and settled in to work.

Sometimes when he was writing, the words and ideas flowed onto the page. That wasn't the case today. He felt like he and Sterling had failed his great-aunt, and he couldn't get that failure out of his head. It wasn't their fault, but in the back of his mind, Connor wondered if they had done enough to try to recruit people.

The work wasn't happening, so Connor grabbed his keys, wallet, and phone and left the house, locking the door before striding toward downtown, needing some kind of distraction and a chance to clear his head.

CONNOR WANDERED through town. He bought a soda and a cinnamon roll from the bake shop and enjoyed the snack before continuing on. He wasn't sure how he managed it, but Connor ended up outside Sterling's home and studio. A woman and her son were just leaving, so Connor took a chance and wandered back toward the studio. He went inside. Sterling was sitting behind his desk, working on the computer.

"What brings you here?" he asked, lifting his gaze with a smile. "What happened?"

"I told Aunt Lucille about our lack of progress."

Sterling nodded. "I see. My guess is she wasn't upset, but quiet. That's the worst, because you keep wondering if you could have done more." He sighed. "I've tried to come up with others to call, but…."

A knock on the door had them both turning.

"I don't have another appointment already." Sterling hurried over and opened the door to a pair of huge guys. Connor stood behind him for support. "Can I help you?"

"We heard you were looking for guys to appear in a calendar. They said it would benefit the community."

"Who told you?"

"Lucille Hillyard called the station. She's been a big supporter for years, and when she called—" The man speaking extended his hand. "I'm Lee Stockton, and this is my partner, Dirk Krausse. He and I are firemen with the Union Fire Company."

Connor stepped forward. "And you want to do the calendar?"

Lee slid closer to Dirk. They were powerful men, but when Lee smiled and Dirk grinned back, they looked like happy teenagers in love for the first time.

"The thing is, we weren't able to get any guys to agree to do it, so we don't know if there's going to be a calendar," Sterling explained. "We have you two, and Connor has agreed to take part, but that's it so far. It's been difficult finding guys willing to join in."

Lee turned to Dirk, who nodded slowly. "I bet Billy and Darryl might want to take part. Darryl is the chef and owner of Café Belgie. We've been friends for a while."

"We asked them, and they said they'd think about it," Connor explained, allowing himself the first rays of hope. "Do you want to come inside? Sterling can go over what he has in mind."

"Okay. Then Lee and I can make a few calls. We know some people. Lucille and the garden club ladies have supported every civic organization in town at one point or another. They're really great ladies, and when Lucille explained that they were having some troubles, we decided we could help."

Lee nudged Dirk in the ribs. "This one wasn't so sure. But I explained that there would definitely be compensation for helping out a good cause." The heat smoldering between them was enough to peel the paint off the walls. Connor was tempted to fan himself. When he turned to Sterling, their gazes locked. It must have been the residual heat, but Connor had never been so happy in his life that kilts were roomy and naturally air conditioned. The temperature in the room must have risen by ten degrees in a matter of seconds. Those two put off enough heat to start fires on their own.

"We appreciate it a great deal." Sterling handed Dirk and Lee each one of his cards. "If you find anyone who's interested, then just have them call me." He smiled. "Is there any particular month that you'd like?"

Lee and Dirk looked at each other and then back at Sterling. "July," they answered together.

"Okay. We'll put you down," Sterling said. "Now we just have to find the guys to fill the rest of the months."

Connor still wondered how that was going to happen, but they had one couple. That was a step forward, some progress he could report to his great-aunt.

"Connor or I will be in touch regarding the details of the photo sessions once we have enough guys to move forward."

"Okay. Dirk and I will let you know if we find anyone else." Lee seemed so confident that Connor actually thought they might have a chance at pulling this off. They shook hands before Lee and Dirk departed.

"How about a beer?" Sterling offered. "I think we need something to commemorate a little success."

"Sure," Connor agreed, following Sterling through to the house.

Sterling pulled open the refrigerator and handed Connor an IPA. They clinked bottles and drank. The beer tasted good, nice and hoppy, cold going down and warming his belly as soon as it hit. Or maybe that was Sterling. It was difficult to tell the difference. The house was cool in the air conditioning, but Connor still sweated, and when Sterling set down his beer and stepped closer, Connor stilled.

His heart raced as his imagination ran forward, wondering if Sterling intended to kiss him. Connor had been kissed before, but he had never really had time for a relationship. For years his focus had been on school, getting his degree, and then securing a tenure-track teaching position. At his age, it had been a challenge. He was always younger than everyone else and had more to prove, so he always felt like he needed to be the best at what he did. Connor studied hard, and the few guys who caught his attention… well, they didn't stay around long once they realized they were too far down on his priority list. Connor tried to remember the last time someone had kissed him, and it must have been a few years earlier. He actually wondered if he'd remember how. What if he was a terrible kisser and after all this buildup in his head, Sterling backed away because he kissed like a dead fish or something?

Sterling was close enough that Connor could feel the heat off his body and smell the citrus of his aftershave along with the earthiness of sweat and the richness of male underneath. The concoction was intoxicating. He knew he should resist Sterling and everything he represented. His life was order and learning; Sterling's was the exact opposite. He was chaos and impetuousness, everything Connor wasn't— and with good reason.

Connor blinked as he stopped his mind from taking a trip down that dark alley of his past.

"Connor," Sterling whispered, softly enough, deeply enough that it might have been a voice used in church.

Connor shivered as Sterling held his gaze, the moment drawing out longer and longer, the tension building. Connor was tempted to lean forward and close the distance between them, driven by curiosity at the taste of his full lips and to know just once what his arms felt like as they closed around him.

"Connor!" There went his name again, flowing past those lips, drawing him closer. "Connor… you're pouring your beer on my leg."

Connor lowered his gaze and the bottle tipped farther forward, sending a trail down Sterling's leg like he had wet himself.

"Oh God, I'm sorry, I…." He backed into the counter, and when he bumped a vase, it tumbled off the counter and smashed on the floor, sending shards of glass, water, and irises spilling out everywhere. Connor stood stock-still, expecting the disaster to grow worse by the second. "Jesus, I'm…." He put his bottle on the counter and stepped away from the mess.

"It's okay. Just stay where you are." Sterling picked up the flowers and set them on the counter on the opposite side of the kitchen, then started picking up the larger pieces of green glass. "It's okay. That vase was something my mother always had around. I used it because she used it, but I always thought it was the ugliest thing." He looked up, flashed Connor a grin, and then tossed away the bits of glass.

"I feel like such a klutz. I…." Connor swallowed.

Sterling began wiping up the water and beer. "Don't worry about it. The floor will clean up." He got a broom to sweep up the remainder of the glass and threw the mess away. Connor stayed out of the way, feeling like the biggest idiot in the history of the world. Sterling turned and pressed a fresh beer into his hand. "I'll be right back."

Connor took his absence as a chance to catch his breath. All of that had been some weird, stupid flight of fancy. If he was going to work with Sterling and get through this project in one piece, he needed to get his head out of the clouds and down to earth where it should be. Besides, his romantic past, limited as it was, had more than demonstrated that he wasn't cut out for someone like Sterling. Connor could see that he had major talent just from the images on the studio walls. Sterling's art was going to take him places. He was certain a small-town college professor couldn't compete with all the outside world had to offer. Sterling was exciting, and Connor knew that for the most part he was boring. The few guys he had dated had all told him so in specific detail.

Sterling returned in a pair of tan shorts that hugged his thighs. When he turned to get something out of the refrigerator, Connor couldn't help staring at his backside, because those pants framed Sterling's stellar ass in way that was almost a religious experience. Hell, with that right in front of him, Connor was certain there was a god. For a few moments, his mind made a serious detour, and he wondered if there was a Roman god of tight gay male asses. Mercury… it had to be Mercury. All his statues had that perfect bare butt that was a pleasure to gawk at, and he was always getting ready to fly off somewhere.

"I made some guacamole yesterday," Sterling said as he straightened up and closed the door. "I also have some chips here somewhere." He rummaged through the pantry and came out with a bag of dark purple tortilla chips. "Here they are."

"I take it we're celebrating," Connor said. "Isn't it a little early for that? We've only got one month covered."

Sterling shrugged. "You celebrate while you can, because the good stuff can evaporate into the ether just as quickly and mysteriously as it appears." He grabbed the bag and the bowl, and Connor took the beers out back into the yard. Sterling set everything on the table and brushed off the patio chairs. His phone chimed, and he grinned and showed Connor the message. "It seems we have two months now. The chef and his partner want September—their anniversary month." He grinned as the phone chimed again. "And here are some others to contact. It seems Lee has been busy." He messaged back and set the phone on the table. "Finally something is going our way with this project."

Connor had to agree and messaged his great-aunt. He told her not to get her hopes up but that they had two months committed to besides the one he had been talked into. Connor still needed to find someone to pose with him, but he'd figure it out. Maybe one of the guys from work would be willing to do it. It was community-minded. His great-aunt responded with a bunch of smiley faces. At least she was happy. "How are we going to set this up? I mean, if we get the guys we need? Bring them here for the sessions?"

"Some of them. I'd like to take as many as I can out in the community, like the firemen in front of the station. The chef in his restaurant. It would make for more diversity in backgrounds, because some are going to need to be done in the studio. That way the pictures will be different enough to be interesting." Connor could almost see Sterling planning his shots in his head.

"But in the studio, you're going to be able to control a lot more of the process," Connor pointed out.

Sterling nodded. "Yes, but there's only so much I can do in the studio, and I can't recreate some of the landmarks around town. The Union Fire Station is the oldest one in town, from the late nineteenth century, so it will make a great backdrop and identify them as firemen even without their uniforms. I'm pretty sure they won't be able to use them. It would probably break a number of rules."

"You're really excited about this." He took a seat at the table and dipped into some of the guac. It was really good. "Are there peppers in here?"

"Just a little for some variation. I like the smooth creaminess of the avocado and then the zip of heat to finish at the end. It isn't too hot, is it?" Sterling took a bite himself. "Sometimes the heat builds up too much."

"I like it." Connor took another bite. "Do you really think we can get enough guys?"

Sterling shrugged again. "No idea. But we're a lot closer now than we were, and Lee did say that he and Dirk knew a lot of people. Sometimes all it takes is for someone in the know to get the word out and things start to happen. You see that in movies all the time, but it's the same in real life. I haven't been back here long enough to have that kind of network."

"I never really had one," Connor admitted. "I'm not the most social of people."

"You don't say," Sterling quipped and then chuckled. "I never would have guessed that." His smile grew wider.

"No need to be mean."

"I wasn't. Not everyone is outgoing and gregarious. Some people are more comfortable working on papers or teaching others."

"I get up in front of classes every day when I'm teaching."

"Yeah, but that's an environment that you control and set the rules for. The interaction is on your terms and within your schedule. You set office hours, and when you're in class, you set the agenda and the schedule. You also control the topics of discussion. So it is interaction, but without the unpredictability of other kinds of social settings." Sterling really seemed to have his number. "There's nothing wrong with that. I had to learn to be outgoing, or else in the fashion world, I'd be chewed up and spit out within minutes. That happened in the end, but I had a successful career up until that point, and I'd like to think my work was good enough for the designers and that the models liked working with me. I also have to be outgoing in order to help draw the performance I need from the models. Sometimes they are super talented and know exactly what to do. Other times it requires more work to get the shots I need. The top photographers can work with the models they want. I wasn't at that level yet, so I worked with the models the client had chosen."

Connor leaned forward. "What happened? I know you had a great career going. I looked you up and saw a number of your images. They were impressive. And then nothing." He wondered if he had a right to ask. "If you don't want to talk about it, I'll understand."

Sterling tipped his beer to his lips and drank most of it, then set the bottle on the table beside his chair. "My ex, Alexander, is a high-fashion model. He works all over the world, and the two of us were going to take the modeling and fashion world by storm. We'd been together four years, and our careers rose steadily that entire time. I took some of his most iconic images, including the ones that landed him on the billboard in Times Square. He was forty feet tall and right there for all to see. The plan was to build on that for both of us." Sterling sat rigidly in the chair, back ramrod straight, his leg bouncing. "The offers came rolling in. Often together, though we both booked separate jobs as well. It was the way of the world. We saw each other all over the globe. If he was working in France, I'd be working in Italy, and we met in the middle in some amazing, exotic locations. It was quite a life. Until it wasn't anymore." Sterling sighed.

Connor nodded and held his tongue.

"I'm just going to say this and get it over with. To make a long story short, I found out that Alexander and I had different expectations about how we should behave when we weren't together. He figured that as long as we were apart, then he could do whatever he wanted with whoever caught his eye. I knew he was bisexual, but we had agreed to be exclusive." Sterling breathed deeply. "I got the two of us tickets to the Cannes Film Festival because both of us were going to be in France and we could attend together. Weather delayed my flight, and that evening I saw him on TV at the festival with a supermodel on his arm… and they were very chummy. The next day, I arrived, figuring he had only gone with her because I couldn't be there. But it seemed my tickets had been given to her and she and Alexander were an item. I saw red and confronted Alexander. All of it was caught on film and played all over Europe. Alexander made it seem like I was crazy, and he went after me in a huge way. The fashion world circled around him, and I found myself out in the cold." Beads of sweat broke out on his forehead. "It turned out that Alexander had been trying to figure out how to tell me that he wanted out and just used this as an excuse to make sure the cheating rat came out smelling like a rose." Sterling leaned forward. "I thought he loved me. Lord knows I rearranged my life plenty of times so I could be with him. And here he was the one who cheated, and…." Sterling finished the rest of his beer and set the bottle aside. "I need another one."

Connor had no idea what to say. He had been quiet because Sterling needed to say his piece, but he wanted to look up this Alexander and give him a piece of his mind.

Sterling trudged away, and while he was gone, Connor took a few seconds on Google to find out who the ex was. It didn't take long. The guy was stunning, with cut cheekbones and the perfect amount of scruff, piercing eyes, and long hair that fell to his shoulders in glorious waves. But there was something else—under it all, a coldness, like the guy was made a marble and what you saw was all you got. At least that was how it seemed to him. Maybe that was what he wanted to see, but looking at picture after picture, that same aloofness was always there, like his soul was missing… and maybe it was never there at all. Connor closed the app and put his phone back in his pocket as Sterling returned.

"Did you find the video?" Sterling asked as he slumped down in the chair. "I'm sure it isn't too hard to find. The internet is like an elephant. It never forgets." He twisted the top off one of his beers and tipped it to his lips.

"No. I wasn't looking for it." He sat back in the chair. "I wanted to see what your ex looked like. Those pictures weren't hard to find. Intense eyes, long, wavy, Fabio-ish blond hair."

"Yeah. You don't need to remind me," Sterling growled. "He didn't always have the hair. A designer wanted it longer, so he let it grow for six months, and damned if it didn't come in as incredibly silky as anything. After that, he let it grow longer and he fucking built a career out of that hair." He finished the beer and reached for another.

Connor put his hand on Sterling's. "You don't need that. It's only going to make you feel awful in the morning, and Alexander is still going to be there in all his vapid glory."

"Getting catty?" Sterling teased.

"You know what they say. If you can't say something nice, come sit by me." He did his best accent to mimic Olympia Dukakis in *Steel Magnolias*. It wasn't that good, but Sterling smiled. Connor counted that as a win.

"You were saying something about his vapidity?" Sterling pressed.

Connor pulled out his phone. "He has great eyes, but look. Behind them, there's nothing there. He's all pretty face, but kind of plastic." He curled his upper lip. "It makes me wonder what he was like in bed."

"Selfish," they said together, and they both laughed.

"So in the end he was no great loss in the lover department, was he?" Connor asked, grinning at the naughty glint in Sterling's eyes.

"Are you kidding? Alexander is the kind of guy who likes to take a very passive role. Sometimes I used to wonder if he'd fallen asleep during sex with the way he lay there. I used to think it was me. I really did. Maybe I wasn't exciting enough for him." Sterling shrugged. "But I loved him, and sex is only part of a relationship. I kept trying, but I guess in the end he found someone who excited him more."

Connor snorted. "Not according to this." He brought up the caption with one of Alexander's pictures. "It's from one of those awful celebrity gossip sites."

"You read those?" Sterling asked, eyes narrowing.

"No, but Google knows everything." He grinned. "Apparently Alexander got dumped by a leggy blond. Theresa something…."

"That's the woman he went to Cannes with," Sterling clarified.

"Then listen to this. 'Alexander Marquart may look amazing in front of the camera, but between the sheets he's as exciting as a three-day-old fish, only without the stink.'" Connor grinned as he met Sterling's gaze. "It seems other people also found the golden-maned boy more of a lazy lion."

That time Sterling laughed until tears ran down his cheeks. Then he buried his face in his hands. Connor thought about turning away to give Sterling his privacy, but he stood instead, then walked behind him and leaned over the chair. He slid his hands down Sterling's chest and stayed there, letting Sterling know he wasn't alone.

"I really loved him, and I thought that we'd have great careers and that he and I would be together, the ultimate power couple."

Connor tightened his hold. "Maybe that was the problem." Sterling stilled, and Connor wished he'd kept his big mouth shut.

"Excuse me?" Sterling snapped.

"Oh, relax." He wasn't going to raise his hackles. "I know you cared for Alexander, and he turned out to be a real schmuck. But listen to yourself. Maybe you were concentrating on your careers and the whole power couple image rather than just being Alexander and Sterling, two guys in love with each other. You could both have had amazing careers, but your lives needed to have more than that. What did you like to do together? What was it that was only for the two of you?"

Sterling stilled and then slowly turned in the chair. "Nothing. He was a model, and I was a photographer. We traveled in the same worlds and had a lot in common."

"Yeah. So why not be best friends and see each other when you saw each other? Skype, talk on the phone… stuff like that. Tell each other catty stories about the other models and find someone with a love of art, like yours. Or…." He scanned the yard. "Someone who loves to garden or spend time on the ocean or make things. It takes more than shared careers to make a lasting relationship."

Chapter 7

"AND YOU know this through experience?" Sterling asked, cocking his eyebrows. Connor pulled his arms away and sat back in his chair. Sterling missed the closeness immediately and wished he'd just kept his smart mouth shut.

"I've dated. I'm not a total loser," Connor protested, and Sterling knew that defensive tone. "Maybe not as much as some people."

"I bared my soul, and since you have all the answers, what makes you an expert?" he teased. "Come on. What happened? It seems we've both been through the man mill."

"I dated in college. I'm not a monk or something." Connor sighed, and Sterling recognized the hurt look all too well. "But nothing worked out. Two of the guys I dated just wanted free tutoring. Perry and I went out a few times, and he started coming to my place. We'd study together, and I'd end up helping him with his work more than I got any of my own done. But I liked him, and he was hot. Like… muscles, and the guy could make his pecs dance the rumba. I thought he liked me, but at the end of the semester, he decided he wanted someone more exciting and he was out the door… and off to his next endeavor with a better grade, and all I got out of it were long nights making up my own work."

Sterling tilted his head. "We all got taken advantage of one or twice in college. I think it's par for the course." He felt for Connor, he really did. To have accomplished everything he had at his age was impressive. He had already gotten his PhD and an assistant professorship. That was quite something and required a lot of hard work.

"More like twice, and I'm supposed to be smart. I figured after that, I'd work and get through school so I could make a living before I settled down." He sighed, and Sterling waited for the real tragedy in this story. "I met David. He was going to be a pharmacist. That requires a lot of dedication. He was funny, and he worked hard too. He also liked to spend time outdoors, so we went hiking on Saturday afternoons and played racquetball. Well, he taught me how to play. When he served, the ball bounced off the wall and hit me right between the eyes. I couldn't see straight for a few seconds, and David was right there. He made sure I was okay and helped me get the blue marks off my face. He was kind and gentle, and then he kissed me for the first time, right there on the court. Things progressed quickly after that, and we were together for four months." Connor held his breath for a second. "Then he found someone else. I suppose I should have expected it. But it still hurt." He wiped his eyes and drank from his bottle. "He left me a note when he cleared out saying that I was too serious and that he wanted someone more exciting now that he was graduating."

"Were those his exact words?" Sterling asked.

"No. Actually he said that I was a good guy but too boring, and that it was time he left school to make his way and he didn't see us as moving forward. He actually used the word boring. Apparently we were together for four of the most boring months of his life." Connor finished his beer. "You know, maybe a few more of these isn't such a bad idea." He burped and then giggled. "Okay, maybe not." He sighed and sat back. "I'm sorry about all this. This was supposed to be a celebration, and because of me, we ended up taking a ride on the old relationship train, stopping at Maudlin and Depression on our way to Drunktown."

"You're funny," Sterling said.

Someone called from outside the gate, and Sterling groaned as he checked the time. He took a few bites of the guacamole to cover his beer breath and went to greet the clients he'd forgotten about. "I'll be about an hour," he told Connor. "When I'm done, we can order some food." He hated to leave Connor in a vulnerable state like that, and he should have checked his appointment book before they came out. He only hoped Connor would still be there when he returned.

"Connor?" Sterling called once the graduate and his mother had left. They had made their appointment to see their proofs and were all set. Sterling wandered back and found Connor where he'd left him, in the same chair, leaning back, eyes closed. He wasn't sure if he was asleep or not, but he quietly gathered their bottles and placed a pizza order before grabbing two more beers and returning to the patio.

"Sorry." Connor sat up when Sterling placed the bottles on the table.

"I ordered a pizza." He checked his messages and grinned. "It seems we may have a policeman and his partner who are interested, as well as an athlete." He thumbed through the messages.

"Not Terry Baumgartner?" Connor asked. "Is he interested? Aunt Lucille is going to flip. He's our local Olympian and won swimming gold in London, I think." Connor whistled as Sterling read the rest of the message, nodding.

"I had no idea." Of course he had been on the other side of the world at that point, working in Asia during those games on a campaign for a designer he couldn't remember. "Then that's awesome. I need to contact both of them and firm things up. Lee sent email addresses and phone numbers. But it's possible that we have four months filled now."

"Good. Then we have more to celebrate, and I promise not to bring down the mood."

"The pizza should get here in about half an hour." Sterling opened the bottles and handed one to Connor. "To a successful calendar." They clinked bottles and toasted as Sterling's phone rang. Connor's did as well, and he wandered off so they each had some privacy.

"Sterling Photography," he answered, not recognizing the number.

"Hello," a tentative male voice began. "This is Terry Baumgartner, and I was speaking with Lee Stockton about the garden club calendar. He gave me your number."

"How can I help you?" Sterling was inordinately pleased to be talking to him. He had photographed famous people before, but never an Olympian, and he was excited about the chance.

"Well, I know I told Lee that I'd do the calendar, but I may have been a little hasty." He paused again. "See… I'd like to do it, but he said it was couples, and I'd only do it with my husband, Red. But he isn't so sure, and I don't want him to be uncomfortable."

Sterling's stomach was already falling. He should have known this was too good to be true and that things were coming together too easily all of a sudden. "What can I do to help? The calendar is to aid the garden club and the community."

"We're both on board with that. The issue is that… well…. Red was in an accident when he was younger, and it left scars on his face. He's a little sensitive about them. I think he's perfect, but if it bothers him, then…."

"If the two of you want to appear together, then we'll photograph you in the studio where I can control the light and shadow to minimize any scarring in the pictures."

"He has a beard, and it covers many of them, but there are some that cross his cheeks," Terry explained gently. "I just don't want him to see the pictures and be disappointed."

"That's not a problem at all. You can tell Red that with a little lighting control and some shading, his scars will fade to the background." That was something Sterling was quite skilled with. "Using light to create the image I want is something I'm amazing at. Please tell him not to worry. After the photo session, the three of us can choose the photo for the calendar. That way he'll be able to have a say in what we use."

Terry sighed. "That's awesome. I think Red is amazing and totally beautiful." The love in his voice was unmistakable. "He doesn't let me take many pictures of him, so I'd love to have him do this with me." He sounded happy now.

"Tell Red he has nothing to worry about," Sterling said, and Terry happily agreed and ended the call.

Sterling set down his phone, breathing a sigh of relief. He had just handled that issue in a huge way. Now he simply had to keep his head above water and keep the people they had on board happy, while figuring out how they were going to get others.

His phone dinged with a message. It was from Terry to say that Red had agreed and everything was good. Sterling answered, and since Connor was still on the phone, Sterling made a call to some of the people Lee had recommended and secured another couple. That was five months covered, with a sixth for the one that would include Connor. They were halfway there, and hopefully the momentum would continue.

Connor returned with a grin. "Aunt Lucille is really pleased. She gave me another number, and I got us one more month. This one is a university librarian." He grinned. "So that makes five for sure."

"Six, and the one I confirmed works construction." He smiled. "You know, if we got a leather daddy and a sailor, we could have the Village People."

Connor chuckled, all smiles. "This is really coming together."

"Yup, and with you for month seven, we're over halfway there." Without thinking, Sterling pulled Connor into a hug and held him there. He felt so good against him, and when Connor lifted his head, their gazes met, and Sterling closed the distance between them. The heat that washed off him was delicious, his scent intoxicating, drawing him nearer. A soft moan from deep in Connor's throat told him this was okay, maybe more than that. Connor was firm in his arms, all muscle, hard and angular, with banked power that made Sterling want to explore the depths of it. He parted his legs, and Sterling slid a knee between them, bringing them more firmly together, their bodies melding, the warmth radiating off both of them creating a bubble of perfection that Sterling wished would go on forever.

Sterling drew his face closer to Connor's, sliding his fingers through his bunny-soft hair. Damn, that was intoxicating and so different from the rest of him. He paused for only a second, giving Connor a chance to pull back before moving the final distance, their lips touching.

That first taste of spicy sweetness from their snack earlier gave him only a bare hint of the man underneath. As he deepened the kiss, the flavor of Connor, just as rich and full as he could have imagined, came forward, threatening to roll right over Sterling, nearly knocking him off his feet.

Connor slipped his arms around Sterling's neck, holding him as he responded, giving as good as he got. This was a new experience for Sterling, and it turned him on no end. God, he had no idea what he'd been missing all those years. He pulled back, gazing deep into Connor's cobalt blue eyes, flecked with purple that grew deeper the longer he held that intense gaze. Connor blinked but didn't make any move to pull back.

"Connor… damn…." He wondered if Connor felt it too. Sterling didn't want to let him go. Having Connor in his arms felt so right. He leaned forward and captured Connor's lips once more. Connor shook in his arms, vibrating as he held him. This time it was Connor who pulled back, stepping away. Sterling refused to break their gaze, and only a sharp rap on the gate pulled him out of the passion haze that had engulfed him.

Sterling swore under his breath as he pulled away, turned toward the gate, and strode over to get the pizza. He paid for it and gave the delivery guy a generous tip before carrying the large pizza back to the table. Sterling wasn't really hungry for anything other than another taste of Connor's lips and the way he felt in his arms.

Connor sat in the chair he had earlier, knee bouncing slightly. As Sterling set down the pizza, Connor got up with a wild look in his eyes.

Sterling wondered if he was going to bolt out of the yard like a scared rabbit. "Come and have something to eat." He opened the box and pulled out a slice, which he passed to Connor.

"I wasn't expecting that," Connor said as he absently took the slice, holding without eating it. "This was supposed to be a project to help my great-aunt. Nothing more than that. Instead it's…." His eyes widened. "Hell, I don't know what this is or what you want."

"You think I'm any surer of anything than you are?" Sterling got a slice for himself, sat down, and took a bite. He ate half the slice before drinking some of his beer. "And as for what I want… I don't know either. My track record in that department is an ex who turned out to be a lying snake who sold me up the river to save his own skin."

"I'd never do something like that," Connor said firmly. "I don't believe in playing games or using people. I have integrity and…." He paused and finally took a small bite, then swallowed before continuing. "How do I know that you… that I… that my judgment in this particular area isn't just complete shit? I'm an academic. I love things I can research and prove, where I can wrestle with ideas and come up with new conclusions."

Sterling smiled and stood, placing the remainder of his slice of pizza on the lid of the box and wiping his fingers on a napkin. Then he stalked over to Connor. "This isn't something you get to control. It isn't researchable, and if you try, you'll get different results every single time." He put his hands on the arms of Connor's chair. "And as for wrestling, well, I'm sure we can accommodate that for you… though the kind that this involves is very different from your usual kind." He smirked and waited for Connor's reaction. "Now as for your judgment being shit, well, that remains to be seen. Mine isn't the greatest in the area of the heart either. However, I will say that what's going on isn't in your imagination. I felt it too. It left me weak in the knees and standing tall in other places."

The tiny scoff from Connor's throat was more than enough proof that Connor understood what he was saying. "Did anyone ever tell you that you have a one-track mind?"

"A dirty mind is a terrible thing to waste," Sterling countered, and Connor chuckled. "Seriously, if something is good, then maybe it's best not to question it too closely. I know how you feel because I'm in the exact same place."

Connor nodded. "Maybe you're right. Lord knows there are things that when studied too closely lose their luster and all we see is the tarnish." Connor then laughed. "God. Now I sound like one of those old fools I work with sometimes who think because they've taught the same theories and facts for fifty years that they're still valid, even when they were disproven decades earlier." He left Sterling wondering what he was talking about, but it didn't really matter. "I guess I didn't expect that a kiss could be like that. I certainly don't have anything in my past to compare it with."

"I don't either." Sterling pushed back and grabbed his slice of pizza, taking another bite before sitting back in his chair. He wasn't sure what to talk about, so he sat quietly and found it was perfectly comfortable. There didn't seem to be a need to fill the quiet with endless talking. Alexander always needed sound, and any quiet he felt he had to fill somehow. Gossip, suppositions, and theories with no basis in fact had all flowed out of him like a fountain of useless prattle. So many times Sterling had stopped himself from telling him to just be quiet.

"Once we have everyone, how long do you think it will take to photograph?" Connor asked.

"Since we're doing couples, I would think a couple hours for each pair spread over a week to ten days. That way there will be time to adjust to schedules and bring people back if necessary. It's also going to be a little different from just portraiture. This project is sort of a hybrid between what I do now and what I used to do, because we want active images and ones that tell a cohesive story. That's going to be the hard part." He grabbed the pizza box and offered Connor another slice before taking one himself. "I mean, we can have guys just stand there together, giving the viewer flowers. Or we can make the images say something, make them evocative. I think some of the images are going to be giving the viewer flowers, while others will be the guys giving each other flowers. It depends." He hadn't quite worked that out yet. "Some of this will depend on the guys and what works between them." A lot of planning and work would have to go into this before anyone set foot in the studio or at the locations around town.

"I can see that." He bit into the pizza. "How did you know I liked meat lovers?"

Sterling snickered. "We're gay men. Of course we love meat lovers. What else is there?"

Connor groaned and took a big bite. "Do you have another appointment this evening?"

"No. Thank goodness. The last couple of days have seen the parents from hell. The kids are often really great, but their parents are enough to make me want to strangle them. Each parent sees their little boy or girl as handsome and perfect, as a parent should. But then they somehow expect me to make little Johnny or Lisa into Zac Efron and Olivia Rodrigo… or whoever the current in-vogue glamorous person is this week. I make their kids look their best, but they want fantasies, and it's so frustrating, especially for the kids, because they can't measure up." Sterling hated those appointments. They weren't so bad when the kids weren't there, but when that was going on in front of them, Sterling wanted to smack the parents. "Thankfully the graduation appointments are for next year, so I'm only getting the early birds right now. In the fall, that will start again in earnest. I have some family portraits on my books and a few other things, but I'll have a slower time for a few months until next year's seniors start booking appointments in a huge way." He was relieved for that. "This year it has been busy, busy, and then yesterday it seemed like my schedule completely opened up."

"That's good that you'll have time for the garden club project."

"It couldn't come at a better time. I have some weddings that I'm booked to photograph in the next few months, but that isn't the mainstay of my business. Basically, that sort of thing I leave to people who do that almost exclusively. That's an art in itself. But I have a few friends of the family who have requested that I photograph their weddings, so I agreed."

"So no appointments on Saturday?" Connor asked.

"No. This weekend my schedule is empty. I was going to try to get a bunch of things done that I've been putting off, and then I thought I would take it easy. We still need to get a few more people to agree to the calendar, and I was going to follow up any more leads we have before putting together a schedule. The thing is, if we're going to get the most bang out of this project, we should have the pictures taken and the photos laid out and everything off to the printer by the end of next month. That way they can get the calendars done in August and the club can start selling in September and through the end of the year. That will give them enough time to get the most out of it. So I'm hoping to schedule the sessions for the end of June, early July." The time frame was tight, but it was doable as long as they secured the last people they needed quickly.

But Sterling was starting to fear that this project was going to be over fast, and then he figured, given Connor's fears and Sterling's luck with guys, that Connor would disappear from his life… and he was going to miss him when he did.

Chapter 8

THE CALENDAR project raced ahead. Between Connor, Sterling, and the guys who had agreed to do the calendar, they had filled all of the slots. The only one open was Connor's counterpart. He had approached a few people he knew, but they had all backed away. None of them had said so, but he figured they didn't want to be involved with a gay calendar. It was their loss as far as Connor was concerned. He and Sterling had developed a fantastic plan and vision for the images, which would feature a number of locations throughout town.

"How is the scheduling coming?" Connor asked as he perused the sketches Sterling had done for each of the pages.

"Pretty well. I only have two more to work through, and one of them is yours." He continued going through his notes. "There is one thing we need to figure out, and that's the flowers. They need to appear in every image, and I think they should be different based on the guys, but I'm not coming up with anything."

"If you ask me, I think you should base the flowers on the complementary color to the background or to the guys. Just let them flow rather than forcing it. Also, I think we need to get the garden club involved. I want to contact Aunt Lucille and have the club members provide flowers from their gardens. That way we can put in the caption for each month who the models are and who provided the flowers, and the ladies get their own recognition."

Sterling pushed his notebook aside, grinning. "That's awesome. There can be bouquets of different flowers and colors, and we can use them as needed. Not fancy roses or florist flowers, just ones from local gardens. It's perfect. I've been wondering how we could get the ladies themselves involved, and that's exactly it." He jumped up, and before Connor realized it, Sterling had kissed him and sat back down.

There hadn't been any more of those intense, knee-buckling kisses since the one in Sterling's backyard, but Connor realized that when they were together, Sterling touched him—lightly, gently, but he touched him—a lot. The touches weren't threatening or intense, they were just there, and Connor looked forward to them.

"I'll call Aunt Lucille tomorrow and have her get in touch with the club. What I think they should do is make the bouquets themselves. Get the ladies to volunteer. That way the flowers in each picture belong to only one of the ladies, rather than a mix that everyone brought. Yes, we should ask them to use different kinds of flowers and to include some that are unique to the area. I'm sure the ladies have some interesting things in their gardens. For Christmas we'll want something holiday-themed, or at least holiday colors."

"Perfect," Sterling said as he sat back down at the table with his sketches.

"What are you trying to do?" Connor asked, leaning over his back.

"Figure out how this thing is going to make sense. I mean, the guys picked their months, so that's rather random… and we'll have the flowers covered once your great-aunt does her magic. I'm trying to think of how the calendar will flow. But…."

Connor patted Sterling's shoulder. "I think you're trying to find something that isn't there yet. You'll know once you've seen the images."

"But…." He continued working with the sketches, and Connor saw him searching. It was frustrating.

"Some things are outside our control. Lee and Dirk were promised July because it's their anniversary. Billy and Darryl wanted May. Those are set, as are some of the others, like me for April. So that's pretty much it. We have some that can float because they didn't have a month preference." He patted Sterling's firm shoulders gently. "Don't struggle with what can't be changed. Maybe once we have the images, we can move some around if they truly don't work."

Sterling sat back. "I know you're right. I just want the calendar to be good, and…."

Connor came around to stand where Sterling could see him. "This is going to be great. I know it. The thing we need to do now is review the schedule for photography. How many shoots are outside?"

"Six. Those we have to let float a little due to the weather and light, so I have the studio schedule set and confirmed. The others have schedules as well, with alternate dates and times that they're available."

"So when do you start?"

"Terry and Red will be here tomorrow morning at ten." There was an excitement in him that built by the second. "I'll need to set up the studio."

"Need some help?" Connor asked, and Sterling slid his hands up his arms, leaving behind a trail of tingles that drove Connor a little crazy. He closed his eyes as Sterling's hands continued upward to his shoulders, then drew him closer. Connor went willingly until their lips crashed together in a wave of desire. He crushed Sterling back into the chair, leaning over him, pressing him against the back of the chair, devouring his lips like they were his alone.

Connor's heart beat staccato in his ears, and he grew hot. Damn, he wanted this man. He straddled Sterling's his legs. He wanted to climb him.

The doorbell chimed, and Connor cursed someone's amazing timing. He backed away and stood straight up. "You better get that. I'll meet you in the studio when you're ready." Connor needed to get out of here so he could breathe and think a few minutes. He turned and went out through the back of the house and into the studio, then turned on the lights in the lobby area and sat in one of the chairs.

It was becoming harder and harder to resist Sterling, and he was beginning to wonder why he was bothering. Sure, he had bad experiences in college. Didn't almost everyone? Guys were self-centered jerks all over the world, and if everyone who crossed paths with one never dated again, then the human race would die out, because Lord knows many women would never have children.

"It was just a delivery," Sterling said as he set a box on the counter. "Come on." He led the way back into the studio, and Connor followed. "Terry is a swimmer, but I don't want to use a water background."

"What about something blue?" Connor asked.

"Red and Terry are going to provide some unique challenges." Sterling set up the lights and had Connor stand in the center of the white backdrop that went down the entire wall and onto the floor. Then he grabbed his camera and snapped a few images, checking the results before changing the angles. "I can add color to the lights that will change the overarching color, but it's going to depend on what works."

He stood back and took a few more pictures, and Connor stood with his hands at his side. "Do something. Have fun with it," Sterling told him.

Connor smiled and turned to the side. "If I'd known I was going to end up in front of the camera, I would have worn my best kilt."

"I think you look stunning just like that." Sterling continued snapping pictures, the lights brightening and then lowering with each shot. "Turn to the side, but look at me… yes… that's it. Lift your head a little. Don't look at the camera, but beyond it. Looking at the camera makes it the focus of the picture. Watching something behind gives the image depth and makes it seem like it's part of a story."

Connor did as he asked, and Sterling kept taking pictures. He simply moved and changed position. Sterling snapped image after image before putting down the camera. Then he turned one of the monitors and flipped through the pictures so Connor could see them. "Just get comfortable with the camera. Don't worry about where it is or what it sees. That's my job. Yours is to move and relax." He showed him some of the first pictures, and even Connor could see he looked like he was about to jump out of his skin. As the pictures went on, he smiled more and his eyes had fewer little lines. "See what I mean?" Sterling came over and popped open the top buttons on Connor's shirt. "Just relax and let yourself shine through. Don't try to hide behind an attitude or anything else." He stepped back, and Connor stared at Sterling, watching him. The camera clicked, and the lights flashed again and again. "Would you take off the shirt?" Sterling asked, and Connor popped the last buttons, parted the fabric, took it off, and draped it over a stool. He was a little self-conscious, but this was only Sterling, and he had said to try to relax. So Connor took a deep breath and let go of his inhibitions as best he could, surprised at how the camera changed things.

Sterling adjusted the lights, softening them, and then picked up the camera again.

"Is this okay?"

"You look amazing," Sterling whispered and continued snapping as Connor moved slowly, turning his body but keeping his gaze to Sterling. "Now look to the side. There's a calendar of puppies on the wall. Watch that…. Perfect…. The cute puppies always get that effect."

Connor smiled and then laughed a little, and Sterling kept taking pictures.

"Am I doing this right?" Connor asked. This was new territory for him.

Sterling lowered his camera and swallowed audibly. "You look absolutely edible." He stared at Connor for a few seconds and then slowly lifted the camera, moving closer and closer, snapping images the entire way. "Now turn gradually toward me."

Connor did as he asked, and Sterling drew away and then close once again. The air in the studio was warm and a little moist. Sweat beaded on his chest. Connor wondered how much longer Sterling was going to keep this up. Finally he set down the camera and walked over to Connor. Without another word, Sterling drew Connor to him. There wasn't an ounce of hesitation in his kiss. A surge of energy roared through Connor like a train, and Sterling drew him nearer, holding him tightly.

"Do you kiss a lot of your models?" Connor teased.

Sterling shook his head. "Only you. Unless you count my ex, which I certainly don't." He kissed him again, and Connor's legs felt weak. Sterling must have felt it too, because he lowered him to the mat, straddling his legs as he cradled Connor's head and shoulders in his arms, keeping him from going all the way to the floor. "I want you, Connor," he whispered.

"Sterling, I...."

He didn't press for more, which surprised Connor. Their breath came in pants, and Sterling's eyes were as dark and deep as the ocean. The room smelled of desire, sharp and musky. Connor knew it was both of them, and denying that he wanted Sterling was impossible. Still, he hesitated, and Sterling slowly released his hold and leaned back. He nudged a stool at the edge of the mat, and it fell to the floor with a bang that made Connor jump.

"God, I'm as nervous as a sheep in a whorehouse." Connor wondered where that reference had come from, and Sterling chuckled as he righted the stool. "Maybe you and I should take our time. See where this goes."

Sterling extended his hand, and Connor got to his feet. "I'd like that." Connor reached for his shirt, but Sterling stilled him. "I also like you just like that."

"Sterling...." His self-consciousness took over under Sterling's heated gaze. He wasn't used to people being so blatant about their attraction to him. Connor didn't see himself as anything special. He was basically a geek who taught history. He loved what he did, and he was passionate about his subject, but he wasn't exciting. Not like Sterling, who had been all over the world. Connor hadn't even actually seen what was left of many of the places he taught about. Studying was something, at least in his experience, that was done largely at a distance, and that was fine with him. He seemed to do better with people at a distance too. At least his past experience led in that direction.

"It's how I felt when saw you. Like some god coming in from outdoors bringing flowers. Don't forget that you were the one who inspired this whole mess." He grinned, and Connor groaned softly, rolling his eyes.

"So I'm responsible for you getting dragged into this project and talking me into standing in front of the camera." He still wasn't sure how he felt about that, but he had committed to it, and he wasn't going to back down. Sterling continued watching him, and Connor reached for his shirt, put it on, and fastened the buttons. There was something about the way that Sterling watched him, his gaze becoming more intense. Part of him liked being the center of Sterling's attention, and yet that naysaying voice in the back of his head kept reminding him that Sterling dealt with models all the time. People who were perfect and paid to look perfect. What if Sterling looked long enough that he found the flaws? What would he think then? Connor knew he wasn't perfect. Quite far from it, as a matter of fact. He turned away so Sterling couldn't see his expression and the worry that he knew had to be written all over his features.

Connor finished buttoning his shirt as he realized that while he wasn't perfect like the models Sterling had photographed, he wanted to be. Or at least he wanted to be for Sterling—he wanted Sterling to notice him. He liked that Sterling wanted to look at him. But he was scared of the fact that one day, Sterling would stop looking and turn his attention to someone else. That always seemed to happen before.

"I need to call Aunt Lucille and arrange for us to have flowers for tomorrow." Connor grabbed his phone, glad to have something to do, and pressed her contact. He wandered away, happy to put some distance between them, because the damned hamster wheel his mind seemed to have climbed on needed to stop spinning.

"Hello, sweetheart," Aunt Lucille said as she answered. "What do you have for me?"

"We have our first photo session tomorrow, and we need some flowers."

"We have set aside a small budget for the project, and I thought we could buy the flowers you need."

Connor explained his and Sterling's idea. "We'd give credit in the photo notes on the calendar for each member that provides the flowers. That way the ladies could have a month too. Can you get them to volunteer to cut some flowers for us? They'll need to be fresh."

"Love that idea. There is a lot in bloom right now, so it shouldn't be difficult. I'll make some calls."

"Good. But we need the first one for tomorrow."

"What colors?" Aunt Lucille asked.

Connor had no idea what to tell her. He turned to Sterling and relayed the question.

"We don't know," Connor said and continued watching Sterling. "Why don't we get enough flowers in two or three colors so we can mix and match them as we go?"

"The more intense the color, the better. That way the flowers won't get lost in the background," Sterling said, and Connor relayed the message.

"I have plenty blooming right now, so stop over and pick what you think you'll need." She spoke quickly. "This is so exciting. I can't wait to tell the ladies at our meeting tomorrow that things are moving ahead." The hesitation in her voice had Connor worrying.

"What's going on? The club *is* on board with this, right?" He suddenly remembered Judy and her reaction to the whole idea. It had never occurred to him that Aunt Lucille might be going out on a limb to make this happen.

"There are some people who will never accept anything new. They want everything to stay the same, and it's that thinking that got us in this position. Well, that and Helen deciding to run off with the treasury. That damned witch with a capital B. Oops...." Connor could see her putting her hand over her mouth. Aunt Lucille was passionate, and you definitely didn't want to get on her bad side.

"Okay. I'll be over first thing in the morning to pick the flowers."

"Come early and I'll make cinnamon rolls." That was a deal. Aunt Lucille's baking was orgasmic, and her cinnamon rolls the equivalent of shooting to the moon. "And I want to talk to you." He should have known—her cinnamon rolls always came with a price. "I understand that you and Sterling have been spending a lot of time together." There was a definite smile in her voice before she cleared her throat. "I know you haven't had much luck with men, so when you come over tomorrow, you and I need to—"

"No, we don't," Connor cut in. "We are not going to talk about that. No way. I can figure out things on my own, especially those kinds of things." He lowered his voice and turned away. "I'm an adult, and I know how things work. It's a little late for the birds and the bees, anyway."

Aunt Lucille scoffed. "Honey, who's talking birds and bees? I'm talking about how to use the damned honey to keep the birds, bears, otters, hunks, or whatever your type is happy and coming back for more." Now she was just being wicked, and Connor tried to keep from coughing up a lung. "I know I never married, but that doesn't mean I don't know what it takes to attract or keep a man. For me, men were like fishing: catch them, reel them in for a little excitement, and then throw them back. Sometimes I caught the same fish twice and I got to see how he grew." She cackled like a loon, and Connor wished the floor would open up and swallow him whole. While Sterling couldn't hear what was being said, Connor's cheeks burned with the intensity of a thousand suns, and there was no way Sterling didn't have an idea of what they were talking about. "You need to make sure your fishing pole is ready and that you have the right bait so you can reel him in and then decide if he's a keeper."

"Oh my God." He peeked at Sterling, who was doing his best not to look like he was listening to their conversation. "Look, if I decide to go fishing, my pole is just fine, and I have plenty of bait, it seems. I don't think you need to worry at all about that. Now, I'll be over tomorrow, and we can have breakfast and I'll pick some flowers. You once told me that the three subjects that are always safe in polite company are the weather, gardening, and your health, so let's stick with those, okay?" He hoped she got the idea that he wasn't the least bit interested in talking to her about his love life.

"Fine, I'll see you then." She hung up, and Connor knew she'd given up way too easily and that this wasn't over.

"What?" Sterling asked, and Connor filled him in—about the garden club part, not the part about his love life. "Your great-aunt will be fine, and she's more than a match for anyone. You know that." Sterling half smiled. "Is she going to get us flowers?"

"Yes. I'll pick some from her garden for tomorrow's shoot. Her garden club meeting is tomorrow afternoon, so she's going to recruit the ladies then. Aunt Lucille said that some of them were resistant."

Sterling came closer. "This is a club, so something like this would need to be voted on. It obviously had enough support to pass the group, so I wouldn't worry too much. There are always people in any group who dissent. It's why I hate group decisions. They go around and around most of the time and get nowhere. If Lucille got approval, then trust her." Connor knew Sterling was right, but he still worried. "What was all that talk about poles?"

Connor tried like hell not to blush again. "Aunt Lucille is a big fan of fishing." He turned away, needing to change the subject. "I thought for tomorrow, I'd try to get spring colors—yellow, some white, and a few purples. Those should work with most other colors, and the irises will be really showy."

"I like that. The more intense the better, except the purples. Lighter colors work better. Sometimes if purples are really intense, they blend into black on film and you lose the color." Sterling went back to looking at the pictures and adjusting the lights. "Will you stand in the center again for me?" He stepped back, looking at the backdrop intensely. Connor stepped on and stood still. Sterling looked through the camera and took a few pictures. "I think that's it. I'm looking for a light that will accentuate certain shadows, and I think I have it."

Connor stepped out of the photographic area. "I can drop off the flowers in the morning. Do you want me to stay for the session, or would you be more comfortable without me here?" He was interested in watching Sterling work and hoped he didn't mind him staying, but he wasn't going to push in where he wasn't needed. The last thing he wanted was to be a problem.

"Please stay. I was hoping you'd act as my assistant. There will be things I'm going to need, and it will slow the session down if I have to stop all the time. If you can help me, that would be wonderful." Sterling shut down the lights, the room growing darker with only the light from the small windows to see by.

"I'll be happy to." Connor headed to the back door and was about to pull it open when Sterling tapped him on the shoulder. Connor turned around, and Sterling pushed him against the door with a kiss that stole Connor's breath and his ability to think. The panels in the door pressed to his back, and he wound his arms around Sterling in order to stay upright. Sterling drew him tighter, deepening the pressure on his lips. When Connor opened his mouth slightly, Sterling slipped his tongue inside, tasting him. Connor groaned softly, and Sterling echoed it right back, the energy between them building until Connor didn't know what end was up. "What was that for?" he whispered when Sterling backed away, their kiss coming to an end.

"I wanted to give you something to think about while you were alone in your bed tonight." Sterling smiled and guided him away from the door. He pulled it open, and Connor stepped outside. "I'll see you in the morning. You have a nice visit with your great-aunt, and we'll figure out which flowers to use when you get here."

Connor was a little surprised. "You really want me to go after that?"

Sterling shook his head, his eyes nearly as dark as night. "I don't want you to go at all, but I'm not going to rush things." He stepped outside behind him. "Drive carefully, and I'll see you tomorrow."

Sterling stood in the doorway as Connor slowly walked down the path and out to his car, half hoping that Sterling would hurry up behind him, take him by the hand, and lead him back inside. Instead, he went home alone, wondering why he didn't just speak up.

"I KNOW I'M embarrassing you, but…," Aunt Lucille pressed as she placed a plate of bacon, eggs, and a cinnamon roll in front of him. How much did she expect him to eat?

Connor just thanked her and took small bites. Under normal circumstances he'd save the roll until last, but the frosting was gooey, so he dug right in.

"How about you stop doing that, then, and leave me alone?" He took another bite and wished he could fill her plate and get her to eat. That way she couldn't talk. But Aunt Lucille settled in with a cup of coffee and an expression that would instill fear in a medieval executioner. "I can handle my own love life." He reached over and took her hand. "I know you mean well, but I have to find my own way in this."

Aunt Lucille shook her head. "No, you don't. I know the guys you dated in college. They were all losers. I knew that as soon as you brought them to visit. They were self-centered assholes. Sterling is not an asshole. In fact, he's been on the same end of the stick as you were."

Connor nodded. "How do you know?"

Aunt Lucille chuckled and then sipped her coffee. "The internet. How else? There were plenty of stories about him and his then-to-be husband,

and there were plenty of articles and posts about their relationship and the breakup. Most took Alexander's side, but a few seemed to include information that Alexander wasn't as pure as the driven snow. Now he's working all over the world, and Sterling is here. It doesn't take much to realize that Sterling was hosed. Not that it changes what most people think. But Sterling knows what you went through."

"I know he does. He told me all about it." Connor finished his roll with its aromatic goodness and gooey sweetness. He wanted another, but he ate the eggs and bacon instead before sitting back in his seat. "I'm going to be fine. I like Sterling, I really do. But you said it yourself. Alexander travels all over the world, and Sterling used to, and once the world forgives him, the offers will come back, I know it. And then if I let myself go for what I want so badly, I'll be the one standing on the outside once again when I'm not exciting enough for him. I can't compete with designers, models, weeks in Paris, Rome, Tokyo, and who knows where."

"Connor—" Aunt Lucille began, but he cut her off.

"Like I said, I have to do this my way. I know you want me to be happy, and you think I'm lonely, but if something is meant to happen, it will in its own time." He had to make her understand. "Please promise me that you won't interfere."

"Me?" Aunt Lucille narrowed her eyes. "Me? I never interfere in your life. You're free to make your own decisions, you know that. I may give advice—fantastic advice if I say so myself—but you are free to take what I say or reject it… at your peril." She got up and tottered to refill her mug, then returned to her chair. "Finish your breakfast and then go on out and pick some of the irises."

"Aunt Lucille," he said softly. There was nothing he could say that would make her change her mind about anything. She was up to something, and Connor knew it was a lot easier to get out of her way and not fight her.

"Don't give me that tone. I'm an old lady, and there are few things in this world that give me more pleasure than seeing you happy. And one of my wishes is to be there when you get married. I learned a long time ago that there isn't going to be a white wedding dress involved, unless that's *your* thing…." She wagged her eyebrows, and Connor about did a spit take with his coffee. "I didn't think so. I do love that RuPaul, though." Oh God. The thought of his great-aunt and drag queens was just too much. "Don't make that pooh-pooh face. I'm going to be thrilled when you marry another man, and I intend to be around to see it." She drank some more coffee and then pushed the mug away. "Decaf. I hate this shit, but the damned doctor says if I want coffee, I gotta drink this stuff for my heart. I swear it would do my heart a hell of a lot of good to have a real Starbucks mocha cappuccino again."

Connor grinned. "Fine. I'll bring you Starbucks if you promise not to interfere in my love life anymore." He stood after checking the time, not expecting her to answer. "I'm going to get the flowers, and then I have to get going." He leaned over to kiss her cheek and then hurried outside.

Aunt Lucille's garden was flourishing, and her iris bed was a riot of color. He cut a dozen iris stems, as well as some roses and peonies, then got one of the old vases she kept in the garage, placed the stems in it with wet paper towels, and popped his head inside to let his great-aunt know he was leaving before hurrying to the studio.

"ARE THEY here?" Connor asked as he strode inside, placing the vase on Sterling's desk. "Do you think these will work?"

"Red and Terry called and will be here in ten minutes." Aunt Lucille and Sterling's father had both asked to watch, but fortunately he and Sterling had put that notion to bed. Sterling bent over the vase, inhaling. "They're beautiful, and I think they'll be perfect. I have everything set up, and the lights will need some minor adjustment, but I think the effect will work." He seemed nervous, his shoulders tight, and Connor put his arms around his waist, leaning against his back. It felt so right that he almost pulled away, remembering his own admonishment to his great-aunt. Sterling was like a magnet whose pull he couldn't seem to resist, and yet he knew he needed to… somehow.

He jumped back at a knock, and then two men entered. He recognized Terry from his pictures, news coverage, and advertisements in magazines and on TV. "Morning! I'm Terry, and this is Red."

Connor was a little surprised at the scars across Red's cheeks. They were older and faded, but still noticeable, and he tried not to react. Terry threaded his arm around Red's and smiled up at him adoringly.

"Welcome," Sterling said as he shook hands with both of them. "I'm Sterling, and this is Connor." He motioned toward the backdrop.

"I have things set up, and I thought we'd start with a few pictures to get you comfortable in front of the camera. Then you can change clothes and we'll shoot the two of you together, shirtless if that works." Sterling was professional and all business. He got the men standing together and took a few test pictures.

Red and Terry seemed to almost circle one another, their movements like they were getting their pictures taken on a cruise ship, stiff and formal. "Relax," Connor said gently. "You two love each other, so let that show." He probably should have stayed quiet, but they continued, and things seemed better.

Sterling showed them the pictures he'd taken so far on a nearby monitor, and Terry brushed his hand over Red's cheek. "I told you they would be beautiful."

"You can't see the scars at all." Red touched his own face and smiled. Then the two of them left to change clothes. They returned in Speedos, with Red in navy blue and Terry in pink. They were stunning men, Terry all sleek, lithe muscle, and Red big and physically impressive, with a chest that could have modeled for a statue of a sexy, robust Zeus or Poseidon. The contrast was quite striking.

"Pink?" Connor asked.

"It's his lucky color. Terry always swims in pink," Red said.

"I brought the medals in case you wanted to use them," Terry offered.

Sterling had them step onto the background and got them into position, handing Terry the bouquet of flowers. As soon as he started snapping pictures, the mood of the room filled with tension that only grew. Terry and Red weren't comfortable, and it showed in the way they moved. Sterling knew it and tried a number of things to shift the energy, but nothing seemed to help.

"Let's take a few minutes," Sterling said, offering both guys water. "I don't get it."

"They aren't models, and this isn't a portrait session either. It's a combination, and they don't know what you want," Connor said softly.

"I don't know either."

Connor rolled his eyes. "I do. This should be sexy, caring, and all about the flowers. They're a gift of love. Remember?" He drew closer. "Those two have enough heat to spontaneously combust, so don't treat them as models. Try treating them as lovers and stoke those fires." He grinned, and Sterling shook his head.

"I should have thought of that."

"You would have." Connor stood a little taller. "But you were trying to do your job, and I was watching everything."

Terry and Red returned, and this time Sterling seemed more relaxed. He picked out a mixture of pale purple, yellow, and white irises and handed the bouquet to Red. "I think we're going to try something different this time. It's just the two of you, so stand slightly to the side instead of straight on, look at each other, forget about the camera and what I'm doing. Just spend some time with each other."

"Should I hand Terry the flowers?" Red asked, looking at Terry with so much love that Connor could almost feel it filling the room. He was afraid to breathe in case he broke the spell.

Sterling snapped image after image. "That's wonderful." Connor moved slightly so he could see the images as they flashed on the screen off to the side. They were stunning. When Sterling glanced over, they shared a smile, a tingle going up Connor's spine. Sterling returned his attention to the guys. "Now, pretend that someone both of you love has just come in and the flowers are for them."

Terry and Red adjusted their hands slightly, moving the flowers forward, and Sterling snapped the perfect image. The two lovers sharing their flowers with the viewer. It took Connor's breath away.

"That's it. Now bring your bellies in, firm and straight. Hold it right there." Sterling snapped an even better image and then another. The expressions were perfect, and Connor leaned closer to the screen without thinking about it. Image after amazing image crossed the screen, and then Sterling paused and put down the camera. "Guys, I think that's it."

Sweat covered Sterling's forehead, and he was smiling brightly. "Do you want to see?" He turned the screen and flipped through the images on his camera. "You two look amazing."

"And one of those is going to be on the calendar?" Red asked.

"Stop," Connor said. "I think that one right there—it's perfect. The two of you have an incredible connection, and yet look at Terry's eyes, the way they're looking just slightly forward, beckoning the viewer closer. It's almost like we're included in the picture. That's exactly the kind of thing we want."

"But my face," Red said softly. "I don't want to scare anyone."

Sterling sighed. "Don't worry." A bit of light accentuated instead of minimized one of the scars. "I can use Photoshop to smooth that out a little and make it recede. Don't worry."

"I love it just as it is," Terry told Red. "It's perfect, and you look so strong, like you've been to battle. Remember, the scars are war wounds. We all have them. Just some are on the outside." Terry leaned closer to Red, and Connor tugged Sterling away and back. Their two models needed a few minutes, and the best thing they could do was give them some privacy.

"What is this for?" Sterling asked.

Connor raised hie eyebrows. "I know you're used to working with models, but what Terry and Red just did is intimate—private. That they let you and me in was something pretty special, but they need a few minutes, so we have to give it to them." He stepped back and hoped Sterling would understand. Sterling found himself some things to do, and Connor wandered off to the lobby area, where he sat in the chair until he heard one of the doors close behind him. Figuring Red and Terry had gone to change, he found Sterling at the screen, perusing the images.

"These are stunning."

"Of course they are. You're a gifted photographer." And he was. "This project is different from anything you've probably done before."

Sterling looked up. "They're making love to each other with their eyes."

Connor nodded. "Exactly, and that's something pretty special." It almost felt voyeuristic to look at the images. "How many times have you tried for an image like that in your professional life? You'd probably have killed for it with professional models."

Sterling raised his gaze. "Hell, I'd kill for that kind of look in my personal life. Forget about professionally. Can you imagine what it would feel like to have someone look at you that way? The devotion, the way the entire world seems to fall away because nothing but the two of them matter." The longing in Sterling's voice was almost palpable. All Connor could do was nod and remain silent. If he spoke, he'd give away every ounce of feeling he had, and Connor wasn't ready for that kind of openness.

"Thank you," Connor told Red and Terry when they returned, dressed in their street clothes.

"You're welcome," Terry said.

"What about the images? What will happen to them?" Red asked. "Could we get some prints of them for ourselves?"

"Yes. The images are copyrighted by me, and yes, you can definitely order prints of them. As for anything else, they won't be used anywhere other than the calendar. Though I know a few magazines… hell, Speedo would probably pay a small fortune to use these in some of their advertising. But that will not happen. These were pictures taken for a specific purpose, and they'll remain that way."

Red sighed. "Good. Posing for a community service project is one thing, but I would be in trouble with the department if any of these were to be published otherwise." He seemed relieved.

"What I'll do is put together some of the best images, and then we can go over them together. You can choose the ones you want and the one we'll use in the calendar. I think we already agree on that one, though we could change our minds. Okay?" Sterling was in full-on business mode, and Connor could almost feel Red and Terry symbolically getting out their wallets.

"What do we owe you for today?" Terry asked.

"Nothing. The session is being donated to the project. Normally a session is much longer, but for the calendar, we're using shortened sessions. If you want to book something for a different occasion, that would be great as well." Sterling gave them each a card. "Give me a call in about a week. I'll have the images reviewed and we can go over them." Sterling shook hands with both men, and Connor did as well. Then they left, carrying their gym bag along with them.

"Man, that was intense," Sterling said as soon as the door closed. His shoulders slumped, and the air seemed to go out of him.

"Yes, it was. But really good."

"You saved it," Sterling told him. "You were the one who saw what was wrong and figured it out." He sat in a chair, his legs apart, head resting back. "Most sessions are like this, high-energy, and it always saps me. I have to put so much out there that when the session is over, I have nothing left."

Connor pulled up another chair and sat next to him. "Is that what it was like when you were working with Alexander?" He needed to know.

Sterling shook his head slowly. "No. Alexander was very different. He was my boyfriend, and we worked differently together. Sometimes, in front of the camera, Alexander came alive, and he was as bright and startling as the first morning sun. Other times he was lifeless, and no one could get anything out of him. At least that's how it was for me. But he has that face and hair that everyone loves, and he's been trading on that for a long time. Initially I worked hard to pull the best I could from him, but toward the end...." Sterling shrugged. "There was only so much I could do, so I took the pictures, and people clamored to buy them."

Connor chuckled. "Who knows? Maybe the vapid look is in now. Remember some time ago when everywhere you looked, all you saw were these models that were so small and skinny that you swore they'd disappear if they turned sideways?"

Sterling rolled his eyes. "It's still that way. Beautiful women with normal, healthy figures, they classify as 'big' models. It's really disgusting. And don't get me started on the guys. Maybe that's why Alexander has done so well. He has a look that's all male, sexy, and all he has to do is walk into a room and heads turn. You know who and what he is." Sterling sighed. "Can we not talk about him?"

"I like that idea." Connor leaned against Sterling's shoulder and closed his eyes. "When is the next appointment?"

Sterling placed his finger under Connor's chin, and he lifted his head. "The rest of my day is clear." The intensity in Sterling's gaze drew Connor like a moth to the flame. "What do you have planned?"

"I need to go in to my office this afternoon. I have some department meetings, and I need to plan the fall term. There are some things I want to change. Freshman history class, the one that many students take because it's required, can be dull and uninspiring, so I try to change the class every year in response to what's happening in the world. I think it's important that my students understand that no matter what the problems of the day are, there really isn't anything new, just a new spin on an old issue." He loved that he could make history relevant.

"Do you want to come over for dinner when you're done?" Sterling asked.

"After our meetings, the department usually goes out to eat. It's a team-building sort of thing and is pretty much expected." Connor had never tried to figure out how to get out of those before, and now all he wanted was to escape. But he needed to make a good impression on the other faculty since his tenure review would be coming up soon and he needed to stay on everyone's good side.

"No problem." Sterling kissed him.

"You never told me when the next appointment is?"

"Tomorrow afternoon at two," Sterling answered before kissing him again. "Will you be here?"

"With bells on."

"Now that I'd like to see." Sterling leered at him for a second, and Connor smiled before being kissed once again. His meeting was going to be a poor substitute.

Chapter 9

STERLING MADE his own dinner and sat at the table with a book, a steak, and a bottle of red. He turned on the television, and immediately Alexander's face shone from the screen, touting some shampoo. Sterling flipped it off again and turned back to the table, eating alone. He picked up the book but couldn't concentrate, his mind turning to Connor.

He wasn't sure what was going on with him. Sometimes Connor seemed so interested, and at others he could feel him pulling away. Sterling understood how he felt. It was hard being rejected, and the things people said during a breakup could be hurtful as all get-out. He finished eating his dinner and took care of the dishes. Sterling wondered what he was going to do for the rest of the evening. Television didn't hold any interest. He thought about going out for a walk, but a roll of thunder changed his mind. Sterling figured he'd go on back to the studio and work on the images from the day.

Thunder shook the house, and the lights flickered and came back on for thirty seconds before flashing off and staying that way. Well, that shot that particular idea. Sterling got the flashlights and candles out of the lower kitchen cabinet as a pounding on the front door sounded over the storm.

Sterling pulled open the door to find Connor there, his shirt soaked and sticking to his skin, kilt drenched, hanging straight down, dripping on the concrete. "What are you doing out on a night like this?" Lightning lit up the sky, and thunder followed almost immediately. "Get inside." The storm was getting worse.

Connor stepped onto the rug, and Sterling closed the door. "What happened? I thought you had a meeting."

"I did, and we went to dinner afterwards." Connor pulled his shirt away from his skin. "But when I was walking home, the sky opened up. I thought I could get there before the rain started." He waved his arms, and a shower of drops fell to the mat.

"Come on upstairs."

"But I'm going to make a mess everywhere," Connor protested.

"Don't worry. The floor will dry." Sterling led the way up the stairs toward the bathroom. He handed Connor some towels and a flashlight. "I'll get you something to put on and be right back." Sterling went to his room and grabbed a pair of shorts and a T-shirt out of his drawers. He returned as the bathroom door opened. Connor peeked out wearing only a towel. Sterling paused, because the sight was something out of one of the dreams he'd had the past few nights. "Connor…." His throat went dry at all the golden skin on display. He had seen Connor shirtless before, but this was different. Only that damned towel clinging precariously to those hips stood between Connor and nakedness. There was something wicked about that, and it was enticing as hell.

"Are those for me?" Connor asked, and Sterling pressed the clothes into his hands and took hold of one of his hands. "What is it you want?"

"I was going to ask you the same thing." Sterling swallowed and drew closer, the heat coming off Connor's skin magnetic. The house was dark, with only the shadowy flashlights and strikes of lightning to cut through. Sterling set his light on the table outside the bathroom before approaching Connor. When he didn't pull away, Sterling encircled him with his arms, tugging Connor closer, holding him tightly. "Is this okay?"

Connor set the clothes aside and hummed his approval as Sterling captured his lips, the energy taking hold of both of them. "I think you promised me something like this."

Sterling nodded, guiding Connor toward his room. They fumbled a little getting the door open. Once inside, Connor's towel fell to the floor, and Sterling ran his hands down his strong back and over the curve of his incredibly firm ass. Sterling growled from his throat, deepening the kiss, getting a good taste of Connor and wanting more at the same time.

Connor was smooth and strong under his hands, and since it was nearly completely dark, Sterling let his hands do his seeing for him. Curves and ridges of muscle danced under his palms as he explored, Connor shivering. "Are you cold?"

"It's not the cold," Connor whispered as he tugged at Sterling's shirt.

He lifted his arms, and Connor tugged off his polo. He must have dropped it to the floor, because it seemed to disappear, Connor's warm hands replacing it. "Damn…." Connor rumbled in his throat, pressing their chests together, melding their heat into a fire that Sterling had no hope or will to douse. He had been looking for something like this for a long time, and now it was in his arms. He turned Connor, pressing him back and down onto the bed.

Lightning lit up the windows, illuminating the room and Connor in his bed. He was as masculinely beautiful as Sterling had known he would be, planes of long, sinewy muscle, wide shoulders, narrow hips, and all man. The light flashed away, and Sterling was left in the darkness once more, his eyes adjusting all over again. Not that it mattered. Connor reached for him, tugging him down until he lay next to him.

Deft fingers stripped Sterling of the remainder of his clothes and pressed him back on the bed. Connor straddled him, his hands roaming slowly over him. Sterling ached to explore Connor.

"Let me take my time. I've wanted to know what you felt like since I saw you at my great-aunt's. Now it's my chance." Sterling held his breath as Connor's hands explored his chest, fingers tweaking his sensitive nipples, sending ripples of pleasure racing through him.

Sterling closed his eyes because they did him no good now. He soaked up each of Connor's caresses like a dry sponge getting its first touch of water. He needed it, wanting more, and Connor gave. It was incredible. Sterling breathed deeply, enclosing Connor in his arms when he leaned forward. Their kiss stopped the world. Everything around them—the house, the storm—all of it disappeared as Connor transported him to another place and time. It was truly like nothing outside the two of them existed.

"I want you," Connor whispered into Sterling's ear. Sterling wasn't sure what he meant until Connor slid down his body, hands and lips blazing a trail of passion that Sterling hoped went on forever. He gasped and grasped the bedding in clenched fists, eyes still closed, the world of their own making taking on even more form and perfection.

Wet heat surrounded him, taking more and more of him, sending Sterling on a flight of ecstasy that went on and on. Breathing became difficult simply because his entire being was centered on wherever Connor touched him. The world began and ended with Connor's lips and hands. So many times, he had built things up in his mind only for reality to disappoint him. With Connor, it was something he couldn't have possibly imagined, and it only got better and better the longer the pleasure lasted.

Sterling took Connor by the shoulders and gently drew him upward, for if he didn't stop it was going to be all over, and Sterling wanted their time together to last.

"What's wrong?" Connor whispered.

"I need a few minutes." He kissed him gently, feasting on those incredible lips once again. "You get me so excited."

"Oh." Connor grinned. "I like the sound of that." He ground his hips against Sterling's, and damned if Connor didn't get him going again. Sterling had hoped for a respite, but that didn't look like it was going to happen. Connor was a live wire, grinding, holding him, pressing their bodies together, building heat that was impossible to put out of his mind.

"You're a minx, you know that."

Connor lifted away, his gaze boring into Sterling's. "Is that a bad thing?"

Sterling closed his arms around him, tugging Connor back down. "No way in hell. It's the best thing I could have hoped for." Damn, he loved that Connor was uninhibited. Now that he had made up his mind, he seemed to throw himself into their passion with everything he had. Sterling's only fear was if he would come out the other side in once piece.

"I want you," Connor groaned, parting Sterling's legs in a display that made it perfectly clear what he meant. Sterling cupped Connor's cheeks, drawing him down, their gazes locking, lips an inch apart.

"How about we save that for another day?" It had been a long time since Sterling had bottomed. Alexander had had no interest in playing the driver, and it had been long enough that Sterling wasn't sure it was something he was capable of. Or maybe it was a residual hangup and now wasn't the time for him to deal with it. If things progressed between him and Connor, then they would need to have a conversation about it, but now wasn't the time to deal with his worries and insecurities.

Connor paused, his eyes filling with doubt. "You don't want…."

"It's just something you and I should talk about before plumbing the depths, so to speak." He tried to make light of it, and thankfully Connor smiled. "It's been a while for me, and…." That was as far as he could open that particular box in his mind, at least for now.

Connor leaned closer. "Okay. Then how about this?" He kissed a trail down Sterling's chest and belly. Sterling held his breath before those talented lips surrounded him, taking him deep and hard, commanding his body, and damned if it didn't obey. Connor played him like a fine instrument.

"Sweetheart," Sterling gasped, his legs shaking as Connor slid all the way down, taking him into his incredible mouth. When Connor took a break, Sterling flipped them on the bed, laying Connor on his back. Finally, this incredible man was all laid out for him. One thing that Sterling knew was that guys tended to give their partners what they wanted to get, and he followed Connor's playbook to passionate results.

It wasn't long before Sterling had Connor whimpering softly and his body rigid with desire in all the right places. He brought their lips together, hips just right, holding Connor tightly, and as the second wave of the storm broke over the house, their own passion reached its zenith and the two of them tumbled over into the abyss of ecstasy as the storm raged outside.

The thunder finally dissipated, the storm moving past as they lay together, rain on the roof obliterating the sound of their attempts to catch their breath. "Are you warmer now?" Sterling asked, and Connor snickered.

"Yes. Though I'm not much drier." He giggled at his own joke.

Sterling rolled his eyes in the darkness and carefully got out of bed to get a cloth to clean them both up before lying down next to him. Connor's head rested on Sterling's shoulder, and he gently stroked Connor's hair as the fatigue of a long day and spent passion caught up with them. Sterling closed his eyes, listening to the now gentler rain, the thunder a distant rumble growing fainter by the minute.

"I hate storms," Connor said into the darkness. "I used to run into Mom and Dad's room at the first sign of thunder. Mom would make room for me and tell me stories until the storm passed. When I got older, I used to hide under the covers, and sometimes I'd go into the basement to find something to do just to try to get away from it."

"I loved them. I used to sit in the backyard looking up at the ridge as the storms gathered. The wind and then the lightning were always just a big show, the thunder another accompaniment. It never bothered me until one really bad storm that brought hail. That was maybe ten years ago. It broke a dozen windows, and I swore someone was attacking the house. The sound of breaking glass seemed to come from everywhere. That really unnerved me for a while. But it's in the past, and it doesn't bother me anymore." He tightened his hold on Connor as they lay there in the dark.

"What were you afraid of?" Connor asked.

"The dark. I never liked it. I always had a night-light growing up. When I got older and Mom took it away, there were times I stayed up all night because I was afraid to go to sleep." He kept his eyes closed. "Mom and Dad lost patience with me, but eventually I grew out of it."

"Most of us are afraid of the dark."

"Yeah. But I was afraid of the dark because I was afraid of the spiders. My monsters under the bed all had eight legs, and to this day I can't watch that second Harry Potter movie because of the spiders. They give me the willies." He chuckled even as the fear threatened to well up. It was irrational, but still there nonetheless.

"Spiders, really?" Connor made wiggly motions on Sterling's belly. "I got a really big spider right here." His movements grew more pronounced, and Sterling giggled and squirmed to get away.

"Tickles… I'll give you tickles." He attacked, and Connor squealed as he found his sides, tickling as he thrashed, laughing like crazy. Sterling backed away just before Connor ended up on the floor. "I'm the king of tickle torture. I had a cousin who used to love to tickle me, and I found the best way to get him to back off was to return the favor. I once tickled him until he threw up."

"Damn, you play to win. Remind me never to get on your bad side in a tickle war." Connor settled next to him.

The night had grown quiet, the storm now past. Sterling was comfortable and happy, but Connor seemed tense. When Sterling lightly rubbed his arm, he jumped and then settled once again.

"Maybe I should go. I'm sure you had things you needed to do tonight. I got caught outside and needed to get out of the storm." Before Sterling could stop him, Connor was out of the bed, searching on the floor for the towel. "I'll return the clothes as soon as I can."

Sterling wondered if he'd done something wrong. Nothing came to mind, which only confused him more. He hadn't said anything wrong as far as he could tell, but Connor was jumpy. Maybe things between them hadn't been as wonderful as he thought and Connor only wanted to get away rather than say anything to him. "Of course." He swallowed hard and slowly got out of bed himself. *So much for the quiet time together.* "If that's what you want."

Connor wrapped the towel around his waist once again, standing in the mostly dark. Suddenly the lights flashed on in the hallway, and Sterling closed his eyes to shut out the sudden brightness. "I think I should go and leave you in peace." He didn't sound so sure of himself this time.

"Like I said, if that's what you want to do." Sterling wasn't going to pressure him or even ask. He had his pride, and if someone didn't want to stay in his bed, he wasn't going to beg them to.

Connor crossed his arms over his chest and stepped back, color rising in his cheeks. "Look, this was…."

"If you say it was a mistake, you can walk home in just the towel," Sterling snapped before Connor could say anything else. "I've heard that before, and I don't need you to say it. I get the picture. You were horny, I was here, and things just happened." Maybe he had completely misread the signals from Connor. Maybe the guy was just horny, and once he'd gotten what he wanted, it was time to go.

"No. It isn't that. Well, I was horny… for you. But…." His arms unfolded and dropped to his side. "Look, I don't know." Doubt rang in his voice.

"And you were worried about what exactly?" Sterling asked, and Connor cleared his throat nervously.

"I don't know. I'm not very good at the relationship part of things." He stepped closer, the towel waving slightly with each step. "I was always good at the sex part of things." His cheeks reddened, and Sterling approached him slowly.

"That was pretty evident."

"Yeah. But it's the afterward part that always gets me into trouble." He swallowed hard. "Guys want the sex, and then afterwards, there's nothing to keep them interested. They find out I'm not exciting, and then it's 'goodbye' or 'help me with my homework'… and they move on to someone else."

"So you were leaving to get a step ahead? Is that what this is?" Connor shrugged. "This sort of thing has happened before?"

"Well… yeah… I told you. Guys think I'm boring." He looked down. "I know I look good because I work at it and go the gym. Guys pursue me, and then they find out that I'm not into football or NASCAR or whatever they find interesting." He shrugged again. "I figured if I left then maybe you and I could be friends and we could work on the project without all kinds of weirdness between us. Things could go back to how they were."

Sterling took Connor in his arms. "And what if I don't want them to go back? What if I'm interested in something more? I'm not some stupid kid in college who doesn't know what's best for them."

Connor sighed. "I know. You're a fashion photographer who's been all over the world. And I'm a history professor. Eventually you'll get bored of me too. Just like everyone else."

Sterling kissed him deeply. At first Connor didn't respond, and Sterling began to worry. Then Connor's arms wound around his neck and the towel dropped to the floor.

"Connor," Sterling whispered as he guided him toward the bed. Sterling didn't think he was ever going to get bored with this man. Now all he had to do was figure out a way to convince Connor.

STERLING LOOKED over all the images he'd taken so far. In the past week, he'd photographed six of the sets of models. The images themselves were coming out beautifully, but something wasn't sitting right with him, and he wasn't sure what.

"Would you give it a rest? You're hovering over that screen like you expect it to provide the answers to the mysteries of the universe." Connor grinned, but Sterling continued staring. "They're all gorgeous. What more do you want? The guys look amazing, and the ladies came through with beautiful flowers." Connor sighed, and Sterling put his arms around his waist and leaned his head against Connor's flat belly.

"I don't get it myself. They should be perfect, but there's something missing. At first I thought it was the colors, but they're all different, and that's fine. The flowers are different, and…."

"The poses? A few are close, but no two are exactly the same." Connor patted his head. "Maybe you're seeing something that isn't there or you're expecting something that isn't possible."

"But…." Sterling grew anxious.

"Look, these images are going to largely be viewed one at a time. When the calendar is used, it will display one image a month. So looking at how each one appears next to the others isn't really helpful. I think you need to stop second-guessing yourself and just go with what are amazing images. They're sexy, hot, and incredibly beautiful. The flowers are front and center, which is what should happen for a garden club calendar."

"Maybe that's it," Sterling said softly, trying to convince himself. He couldn't put his finger on it anyway. "The images are gorgeous, and the guys picked the best ones."

"Good, and I found someone willing to pose with me. He'll borrow one of my kilts. He's an American studies professor at the college, and his wife is thrilled that he'll be part of the calendar. Cotten says she's preparing to buy a number of copies that she can send to her family." Connor snickered. "Cotten told me that his wife and her sister are very competitive. Apparently her husband was featured in an ad for some gym, so she's thrilled that her husband is going to be a calendar guy. I guess that beats a gym ad." They shared a grin.

Sterling was happy Connor had someone to share his month with, but he was jealous as well. Yes, it had been his idea for Connor to take part, and it was his idea for Connor to find someone to do the pictures with, but the idea of another guy, straight or not, being that close to Connor, even holding him, made his blood boil. Not that he could say anything or let on how he felt. This was what he'd wanted. "That's good, then. Find out when he's available. I have all the others scheduled. I'm going to be busy in the next couple of days, but I need to get these images solidified so we can move ahead with the rest of the project."

"I understand." Connor seemed excited. "I think I'm looking forward to this."

"I'm a little surprised. I know I talked you into it."

Connor nodded. "Yeah, you did at first. But after seeing your work…." He paused. "I was afraid that this was going to be cheesy—a beefcake calendar with flowers—but it's more than that. The images are gorgeous and loving. I don't know how many copies the club is going to sell, but it will be something we can be proud of." He slid his arms down Sterling's shoulders and over his chest, leaning in close. Sterling liked that Connor had taken to touching him. He really was a tactile guy. Sterling placed his hands on Connor's and closed his eyes. Sometimes the hardest thing was to simply let himself be happy.

"I'll call him," Connor said and stepped away, only to return a few minutes later. "How about Friday at four? Does that work?"

Sterling smiled. "If everything works out, the rest will be done by then. The two of you will be the last ones, and then the photography will be completed. I'll put together a mock-up, and we can show it to your great-aunt before we finalize everything and get it all ready to send off to the printers." He was in two minds about this project coming to an end. "Have you given any thought to what you might like to do when this is all over?"

Connor chuckled. "You mean after I go back to my nice quiet life and my great-aunt moves on to her next project? Probably plan my senior seminar for the spring and dive back into my research."

That hadn't been exactly what he had been asking, but it seemed he had his answer. Connor had said that with his previous relationships, he had immersed himself in work, and that seemed to be what he intended to do now. Sterling noticed that there was no mention of the two of them dating or going out. Anything like that was gone. "I guess I'll be doing something like that too. There will be portrait appointments, and I'll go back to what I was doing before." Right now, that prospect sounded about as exciting as cleaning up the goose poop in the local park.

It wasn't that Connor hadn't warned him. As Sterling saw it, he could either make the best of what Connor had said and deal with it, or he could do his best to get Connor to realize that there was more out there than work. "I guess it isn't every day that you get a project dumped into your lap that turns out to be fun."

Connor squeezed his shoulders. "You can say that again."

Sterling closed his eyes, enjoying the touch and the way Connor's hands felt. He liked the closeness, the intimacy, but it apparently had a time limit on it, and Sterling needed to figure out what he intended to do about that.

Chapter 10

"OKAY. THANKS, Cotten, I understand. There really isn't any way you can do the photoshoot with your arm in a sling. Don't worry about it. I hope you feel better, and I'll see you on Monday." They spoke for a few minutes more, and then he hung up.

Connor called Sterling, but it went right to voicemail. Great. He was supposed to be at his place in half an hour, and the other half of April wasn't going to be able to make it. They were a person short, and Connor wasn't sure where he was going to find someone to fill in, let alone in the next half hour.

Connor grabbed the garment bag he had already prepared and carried it out to his car. Maybe Sterling would have some ideas. He locked the house and drove over to Sterling's, grabbed the clothes, and headed inside. Laughter greeted him as soon as he entered, and Grant came around from the studio with Connor's great-aunt next to him.

"A little birdie told me that today was your photoshoot, and I wanted to be here to support you," Aunt Lucille said innocently. Connor knew she was anything but. Somehow, she had decided to butt into the process.

"You just couldn't stay away?" he asked her. "Damned matchmaking granny… or auntie." He narrowed his gaze, but she simply flashed him a look of complete confusion that Connor knew was as fake as her hair color.

"Where's your partner for this little shindig?" she asked.

Fortunately Sterling joined them at that point.

Connor locked his gaze onto Sterling's. "Cotten broke his arm, and it's in a cast and sling. He's in pain and isn't going to be able to do the shoot. Apparently it's pretty bad."

"How did it happen?" Sterling asked.

Connor glanced to the others and then back to Sterling. "Well, it seems his wife found the calendar idea really exciting… if you know what I mean. They were making good on that excitement, and things got a little out of hand. From what I understand, Cotten's wife likes a little role-play." This was so damned embarrassingly fun, especially in front of his great-aunt and Sterling's father. "I don't know all the details and really don't need to. But it seems that things got a little slippery and they weren't careful enough, and he fell…." Connor tried to keep it serious and matter-of-fact. "Well, he tried to catch himself and broke his arm. The thing was…." He stepped closer to Sterling and lowered his voice. "In order to set his arm, the hospital had to…." Connor could barely keep it together. "Carrie was really into it, and when he got hurt, she couldn't find the key to the collar-and-hood piece he was wearing…."

His great-aunt broke first, followed by Grant, their laughter spilling through the whole group. "My goodness. I bet the emergency room people were shocked," Aunt Lucille said.

Connor shrugged. "According to him, they cut him out of the paraphernalia, set his arm, and sent him home. Carrie, on the other hand, forgot she was still in her leather corset and apparently raced into the emergency room with her riding crop slipped into the pocket along the side of her boot." He couldn't hold it in any longer and doubled over. Poor Sterling was crying, he was laughing so hard. "The ER staff asked Cotten at least a dozen times if his wife had hurt him on purpose, and one nurse whispered that she could quietly call someone if he needed help and was too afraid to ask for it in front of his wife. Cotten is six two, and his wife is about five foot and weighs maybe a hundred pounds."

"And he told you all this?" Sterling asked.

"Well…." Connor snickered.

"No way. You liar." Sterling lunged for him, grabbing Connor and tickling him until his knees gave out and he slumped to the floor. "You made all that up."

"It was a much better story than him slipping in the shower." He squirmed to get away, but Sterling held him tighter. "We have things to figure out." Connor wasn't sure if the tickling would return, and he'd just as soon avoid it if possible.

"Yes," his great-aunt said, straightening up. "Your story was quite funny. But we have a problem. If Cotten has a broken arm, then we don't have our last model." Connor knew that look. She was amused but shifting to all business.

"Okay. Let me think," Sterling said as he went to his computer. "I could call one of the other guys to see if they'll pose with you for the last image. We could change his hair and he'd be dressed differently. With some creative lighting, maybe people wouldn't notice." He began looking through the other images. "Maybe Billy or Sebastian. They were good, and with a little styling...."

"You do it," Aunt Lucille said. "You pose with Connor. He has the kilts with him, and the two of you could do it. I've taken plenty of pictures in my life, and if you set up the shots, I can take them."

"When did you work as a photographer?" Connor asked.

Aunt Lucille sauntered up to him. "Honey, at my age, there are plenty of things I've done that you don't know about—and just for future reference, if you decide to tell that story again, collars generally have quick-release links for safety reasons." She turned to Sterling, and Connor stared after her, suddenly unable to breathe. "We should get started. Why don't you set things up while Connor goes to change? Then he can help you into the kilt and we can get moving."

Sterling looked like he had whiplash. "I...."

Connor took his arm. "Trust me. Don't fight it. You'll only lose, and it isn't worth the effort." He leaned closer. "Besides, it'll be really hot."

Sterling snorted. "Really. You and me, posing only in kilts for the calendar, with your great-aunt behind the camera. Yeah, that's going to be as hot as Alaska in January." He rolled his eyes.

"Come on. Just ignore her and your father and...." He saw Sterling's point. The other pictures were truly electric, and the couples had chemistry. Even the two straight guys had gotten into it and connected with each other. "We'll do the best we can." He picked up the garment bag. "Go get things set up, and I'll change." There really was no use fighting her. When Aunt Lucille got something into her head, particularly when she was convinced she was right, there was no moving her. They just needed to get out of the way.

CONNOR STEPPED out of the bathroom in his best kilt, sash over his bare shoulder and across his chest. He wasn't sure if that was what would work, but he thought he'd give it a try. Connor had left one of his other kilts for Sterling. The one he wore was traditional for his clan, and the other was a universal tartan, but he thought the colors would look good together.

"Very nice, son," Grant said.

"Thanks, Grant. I hope this is what Sterling was looking for." He entered the studio area. Sterling was adjusting the lights, and he stopped, his gaze falling onto Connor like a weight. "Are you ready?"

"Yes."

"I left yours in the bathroom if you're ready to change. I can help you with it to ensure it's worn properly."

"Okay." Sterling's voice was short and tight. Connor waited until he was done before accompanying him to the bathroom. Sterling stripped off his clothes. "Do you really wear nothing under?"

"No. I do because I wear them to school. Some guys don't. I think it's a personal preference." Sterling kept his briefs on, and Connor helped him into the kilt, ensuring the overlap was across the front with the end at the right side. "I don't have a sash for that one."

"It's okay. The difference will be good." He fussed with the fabric. "This feels weird to me." Sterling turned to try to look over his shoulder.

"What? You afraid the kilt will make your butt look big?" Connor teased. "Come on, you look stunning." He placed his hand on Sterling's chest. "You look really hot." He closed the distance between them. "Maybe I should have told you to wear nothing." He ran his hand up Sterling's leg. "Easy access is really something."

Sterling shivered. "You know your great-aunt and my father are going to wonder what we're doing, and one of them is going to come check that we're okay." That was definitely a ball-shriveling idea.

Still, Connor sucked lightly at the base of Sterling's neck. "But I like it in here. It's quiet, we're alone, you're sexy as hell, and…."

A loud throat clearing on the other side of the door had Connor pulling away.

"That's perfect. I think you look great." Connor straightened his own kilt and the sash before opening the door and stepping out. Sterling came after him, passing Grant on their way to the studio.

Aunt Lucille stood near the camera as he stepped in front of the background. "I have these," she said, handing Connor a bouquet of cream-colored peonies. "They should be wonderful."

Sterling joined him and got Connor into position. Then he checked the viewfinder before handing Lucille the camera and stepping onto the mat himself. "I'm not sure how this is going to work, so we'll take it slow." He changed his mind and turned the monitor to face them. "That's better." Sterling got into position, standing with Connor, the flowers between them.

Aunt Lucille took a number of pictures, and Sterling adjusted their positions after each one. Sterling wasn't comfortable, and neither was Connor. The ease they shared in the bedroom did not translate to the camera. He kept watching Lucille and then his father. Connor picked up on Sterling's tension, and it only added to his own.

The last time he had been in front of the camera, it had been him and Sterling playing, just the two of them, and eventually he'd gotten comfortable, but that wasn't happening this time. Connor was uneasy and kept thinking about his great-aunt watching him.

"This isn't working at all," Sterling finally pronounced, and Connor took the flowers and stepped away, placed them in a vase, and sat down.

"Tell me about it. You two are as jumpy as a virgin at an orgy," Grant observed.

"That isn't helping, Dad," Sterling countered.

"Smile, for goodness' sake. A real smile. Not those forced ones you've been flashing at that camera. It's like you're both holding dead fish rather than flowers, and when you look at each other, there's nothing." He stalked toward Sterling. "This is a handsome guy. You should be attracted to him, want to jump his bones or whatever it is two guys do. It certainly didn't look like that."

"I'm not comfortable in front of the camera," Sterling countered.

Grant shrugged. "Big fucking deal. It's one picture. Whoop-de-doo. What do you tell your sitters when they're not comfortable? You get them used to the camera and make them comfortable. Do that to yourself. And if that happens, Connor will respond to it, because he's picking up on your nerves." Man, he was a little up in Sterling's face. "You can do this, boy. I know you can. Just make it work."

Sterling's shoulders slumped, and Connor stood next to him. "It will be okay. Maybe it's the location. Let's try outside in the yard—change the location and the energy." He leaned close. "Just let go of whatever is holding you back. You look amazing, and we're going to take good pictures. I promise you that."

"Whatever you think," Sterling said.

Connor wondered if there was something else wrong. "Would you give us a second?" he asked the other two.

"Let's go have some tea," Aunt Lucille offered, and Grant led the way out of the studio and into the main house.

"What's really bothering you? I know you weren't expecting to do this. Is it the sudden change?" Connor grabbed a chair and sat across from him.

"I've never wanted to be in front of the camera," he said in almost a whisper.

"This is up to you. If you don't want to do it, then don't. I'll try to find someone else." Connor leaned forward, and Sterling clutched his hands tightly.

"I don't want you to do it with anyone else. That's the problem. I don't feel comfortable in front of the camera, and yet I don't want anyone else to pose with you while you're half dressed. I know it's dumb, but there it is." He sighed loudly.

"Then you need to decide what you want more," Connor told him gently. "Figure out what it is you really want and then join me outside." He stood and grabbed one of the chairs. "I'll be outside when you're ready." Connor wasn't sure what Sterling would decide, but it was up to him. If he didn't want to be photographed with Connor, then it was his decision.

"Sweetheart," Aunt Lucille said as she came out the back door. She must have been watching and was ready to swoop in and come to the rescue.

"I'm fine." He smiled to cover his worry. "Sterling has some things he needs to figure out."

"Like when he's going to grow a set of balls and listen to his heart?" she snapped, and Connor groaned, but he couldn't argue with her.

"When did you start talking that way?" he quizzed. "I don't remember you swearing so much."

Aunt Lucille lowered herself into one of the cushioned patio chairs and slowly sat back. "Most things about getting old suck. You can't do the things you always loved, everything hurts most of the time, the best foods repeat on you something awful, and going to the bathroom can be an occasion. But one of the good things is that you get to say the things you always wanted to and be damned. I never swore in front of any of my nieces or nephews or any of you kids. But fuck that. I spent a lot of years biting my tongue. I wanted to tell your father he was a stupid piece-of-shit jackass for how he treated you, and I wanted to tell my brother that he was as smart as a box of rocks. But I kept quiet. Now I don't have to do that shit anymore." She drank from her glass of iced tea, and Grant came out to join them, sitting next to Aunt Lucille. They clinked glasses in some kind of silent toast and then drank, smiling at each other. For a split second, Aunt Lucille looked the way she must have when she was in her twenties.

Connor wasn't sure he wanted to see his great-aunt smitten with anyone and did his best to put it out of his mind.

"What's he doing?" Aunt Lucille asked Grant, who shrugged.

"Sterling needs to few minutes to make up his mind about something." They drank their tea, and Connor watched the studio door.

Finally it opened, with Sterling stepping out, still in the kilt, carrying the camera. "You still up for this?" he asked and handed it to Lucille. "The pictures will automatically transmit back to the studio system, but out here there isn't going to be a screen. We'll review the shots later." He turned, surveying the garden. "How about over there? It has a great background with the tree and the ivy."

Connor got up and took the chair with him. "I have an idea. Okay?"

"Have at it," Sterling agreed.

Connor set the chair off center from the large trunk. The background was deep green and lush, and he liked it. Grant went inside and returned with the flowers, which he handed to Sterling. "What are we doing?"

"Aunt Lucille, stand right here. Sterling, sit down and hold the flowers." Connor arranged the kilt so it fell open just enough to show some of Sterling's leg and hid the chair. Then he stood behind him, squatting slightly and leaning forward, sliding his arms around Sterling's shoulders and down his impressive chest. "Go ahead and start," he told Lucille, who began taking pictures. Ignoring her completely, Connor leaned close to Sterling. Click… click.

"Forget her and everything else but me. Think about how good this picture is going to be and what you and I are going to do tonight once this is over and I get to have you all to myself." He whispered so only Sterling could hear and slid his hands lower, resting one on Sterling's belly and the other on the flowers. Click. He turned slightly so he could see Sterling, who shifted toward him. Click… click… click. Connor raised his gaze and slid his free hand to the side, resting his arm against Sterling's chest. Click… click.

"Okay, boys," Aunt Lucille said. "You can stop eye-fucking one another. Good God, get a room. I don't know how much of this my old heart can take." She handed Sterling the camera and sat down in her seat before draining half her glass of tea.

Connor didn't move, watching over Sterling's shoulder as he quickly reviewed the images. "These are still transmitting. We'll need to look at them on the larger screen." He set the camera aside, and Connor straightened up. He could use something cool to drink—hell, maybe a beer… or four. Sterling took the camera inside, returned with two bottles, and handed one to him.

"When can we look at them?" Aunt Lucille asked.

"In a few minutes. I want to give them all a chance to transmit. They're big, detailed files, so it always takes a little bit, especially from out here. It will be faster now that the camera is closer."

Aunt Lucille tapped her foot, and Sterling took a pull of his beer and then went back inside. He must have checked the pictures, because when he returned, he was grinning and handed Connor a tablet. "Take a look."

Connor went through all of them from the first session in the studio and then outside. The outside pictures were much better, and as the images changed, they got hotter and more intense. He kept thinking he had the image until he got to the last one with his bare arm resting on Sterling's chest, their hands clasped around the flowers. Sterling's eyes burned, but it was Connor's own image that stopped him cold. He closed his eyes and turned away from the naked emotion on display.

"That's the one!" Sterling nearly knocked the tablet out of his hand.

Chapter 11

STERLING HEAVED a sigh of relief as he sent the requested email and made the call. "Lucille, can you look at the mock-up I sent you?" He waited as she opened the email.

"I have it." She hummed as she opened the file. "Oh…," she breathed.

"Yeah. What I need you to do is check over the attributions. I need to make sure that the ladies credited for the flowers are correct. I have double-checked the models and verified the spelling of all their names."

"Okay. Hold on." She set down the phone, and papers rustled. "I have the list of who provided what." She went through each month and verified the name and the spelling. Sterling corrected a few misspellings in the file and confirmed them with her.

"That's perfect, then. Go ahead and delete that file. It's not any good. I'll send you a new one as soon as I'm finished. I ask that you don't share it with anyone. I don't want electronic versions of the images out in the general public. That way we can build some anticipation and they won't be leaked."

"Very well, but…."

"Lucille, I want to caution you. I am allowing the garden club to use the images provided on their calendar, but they don't own them. You can't reproduce or share them other than on the calendar. No one can make or distribute copies of the images. They are copyrighted. Do you understand that? I will provide images that can be used for promotion." Sterling was adamant about that. He needed to keep control of his work. "The use of them has been donated. The pictures themselves are still my property." He hated to be a dick about it, but she had to understand.

"Very well. I'll make sure the ladies in the club know that. It's what we already agreed."

Sterling was grateful there was no issue. "Great. I'll finish this up and get the files sent to the printer. After that, you need to order the printed copies and take it from there. Have you thought of how many you want to start with?"

Lucille chuckled. "I've taken orders from some of the ladies, and I already have fifty sold. I was thinking that if we sell five hundred total, we'd make almost three thousand dollars, and the club could be well on its way to a sound financial footing. That's all I ever wanted."

"Good. Then we will have accomplished what we set out to do. I suggest that you get some businesses and bookstores to sell the calendar."

"Way ahead of you. I have two bookstores in town, an antique store run by a member, and a couple of art stores that will sell it for us. I'm also working on a few bookstores in Mechanicsburg and even Camp Hill. There is some real interest, which is a little surprising to me. We've had a number of businesses who have declined to carry the calendar because of the subject matter, but no one has been nasty about it." She cleared her throat. "Well, one person has been. We approached the Downtown Gallery, and they weren't particularly nice. But then that's the outgoing mayor's business, and he's always been a self-righteous asshole of epic proportions."

"That's okay, I guess."

"We also have a booth arranged for the Harvest Festival in the fall, and I'm hoping we can sell some there, as well as at our Christmas sale. We have outlets and opportunities for sales." She really seemed to have a plan.

"Do you really think that people here in Central Pennsylvania are going to welcome this kind of calendar?" Now that it was done and ready to go, Sterling was worried. This area wasn't seen as progressive, usually. But Lucille seemed confident, and she would know the people of this area and the potential customers better than him.

"Yes. I've already sold fifty, and there are plenty of ladies who will want a little extra heat in their lives." She chuckled. "We'll be fine, and regardless of what happens, we'll have folks talking about the club, and that's something we wanted as well." She seemed excited. "Is there anything else you need from me?"

"Not right now. I have all I need, and I just have to put the finishing touches on the files and I'll send them off to the printer."

"Excellent. I've already left instructions with them to go ahead and print as soon as they get the files." He could almost see her rubbing her hands, ready to move ahead. Connor's Aunt Lucille was really something else. He had seen his father making eyes at her. While he wasn't sure how he felt about it, he knew he needed to make damned sure that Lucille wasn't going to end up just another notch on his father's retirement community bedpost.

"Then I'll get the files sent and let you know when they're there."

"Perfect." The way she drew out the word had him wondering if there was something else. "While I have you on the phone—are you and Connor still seeing each other?" She didn't wait for an answer. "I don't know if he's told you, but Connor has spent most of his life in school, one way or another. He's a good, kind, gentle soul, and I don't want him hurt."

"I know—"

"But I think he needs someone who is going to take the lead. All I'm saying is that if you're interested—and from what I saw through that camera lens of yours, you are—just be willing to go after what you want."

"Are you saying Connor won't?" Because that hadn't been the impression he got. But Connor tended toward hot and cold, and Sterling had to try to figure things out. It wasn't like Connor was a tease. After their photo session, he had stayed the night and the two of them had steamed the old wallpaper down.

"No. He knows his mind most of the time. I'm saying that when things get a little unsure for him, he retreats to work and his classes. Those are safe and predictable. We all know that life and the rest of what comes with it is anything but predictable." Sterling couldn't argue with that. "I think I've said enough, and Connor would snatch me bald for talking to you...." Sterling could see that and let the subject drop. There had probably been too much said already.

They talked for a few minutes more about the calendar arrangements. Then they hung up, and Sterling got to work doing a final check on all the information before sending the files to the printer.

As soon as that was done, he sent a copy to Lucille to let her know the ball was in her court. The printer got right back to him to say that they were prepping the files and would be moving forward. Sterling had done his part, and the project was complete from his perspective. Now all he had to do was sit back, wait for the results, and figure out what to do about Connor. One thing was for sure—he wasn't going to just walk away. But how was he going to keep Connor from retreating to his work and pushing him away?

Chapter 12

CONNOR'S PHONE rang, and he picked it up off his desk. He had gone to his office to try to get some work done. The paper he'd been working on had been coming along but was now at a complete halt, and he had hoped that a change of scenery might help get the words flowing again. But it wasn't working. When he saw the call was from Sterling, he smiled, a little warmth running through him. "Hey, how's it going?"

"I finished the pictures, checked all the copy, and got your great-aunt's approval. I just sent the files off to the printer, and I was wondering if you might want to celebrate?" He sounded so upbeat.

Connor looked at his screen with that damn blinking cursor that was going nowhere. "Sounds good. I'm trying to finish up this paper." He was determined to get this draft completed. "It's Thursday, right?" He blinked as he pulled his attention back fully into the real world. Sometimes the days ran together when he was working. Hell, sometimes *weeks* did when he was deep into a writing project.

Sterling chuckled. "Yes. How about we get together on Saturday for dinner? I can grill some steaks, and we can eat in the backyard."

"Sounds really good." Connor sighed to himself and smiled. He liked that Sterling hadn't backed away and that even though the project was over, he was still interested. That was nice. Connor had wondered if, when they were done with the calendar, Sterling's interest would cool and they would drift back to their separate worlds. That could still happen, but it was nice that Sterling was making an effort.

"Then I'll see you Saturday at six." They agreed as Connor got another call. He said goodbye to Sterling and took the call, expecting it to be a pain-in-the-butt telemarketer. They had become the bane of his existence lately.

"Hello." He expected to hear nothing or maybe a few clicks.

"Connor Hillyard?"

"Yes," he said warily, looking at his screen, where the cursor still blinked at him like a mocking schoolboy.

"I'm Weston Marcus, the current deputy mayor, and I wanted to approach you to see if you might be interested in running for office." That got Connor's attention. "As you know, the current mayor, Phillip Randall, is not going to seek the office again, and we see this as a chance for fresh ideas and younger blood in city government. You're a much-loved professor, and you have a very vocal champion." Connor rolled his eyes as he wondered, sarcastically, who that could be. Aunt Lucille had to be at it again. "We know of your community-mindedness and would like to have you in a leadership position."

Connor was flattered. "But mayor?" he asked as his heart beat faster. Connor had always been interested in his community, and he could do a great deal of good as mayor. Excitement at the idea raced through him.

"Yes. I'm not interested in the position." Weston paused. "I was approached to run, but my wife is expecting our second child, and our oldest has health issues that require a great deal of care. I don't feel as though I'm able to give more than I already am. We have an excellent council with experienced members who care about this community, but none of them is in a position to step into the mayoral role. When your name was mentioned as a possibility, we looked into your background and interests and thought you would be an excellent choice." He seemed so positive.

"You do know that I'm gay?" Connor said matter-of-factly. "I won't hide that or go back into the closet."

"One of the other council members is gay. It hasn't been an issue, and no one would ask you to be anyone other than who you are."

Connor swallowed hard as he thought it over. "But I don't know how to run a borough."

"You don't have to. The mayor heads the council and presides over meetings, has the power to declare an emergency, and signs ordinances. The council as a body hires a borough manager to run the day-to-day business of the borough. The mayor is an important position and one of leadership and being the public face of the borough." He paused. "May I be frank?"

"Of course," Connor agreed.

"Up until now, the face of Carlisle has been a man who's been in the office for twenty years and isn't up to the job. When he was elected, the government was organized differently, and the mayor didn't have a huge role in borough government. The council ran the government, and he had an ancillary role. He's proven he isn't able to handle the position it became. The council doesn't trust him and is being bogged down in petty issues rather than the ones that are truly important. His not seeking office is a godsend, but we need new blood and new ideas. Will you at least consider it?"

Connor's heart beat a mile a minute, and he was too excited to sit. This had been what he had always hoped to do: be a leader and be able to give back to the community. "Of course I will." He had taught a History of Local Governments course a few years earlier, so he understood how they worked historically. The modern incarnation couldn't be all that different. "But what about my job?"

"The mayor isn't a full-time position. It's a council leadership position. The borough manager runs things day to day. You will be part of the various committees, which have regular meetings once a month. I know it's a commitment, but part of what I'm here for is to work with you and support you." Connor liked Weston already. "Please say you'll consider it."

Thoughts and alternatives raced through his mind. This was something he wanted to do, and it would allow him to give back to the community in a meaningful way. He had hoped that someday the opportunity would present itself, and here it was. Part of him urged caution, while another argued for him to jump at what he wanted. "What do I need to do to get on the ballot?" he asked, and Wesley whooped a little before going into the details about gathering signatures and contacting people to help him. "Okay, let me think about it and I'll get back to you on Monday." There was a lot to think about, and no matter how much he might want to jump in with both feet, this was a decision that would require some thought. He needed to take the time to consider his options.

"Thank you. Please let me know if you have any questions." Weston gave him his number to make sure Connor had it, and they ended the call.

Connor set down his phone and wondered what Sterling would think about this development. It took him a second to realize that his first thought wasn't what *he* wanted, but what Sterling might think of what he wanted to do. Connor knew he had a history of throwing himself into his work and ignoring the other things in his life, but this felt different. He worried that Sterling would be unhappy and not like that he was considering running for mayor. He wanted Sterling to be happy, and he wanted—"Jesus Christ," he said out loud as he realized he not only wanted Sterling to be happy, he wanted to be the one to *make* him happy. Damn it all to hell, why couldn't things just be simple for once in his life? Was that too much to ask for?

He sighed and turned his attention to the damned mocking cursor and tried to make some headway, but thoughts of Sterling kept getting in the way.

FOR THE next two nights, Connor tossed and turned. During the day he tried to work and managed to make progress, but the idea of running for mayor and his attempts to finish his article, combined with thoughts of Sterling, kept his mind on a weird Ferris wheel that wouldn't stop turning.

Shortly before he was supposed to meet Sterling, Connor dressed and got ready to go. He hoped Sterling would understand why he wanted to run for office. Maybe it was a little farfetched. After all, he was delving into local politics in a big way, but the mayor's position was what was available, and Connor thought he could do a good job.

He checked himself in the mirror and then left the house. He decided to walk to Sterling's and took his time going through town. The sun was out, and as he passed through the downtown, the town seemed different to him. He saw the things that made it different and special, like the old courthouse and the church on the square where George Washington had once worshipped. Connor turned down Pomfret Street and then toward Sterling's, where he walked around the side and to the studio. Sterling was moving around inside, and Connor knocked before going in.

"Hey, Connor, look at this," he said brightly, practically bouncing as he came over to hug him. "I got an electronic mock-up of the calendar earlier today. Your great-aunt approved it, and I'm told the printing has begun." He grinned and sat down, paging through the calendar for next year.

When they came to April, Sterling paused and took Connor's hand. "I think I'm most proud of that picture because it was your idea." He squeezed Connor's fingers, but Connor could only stare at the image.

"Oh God." He hadn't given the calendar a thought. "I should have called you, but I wanted to surprise you in person, and I didn't think about the calendar because I didn't know it had moved this fast, but… I have some big news… that's going to make a real mess."

Sterling turned. "Don't tell me the college said you can't do the calendar. I thought they were fine with it since it was for the community." He got to his feet. "I can't turn this back now. It's already in the printing process, and it would cost the club more money to pull it back, and then everything would need to be redone." Sterling's eyes were almost cartoonishly wide, and Connor might have seen smoke coming out of his ears.

"It isn't that. And I haven't even told Aunt Lucille because I haven't made up my mind, but I guess I have now." He slumped into the chair near the desk. "I was asked to run for mayor. The current mayor, Phillip Randall, isn't running for reelection, and the deputy mayor asked me to run for the office."

Relief seemed to wash over Sterling, and then he grinned. "I think that's a great idea. You should do it."

Connor gaped at him. He'd had this whole speech prepared to try to convince Sterling that it was a good thing, and here Sterling was on board already. It left him a little speechless.

"I mean it." Sterling was up and had him in his arms before Connor could process everything. "You'd be a great mayor, and I'd help you. I bet your great-aunt would too." His enthusiasm was almost overwhelming.

"Hold it," Connor said. "I haven't made up my mind yet, and if you recall, we were just going over the sexy gay calendar that I'm in. It's bad enough that I know I'm going to have students who will want me to sign their calendars as Mr. April, but do you really think Carlisle is ready for a pin-up mayor? Those are words I never thought I'd utter."

Sterling rolled his eyes. "Are you going to let that stop you? It was for the community and the garden club. You weren't paid for it. You donated your image and your time to do this for the club and your great-aunt."

"I know. But can you hear what the news will make of this?"

"Look, go on down to Borough Hall and into the council chamber. On the wall are pictures of the former mayors. Let me tell you, some of those guys should have worked in a dairy, because they could have curdled the milk to make cottage cheese just by looking at it." He shivered. "Heck, we could have that picture framed and put on the wall for your picture. That room could use a little sexiness, because it's about as interesting as my dentist's office." Sterling grinned. "Come on. I know you want to do this. You put aside your misgivings to do this calendar because it would help the community, and now you have a chance to make a difference in a huge way. You can't turn it down."

Connor was speechless. Sterling actually understood what was important to him. Damn, no one else ever had. He jumped into his arms without a second thought. "You really think I should?"

"Hell yes." Sterling smirked and then took his lips. "Just think—I could be kissing a future mayor."

"YOU KNOW, we really should get something to eat," Connor said a couple hours later. They had ended up in Sterling's bedroom and were both sweaty, sticky, and sated. At least Connor hoped so. He was deliciously sore in a number of places and stretched languidly after sitting up. His stomach rumbled.

Sterling tugged him back down on the bed. "So, Your Honor, was that good for you?"

Connor groaned. "I'm not Your Honor yet, and yes, that was wonderful." He tried not to yawn. "You really think I should do this?" He had asked before, but it was a huge decision. "It's going to mean a lot of extra time and dedication." He worried he might not be up to the job. "I always figured at some point I'd run for council, but this seems like a big step."

Sterling closed his arms around him. "This is your decision. If you want to do it, then I say go for it. You'd do a great job and would be a wonderful representative for this town. But if it isn't something you really want to do, then don't. I know someone came to you, but that doesn't mean you have to say yes just because you were asked." Sterling lightly stroked his arm. "Make your decision about what you want, and then go for it. And if you decide to run, I'll take pictures of you for the campaign in front of Borough Hall and around town. My dad has had experience with this sort of thing. He was on the school board a number of years ago. So maybe he can give you some advice."

Connor smiled and snuggled closer. He hadn't expected this kind of support from Sterling… or anyone else. His great-aunt would probably tell him to wait. Connor hadn't made up his mind what he wanted to do, but knowing Sterling had his back went a long way. "I need to tell my Aunt Lucille."

Sterling's belly rumbled. "How about you call her and see what she says? I'm going to dress and get the grill started." He leaned over and gave Connor a kiss. "You go ahead and make your call. Then come on down." He climbed out of bed and found his clothes, which were spread around the floor, and then left the room.

Connor located his phone in the pocket of his pants, which he'd flung over the back of a chair, and called his great-aunt.

"To what do I owe this pleasure?" she said.

"As if you didn't know," Connor retorted.

"I have no idea what you're talking about," she said, evidently confused.

"You haven't been talking to someone on the council?" he asked. "Because I got a call two days ago." He had suspected that she had been talking him up, but apparently not. "You really didn't use your network of friends to put a bug in the ear of someone on the council?"

"No. What's this all about?" she asked a little tersely. "You're accusing me of something that I haven't done."

"Hardly, Auntie," he said gently. "I got a call a few days ago from the deputy mayor, and I've been asked to run."

"For what? I know the mayor isn't running again. Is the deputy going to run, and did he ask you to step in as deputy?"

"No. He asked me to run for mayor. Weston has family issues and doesn't feel he can take the higher office. He asked if I'd run for the top job, and I'm tempted." He wasn't sure about her reaction. "I thought at first that you might have put me up for it, but you haven't." Which meant that he truly had done this on his own. Connor didn't know who had mentioned him, but he was very pleased that someone had thought enough of him on his own merits.

"I didn't and I wouldn't," Aunt Lucille said flatly. "I know this is something you'd like to do, but is the timing right? Your tenure review process will start soon, and there will be plenty of work to get that ready. You have your classes. And what about Sterling? If you do this, you aren't going to have much time for anything else."

Connor was a little taken aback. He had expected resistance from Sterling, but his great-aunt had always been supportive of what he wanted, sometimes pushing him into things when he was hesitant. To have her take the other approach was a little surprising. "You think I shouldn't run?"

"I didn't say that. I just want you to make sure you aren't spreading yourself too thin. What does Sterling think?"

"That he's been kissing a future mayor, and he's pretty excited about it. Sterling offered to help take pictures through town that I can use, and to design fliers and other campaign posters and literature. He also said he'd get in touch with Grant for some help. He was on the school board." Connor's excitement rose again. "I think I really want to do it. But I can't without support. I know it's going to take time and effort, but as far as tenure goes, this is going to help me, not hurt. You know I'm all about helping the community—you taught me that."

"Yes, I know." Aunt Lucille seemed strung tight. "And I'm not telling you not to do it but to make a careful decision. If you want to run, I'll support it. You know that. And Sterling seems like he'll be there in your corner."

Connor put the phone on speaker and began getting dressed. Talking to his great-aunt while he was naked just seemed wrong on so many levels. "I think he will be. But this is my decision."

Aunt Lucille cleared her throat. "Yes, it is. But are you running away again? Sterling is a nice young man. I like him, and I think he's good for you. I'd hate—"

"Auntie, I'm not running away, and if I were, it would be my business. I know you think I'm lonely and desperate, but—"

"I do not," she snapped. "What I think is that I saw the way he looked at you and how you looked at him. I was there taking those pictures, and the two of you steamed up the lens. Do you know how rare that is?" She cleared her throat again, and Connor wondered if she was coming down with a cold. "I never found that, and I would have given anything, when I was younger, to have had someone look at me like I was the center of the universe and everything revolved around me." She rarely opened up about her love life or her romantic past, so Connor was getting a glimpse into a life he knew little about.

"I understand. But Sterling was supportive, and he said I should do it." The truth was that Connor had been worried about the same thing. The reason his great-aunt's words hurt so much was because he had asked himself those questions. Maybe she was right, and running would be biting off more than he could chew. Connor didn't know. "There's no one else running, and it's a great chance for me to really make our community better. When I walked to Sterling's, I looked at the town differently. I see things now that I haven't before. Like how the areas around the college and the downtown are so separate. We need to more fully integrate the college into the town. The college has a lot to offer, and so does the town.

But they keep things to themselves and don't support each other the way they should. They need each other, but they're separate in many ways. The trees downtown are a mess. The streets need work…. There's a huge number of things that need to be done, but they aren't happening. I'm not sure why, but I want to help. I know I don't know everything, but I'll get up to speed. I'm a good study." He smiled as Aunt Lucille chuckled.

"I know you'd do a good job. But take some time and think about what you want. I won't stand in your way and will be out beating my drum to help you if you decide to run."

Connor sighed. "But you don't think I should."

Aunt Lucille didn't answer right away. "This is one of those areas where I don't think I should have an opinion. I know what I would decide, but that's what would be right for me and not you."

Damn. Connor pulled on his pants and then wiped his eyes. How in the hell did he get so lucky as to have her in his life?

"I'll only ask that you think about it hard, plan it out the way you would one of your classes—with alternatives depending on how things work out—and once you know what you want to do, then go for it with your usual energy and enthusiasm."

"I will. You know that. But if I decide to do this, I wanted to be the one to tell you."

"Then you've decided already?" Aunt Lucille said. "You had made up your mind before you called me." She didn't sound disappointed. "Let me guess, it was Sterling's support that tipped the balance." And just like that, he could almost hear the smile in her voice.

"I know what I want to do, but there are ramifications that need to be considered. I told Weston that I'd give him an answer on Monday, and if I go forward, then I have to gather signatures to get myself on the ballot." At that point, the work would begin.

"Let me know what you decide," she said, and Connor promised that he would before ending the call and finishing getting dressed.

CONNOR FOUND Sterling manning the grill. "Is there anything I can do to help?"

"No. I have some fresh vegetables and a fruit salad all ready to go." He turned the steaks and closed the lid of the grill. "What did your great-aunt say?"

"That she would support whatever my decision was." That was as close a summation as he wanted to give. And it sufficed. His great-aunt would be there if he decided to make a run for the mayor's office. That was what counted. The rest would fall into line. "I still need to make up my mind." He slipped his arms around Sterling. "But I appreciate your support." Now he needed to figure out what his future could possibly look like.

Sterling snorted softly. "I know what you want to do. I can see it in your eyes when you talk about running. They light up. So go ahead, make your decision, and then go forward. We can talk to my father tomorrow and put together a strategy for your campaign."

"You think you know me so well." He leaned his head on Sterling's back.

"I know when your eyes go as deep as a well. It's pretty obvious that this is what you want, so do it. If someone else enters the race and you lose, then you tried. And if you win, you'll do a fantastic job. Go for it, and let the chips fall where they may."

Connor swallowed hard. "But the calendar, and…."

"You know about it. The calendar isn't going to be a surprise. Figure out how you want to deal with it." Sterling slowly turned in his arms. "We'll build your campaign around a desire to serve the community. The calendar is only another way you've been supportive. If someone wants to go after you for it, then we'll turn it back on them."

This was what he really wanted, and Connor felt his decision settle around him like a warm coat. Once he had decided to go for it, his indecision and nervousness fell away. This was right, and with everyone's support, he might just get elected and everything could work out.

Chapter 13

"The calendar is for sale," Lucille said as soon as Sterling picked up the phone. "We got the first batch today, and the preordered copies have been delivered and paid for. We have it on the club website, and one of the ladies is good with Facebook and all that social media stuff. She put it up, and we're getting emails already. The outlets have the calendars, and we're sending people there. I'm not expecting a run on them, but it's good to know that they're out. I've also been told that there will be an article in the *Carlisle Observer* tonight, and apparently the Mechanicsburg paper is going to print something as well, since a lot of our members are from that area. That should help us too."

"Excellent." He sat back in his desk chair. "Have you told Connor, or should I let him know?" Over the past month, Connor had been a very busy man. He and Sterling's father, along with a number of people from his dad's community, had been out gathering signatures. Sterling had canvassed his own neighborhood. "He's out at the farmer's market meeting people and shaking hands." Connor had been doing that each week.

"I know he's been busy."

"Yes, he has. He turned in the petitions to the election commission, and they called to certify that he had enough and would be on the ballot. So the campaign has really started. He makes sure to attend any public gatherings and goes to the farmer's market each week." Sometimes Sterling went as well, just to watch Connor in his full Scottish regalia.

"And how are things for you?" Aunt Lucille asked, and Sterling hummed softly.

"Going well. I'm busy." He knew exactly what she was fishing for and purposely didn't give her any information. He and Connor saw each other at least three times a week, and Connor usually stopped by the house once the market was over. Sterling liked that they had a routine. It meant that even though they were both busy, they had special times when they could see each other.

"I meant how are you and Connor getting on?" she pressed.

"We get along great, though I contend that Connor should wear pants sometimes, especially when it's raining cats and dogs and it's windy. We don't need another Marilyn Monroe moment. I was afraid that Connor was going to get a ticket for indecent exposure. How would *that* look in the papers?" He grinned at how he'd sidestepped her question.

Speaking of Connor, he heard the side door open, and then the man himself stood in front of him, windblown hair, skin kissed by the sun, eyes bright with excitement, cheeks flushed, a smile on his lips.

"No, I meant has there been any tension between you? I know that things like this can put a strain on things, especially something new." It was sweet that she was concerned, while maddening as all hell at the same time.

"I understand, and if Connor wishes to speak with you about our relationship, that's his business. But if you want to know something, you should ask him. I'm not going to tell tales out of school." There were enough balls in the air already—they didn't need secret communications and back-alley talks. Even though Connor was in the room, he still didn't feel comfortable talking about their relationship with her. It was private and special, and he didn't want anyone intruding. Sterling was damned possessive about what they had.

"Fair enough," Lucille said rather happily, and for a second before she hung up, Sterling thought he might have just passed some sort of test.

"Was my great-aunt giving you the third degree?" Connor seemed amused. "You know she's like the Spanish Inquisition when it comes to extracting information. And the worst part is that she does it with a damned smile."

"Tell me about it. She asked, but I gave her the runaround. I'm pretty sure she liked it." He grinned, and Connor came around behind him and placed his hands on his shoulders.

"Don't be so sure of that. Sometimes with Aunt Lucille, it's what you don't say that has more meaning. As a kid I was almost scared to tell her anything, and I could never hide anything from her, ever. I swear she has ESP or something. But I did hear what you said at the end, and I'm grateful for it." He leaned closer, and his scent filled Sterling's nose. "I feel the same way. I don't want her interfering or butting into what we have."

Sterling sighed and closed his eyes, reveling in the calm that came over him when they were together. "How did meet-the-public go?"

"Good. I shook quite a few hands and talked to a lot of people. There are a huge number of folks who feel like I do, that things have been stagnant for a long time and that they need to change and move forward. People want parks with working playground equipment and streets that are cleaned and in good repair, not potholes and ruts. They want the borough to manage the street trees rather than just letting them go." He sighed. "And they want more jobs, good ones, and to somehow bring people back downtown. They love their town and want it to be better, but they aren't sure how to do it."

"Sounds like a big job," Sterling whispered. "It's a good thing the guy running for mayor has lots of energy. He's going to need it."

"Actually, I need some energy now. I'm really hungry, and I thought you and I could go out for dinner. I've talked to people for three hours. My throat is parched and my stomach thinks my throat's been cut."

"Colorful," Sterling commented. He saved what he was working on and locked the computer. "Why don't we walk over to the Molly." He checked his calendar, grateful he didn't have an appointment this evening, locked the door, and they left through the house, with Sterling grabbing his wallet and a cap. Then they walked the three blocks to the tap room.

Inside they had to wait for a table, and one opened up by the front window. They sat down and looked over the beer selection. When their server approached, they ordered their drinks and then glanced at the food menu.

"Oh my God!" An excited female voice cut through the restaurant like a knife. Then she drew closer, carrying a bag. "It's you—both of you." She grinned and pulled one of the calendars out of the bag. "I just saw it at the bookstore down the street and bought it because it was so *hot*." She fanned herself. "And then here you are." She opened the calendar to April. "Would you sign it for me?" She passed it over, and Connor took the calendar and the pen she thrust in front of him and signed it. Sterling did the same.

"I'm glad you like it," Connor said.

"Are you two, like, a couple? Are all these guys couples?"

Connor smiled. "Yes, we are dating, and the calendar brought us together." As soon as he said that, she sighed. "But not all of the guys are couples, though a number of them are. All of the guys are local." He smiled again as the server brought their beers.

Sterling hoped the lady would excuse herself, but she stood near the table, bouncing on her heels. "How long have you been dating?"

"A few months. Tonight is our date night," Connor answered patiently. Sterling loved how he gently asked her to move on without saying the words.

"Of course. You guys have a great evening, and thank you." She held the calendar to her chest. "You guys are really hot, and I love this. I can't wait to tell my roommates that I met you." She hurried away.

Connor's smile faded, and he seemed to pull into himself as soon as they were alone again. "I hope that doesn't keep happening all over town. I expected this to happen a few times, but not right away." Connor seemed a little pale.

"Come on. She was excited, and you can't tell me that wasn't a little fun. How many times in your life do you get squeed over something?" Sterling couldn't help smiling, and even Connor couldn't keep the corners of his mouth from turning up. "It's one heck of an ego boost."

"Yeah." Then the smile slipped from his lips. "Can you imagine how my students are going to react?" he asked morosely. "I'm going to have to put up with that for months."

Sterling lightly bumped Connor's leg under the table. "Drama queen much? It was one person, and she just bought the calendar and happened to see us. It's not that bad, and it isn't like everyone who gets one is going to go through town looking for the guys. It's meant to be fun." He leaned over the table, hating that Connor wasn't happy. "And we did have fun. Remember the day that picture was taken? That was one of the hottest things ever. People like it, and if there's some excitement about the calendar, then that helps your great-aunt, who is hoping to sell five hundred of them." That seemed like a lot to Sterling. He hoped things turned out well.

"You're right. I'm probably overreacting. It isn't like I'm one of the Beatles and people are trying to rip my clothes off." Finally he smiled again.

"Maybe just a little," Sterling told him. "Relax. We did something good, and it will help the town in the end. That's the goal." He was quickly realizing just how private a person Connor was. He wondered how he was going to survive in the public eye if he got elected. "I was just thinking… when is the election filing deadline?"

"For mayor, ten days. So far I'm told that no one else has inquired about running." Connor seemed to relax. "So if I wait it out just ten more days, then that's pretty much it. Someone could try to mount a write-in campaign, but those so rarely work." He bounced in his seat a little. "I want this so bad. I've been walking through town, and there are so many things that need attention." He sipped his beer and put the glass down again, leaning forward. "Your dad has been a huge help." He seemed to remember something. "Oh, did I tell you? Apparently your dad and my great-aunt went out gathering signatures together."

Sterling nodded. "I take it Aunt Lucille didn't tell you that she and my dad also went to dinner last week." He bit his lower lip. "It seems your great-aunt is tight-lipped, and my father gossips like crazy." He smiled. "Dad took her to the Outback Steakhouse." He rolled his eyes. "Yeah, I know, but Dad's kind of clueless when it comes to food. Your great-aunt had a good time, from what he said, and then afterward Dad took her for a walk by the creek to look at the stars. He says it was very nice and declined to go into any more detail." That alone was telling.

"They were making eyes at each other when they were at your place for the photoshoot. I saw your dad watching her like a hawk."

Sterling groaned. "God, I hope my father isn't playing games like he does at the home."

Connor lifted his beer, and Sterling envied the glass as it contacted Connor's lips. Damn, he wanted to taste him right now. Sterling shifted to get things more comfortable and drank his own beer. When the server returned, they ordered dinner and resumed their conversation when he left.

"Do you really think they're serious?" Connor asked. "I know I should stay out of it. Aunt Lucille is an adult, and Lord knows she's capable of taking care of herself. But you said your dad is kind of the community stud, and I don't want him studding all over my great-aunt." Connor cocked his eyebrows.

"I don't want to think of my dad studding it up with anyone. I mean, he's my dad. I much prefer to believe that I was delivered by the stork than thinking about my father doing the horizontal hula with anyone." He shivered. "I know it's a stereotype, but I don't want to consider that aspect of him and my mom. It's just squicky. I know they must have done it because they had me. But…."

"Yeah… I know." Connor finished his beer and ordered another as the food began to arrive. "There's something unsettling about the people who read you bedtime stories and kissed your knees to make the hurts better actually having sex." He shivered. "They're people, and of course they had sex. It's fun and hot and, well, everything. But…."

Sterling put his hands up. "Okay, that's enough. Let's talk about something more pleasant."

Connor thought a second. "I agree. I have an appointment for a root canal next week. Let's talk about that." He flashed a smile. "Or we could talk about the campaign. Regardless of whether I have an opponent, I want to run some kind of campaign so I can meet the people of the borough and learn what their concerns are. Your dad suggested an interview with the paper and maybe a meet-and-greet somewhere that's open to everyone interested. He said that he'd look into a location we could use."

"That's awesome. And I think we should get you dressed up in your best tartan and take some pictures in front of the old courthouse and Borough Hall. Make you look like mayoral material. We can build a campaign website. It will give you a forum to get your message out and to respond to things that are happening in town. Make your positions clear. Though if I'm being honest, there's one particular position I'm interested in." Sterling leered, and Connor set down his sandwich with an exaggerated roll of his eyes.

"You're always thinking about that. Not that I'm complaining, but I don't want to be overheard." He continued eating, and Sterling dug into his chicken sandwich as a throat cleared nearby.

"Can I help you?" Connor asked with more genuineness than Sterling could have managed. All he wanted was a quiet evening out together. Sterling figured he was going to have to get used to this.

"Phillip Randall," the man who'd interrupted said without extending his hand.

Sterling narrowed his gaze. He was a little perturbed at yet another interruption. "Do you know us?"

"I'm the current mayor," he said, and Sterling met Connor's gaze.

"That's nice. Is there something you wanted?" This guy seemed to think he was important enough that everyone should know who he was, or else he was playing dumb. "I don't know of any business you could have with us."

Randall seemed a little taken aback, which was exactly what Sterling was hoping for. "I understand that Mr. Hillyard here has decided to run for mayor."

"Yes, I have. I filed my petition for the office a few weeks ago." He set down his glass. "Is there something you wanted? Do you have any advice on the office?" He smiled, but Sterling knew it was cold. Outwardly Connor was being nice, but there was nothing beneath.

"I...." Suddenly the man didn't seem to know what he wanted to say.

"It's nice to meet you. My great-aunt has told me a lot about you." He grinned with a hint of devilry. Connor's great-aunt probably had, and Sterling was sure that she had had nothing nice to say. "I'm here with my friend, and we were just enjoying our dinner. It was nice of you to stop by. Maybe we can have a chance to speak soon."

The mayor didn't take the hint. "I've seen you in the square talking to people and meeting folks. You need to know that there are many obligations in this community and that nothing is as easy as you seem to believe it will be. But then, if you're elected, you'll learn just the kind of tightrope the mayor's job can be."

"I'm sure I will. Though I believe that listening to the people of Carlisle and making sure the business of the people is what gets done will lead to the right outcomes." Connor's jaw hardened. "I believe that the mayor and all the town leaders should be interested in what's best for the town. There will be difficult decisions, and some of them won't be popular, but there are times when hard choices have to be made whether they are popular at the time or not." Damn, Sterling loved the way Connor held himself. It was sexy seeing him standing toe to toe with this guy.

"I wish you well," he finally said and turned away from the table. He walked back across the restaurant with a piece of toilet paper stuck to the bottom of his shoe. Sterling did his best not to pay attention to it. Laughing was adolescent, and yet it was still funny.

"That was weird. I wonder what the heck that was about," Connor commented softly. "Did he seem kind of creepy to you? Your dad said he ran unopposed the last time, and a couple of elections ago he had a worthy challenger who ended up dropping out a few weeks before the election. He thought there was something to it, but didn't know what it was." He held Sterling's gaze. "I get the idea that he's one of those guys who will play dirty if he thinks it will get him what he wants."

"That's been the rumor for a long time. I think that's part of how he keeps getting reelected. There aren't many people who want to go up against him. And I'm a little surprised that there aren't more people getting into the race, since he's said he isn't running." Sterling leaned closer. "If you talk to him again, be nice but not friendly. You don't need him as an ally—or an enemy either."

"Aunt Lucille told me that he and his wife want to relocate to Florida, so I doubt he's going to be around here for very much longer. Which is a relief. The last thing the town needs is a former mayor making trouble whenever the town decides to go in a different direction." Connor asked for the check when the server returned, and he brought it right away. Connor grabbed it first and paid with his credit card.

"Do you want to go for a walk?" Sterling asked once they were out on the sidewalk. It had been a sweltering hot day, but with the setting sun, the temperature had eased back and the sidewalk was in the shade.

"Sure," Connor agreed, and they headed toward the college, stepping off the sidewalk and under the huge trees that shaded the quad. "I love this part of campus. It's beautifully shaded and so green."

"I haven't spent much time on campus." Sterling turned to Connor. "I've been thinking, and I have to ask. Are you really sure you want to delve into politics? It's not that I don't think you should do it. I just want to make sure you're okay with all it's going to entail." He was proud of Connor for what he was doing, but he wanted to be sure he was comfortable opening his life to scrutiny.

"Let me explain. These red Adirondack chairs are a staple of the campus. They move all over as the students gather." Connor ran his hand over the back of one of the chairs. "The previous president thought of the idea, and it has been a huge hit."

"I see."

Connor sighed. "The current president didn't like them and wanted to remove them because they tear up the lawn. The students made their desires known, and the chairs stayed." He grinned. "Sometimes the people just need to stand up and say what they want. Of course, the current leader of the college is an idiot, in my opinion. Thankfully, the board of governors is excellent, so they keep her in line."

"Why not fire her?"

"Too big a payout of the contract. She has a year and a half and then she'll be gone." Connor sounded happy. "There's politics everywhere.

The faculty didn't like this candidate for president, but the board did, and now the board is paying the price for their decision. But it's the right thing to do because they love the college and want it to be successful." He paused. "See, politics is everywhere whenever you deal with other people. When I go for tenure, it's another political exercise." He shrugged.

"I get it." Politics was part of Connor's everyday life. To Sterling it was something mysterious and daunting, but to Connor it was business as usual. "This is something you thrive on." And he supposed that if Connor wanted to do some good in the community, there was going to be a political aspect to it. He even supposed that Connor's great-aunt had to deal with politics when it came to the garden club.

"And I bet there was a great deal of politics in the modeling world. Some people are in, others are out, groups and cliques form to advance themselves and hold others back. Politics is part of daily life."

Sterling nodded, realizing he had gotten on the bad side of the politics. "I suppose." He hated that Connor understood what had been happening maybe better than he did. Heck, if Sterling had understood the situation at the time and how he'd appear, he might have acted differently. Then maybe he'd still have his career and Alexander would be on the outs. He rolled his eyes at his own naiveté. Alexander was one of the super-beautiful people, and that carried a ton of weight in that world. It was what everyone made their money on.

Sterling didn't realize he was brooding until Connor snapped him out of his thoughts. "I'm sorry," Connor whispered. "I shouldn't have brought it up."

"It's not your fault. And I see your point."

Connor stepped back, his hand over his mouth. "Oh God, was I just mansplaining? If I was, I didn't mean to."

Sterling gawked. "Mansplaining?" That was a new one.

"Yeah. It usually happens with women, but I suppose it can be with guys too. Let's say someone doesn't understand something… to make it simple, say Aunt Lucille has an issue, and whether she asked for my help or not, I explain her problem to her and what I think she should do like I have all the answers. You know, like on one of those Master Mind quiz shows where the experts have to explain their answers because they're soooo smart." His voice went up an octave, and Sterling laughed. "Sometimes I have a way of slipping into educator mode."

"Sweetheart, I promise you, if I find you mansplaining, or gaysplaining… or any kind of 'splaining—God, I just sounded like Ricky Ricardo—" He put his hands on his head for a second. "—I promise I'll tell you." He smiled and tugged Connor to him. "Come on, let's keep walking and you can 'splain all you want." He chuckled and took Connor's hand for the rest of their walk.

Chapter 14

"Have you seen this?" Cotten asked as he strode into Connor's office at the college the following Monday morning. "It's from yesterday, and Carrie said I should save it for you. It seems your little calendar is causing quite a kerfuffle." He held up the Local section of the Mechanicsburg newspaper. "'Garden Club Goes Gay!' Don't you love the headline?" He snickered.

Connor practically snatched the paper out of his hands. "Good God." He didn't know whether to smile or not.

"The article is actually very positive, and they talk a lot about the fact that the money is for projects around the community, but there's also a hint of snark, which makes it really good." He grinned, and Connor groaned. "What's with you? This article is going to sell a ton of calendars."

"I know. Aunt Lucille is going to be thrilled. I think I'm worried that my students are going to see me as Mr. April rather than as their history professor."

Cotten sat down in the wooden guest chair, leaning forward. "What's going to happen is that your classes are all going to fill up and you'll be beating them off with a stick. Besides, this is a local thing. Today it's the calendar, and tomorrow the headline will be that someone's cow gave birth to a chicken." Cotten had a way of putting things in perspective. "Relax and enjoy the fact that you did something good. And just so you know, Carrie bought a copy and declared that every month was April." He stood back up. "It's a great thing."

Connor smiled. "Yeah, it is, and it's going to be a success." That sank in, and he smiled, really smiled. "Can I keep this?"

"Sure." Cotten stood slowly.

"How is the arm? I should have asked earlier."

"It's healing well, and I should be able to just wear the sling in a week or so. You know, if they decide to do a second version of the calendar, definitely keep me in mind, okay?" He left the office, and Connor shook his head before reading the entire article. Then he picked up the phone.

"Connor, sweetheart, I'm a little busy right now. The outlet in Mechanicsburg has no more calendars, and the bookstore in Carlisle is almost out. I have to run to check on the other stores and deliver calendars." The excitement in Aunt Lucille's voice was amazing. "Grant is picking me up in five minutes, so I have to go. Love you, honey, and I'll call you this afternoon." She hung up, and Connor snickered as he called Sterling.

"Did you see the paper?"

"Yeah…. Garden Club…. Hot Stuff," Sterling chuckled through the phone at the headlines. "I saw Mechanicsburg's too. This is going to sell calendars. I was so worried that it wouldn't work, and…." Sterling choked up, and Connor did the same. "It feels good to do something right."

Connor nodded, even though he was alone in the room. "Aunt Lucille says she's already out delivering more."

"Dad is taking her, apparently. This is going to work out, and the club is going to be able to continue their mission. That's what we set out to do, and it looks like it will happen."

That was right. What more did Connor want? It was perfect. "Yeah. It's going to be okay." His office phone rang, so Connor said goodbye.

"Wait—will I see you tonight?"

"I have so much to do. Wednesday? Do you have appointments?"

"I'll see you then." Sterling hung up, and Connor answered the other phone, happy that everything was good.

CONNOR SHUT down his computer, pleased that his article was finally done and reviewed. He'd just sent it to the editor, and now he was waiting to hear what they thought. But it was done. What he had supposed would be a quick article had turned into something much different than he originally anticipated. Connor chuckled as he realized a lot of things in his life had gone that way lately.

He and Sterling had expected to work on the calendar project together and then go their separate ways. It was only supposed to be a project to help his great-aunt, but along the way things had changed. Now they were dating, and Connor didn't want to go back to the way things had been before. His life had been lonely and kind of black and white. Now his life had color and texture. Hell, he was happy. The only thing that nagged at the back of his mind was just how long this could last. After all, he'd heard once that you could have a hot job, a hot place to live, and a hot lover, but not all three at the same time. It was one of the laws of the universe. And right now, he liked his small home, Sterling was definitely a hot lover, and if things continued, he was in line to be mayor as well as a professor. The universe was going to kick in, he just knew it. The only question was where the foot was going to land, and he hoped to heck it wasn't in the balls.

"STERLING?" CONNOR called as he walked through the gate into the backyard. The scent of grilling meat drew him in, and all he had to do was follow his nose.

"Dammit," Sterling's voice drifted to him through the open windows. "That bastard!"

Connor picked up the pace and called once again. "What's wrong?"

"Have you seen this?" Sterling asked as he opened the back door and practically tugged Connor into the house. "It's *Pennsylvania Live*, one of the online local news outlets. It seems that they've picked up on the calendar and decided to write an article. Only their headline is…." Sterling turned the screen so Connor could see it.

"Calendar Boy for Mayor!" it read. Connor felt his stomach fall to his feet and bounce back. For a second he thought he was going to be sick. The article included an image of their calendar page. Connor stepped closer to read the article, which explained that Connor, who had posed for the Cumberland County Garden Club calendar, was also running for mayor of Carlisle. It was surprisingly factual, given the inflammatory headline.

"Okay…." Connor tried to keep his nerves under control. "It isn't that bad… really."

"The article is pretty decent. It even gives you credit for doing the calendar to help the community. It's the comments that made me angry, and I suggest you don't read them. Most of them are from people outside of Carlisle and don't count anyway. There are some that are very positive, but others are downright mean, and even more are just stupid."

Connor scrolled down to read a few and then stepped away, relinquishing the mouse like his hand had been burned. "Should I just bow out?" he asked, almost to himself, and it took him a second to realize he had said that out loud.

"Hell no," Sterling answered. "You can't let the small-minded people of the world get to you like this. They will always be out there. And… really. You haven't hidden that you were gay, so there's no angle there. The calendar is out there for everyone to see. It's no secret. Please. This will blow over in a day or two, and then things will return to normal."

"Yeah. But people aren't talking about you like this," Connor said, lowering himself into a chair. "I probably should have seen something like this coming."

"You did, in a way, but I didn't see something like this happening. Honestly, I thought the calendar would sell a number of copies because it was the garden club, but I wasn't expecting this type of splash." Sterling slipped his arms around Connor. "It's going to be okay. This is going to be good for your great-aunt and the calendar sales, and it will probably be good for your campaign. You just got more advertising than you could ever have been able to afford." He scrolled down to the end of the article. "They actually included some things that you put on social media about what you stand for and hope to accomplish. This is a good thing."

Connor wasn't so sure. "But the headline…."

"Will grab attention." Sterling hugged him tighter. "I'm not going to step back from this because things get a little rough. When I encouraged you to do this, I said I'd back you up, and I will. No matter what."

Connor closed his eyes and leaned back against Sterling, soaking in his warmth and strength. Sterling was right—if Connor wanted to do this, then he was in for the long haul. "I'll be okay." He sighed. "The thing is that I want to be taken seriously, and not just because I did the calendar." He wasn't expressing things the way he wanted. "I don't want to be the calendar-boy mayor. I want to be the best leader the borough of Carlisle has ever had."

Sterling hugged him tighter. "You do realize that you can be both."

And just like that, Sterling took a firmer hold of his heart. He was right. Connor didn't have to be defined by one picture in a service calendar. He was more than that, he knew it, and it seemed so did Sterling. "Thank you." He put his hands on top of Sterling's and held them there.

"It's just a few more days and then the deadline will pass and you'll be the next mayor. The attention regarding the calendar will fade, and life will settle into whatever the new normal will be." Sterling sniffed, and his arms jerked away. "Damn it all, I forgot about dinner." He raced away to rescue whatever was on the grill.

Sterling returned with four hockey pucks on a plate. Apparently they had once been burgers, but now they were burnt offerings to a Grecian god. Sterling carried the plate into the kitchen and thunked the ashes of dinner into the trash. "I'm sorry."

"It's okay. We'll figure something out." Now it was his turn to hug Sterling. "I can order something and have it delivered. It's not a big deal. Go on and turn on the television. Sit down and relax. I'll be right in." Connor held him a few moments longer, and when Sterling left the kitchen, Connor called the tap room and placed a delivery order.

"Connor," Sterling called as though he were in distress. Connor hurried back to find Sterling had been watching the local news.

"I wasn't going to run again. But after consultation with my wife," Mayor Randall was saying to a reporter, "I have decided that I have to run for another term as mayor of Carlisle. It's obvious that the people need me, and someone has to stand up for decency in our community. The current candidate for mayor has already proven himself unworthy of the office. The people of Carlisle deserve someone with integrity—"

Sterling snorted loudly, cutting off the rest of what he said. "That man wouldn't know decency if it bit him on the ass," he practically shouted, and Connor tried to hear what else was said, but the interview ended, and he slowly lowered himself into one of the chairs.

Connor felt as though his legs had been knocked out from under him. "I'm not decent? Unworthy?" He blinked and ground his teeth.

"That man is an underhanded snake who isn't worthy of anything. Don't you pay attention to a single thing he says. Phillip Randall running for office on a decency platform is like Satan himself running on truth, love, and puppies." Sterling's voice rose, and Connor smiled as Sterling hugged him tightly. "He doesn't know what decency is, and he certainly isn't the standard for who is worthy of office. If he's just decided to run, then he has to file everything in a few days."

Connor sighed. "I guess I had figured that with no one else running, getting the job would be smooth. But I suppose that nothing worth having is easy." He put his head on Sterling's shoulder. Sterling's scent surrounded him, and in seconds, the beginnings of desire coursed through him. This man made him feel good, even when the world seemed hurtful. Connor wanted Sterling—it seemed he always wanted Sterling. At work he found his mind traveling the blocks to Sterling's studio, wondering what he was doing, rather than where it should be, on his work. He tightened his hold, taking comfort in Sterling's strength and the way Sterling held him in return. The heated desire soon backed away to a simmer, still there but less urgent as he simply let himself accept the comfort and care so freely offered.

"Look, you've already started campaigning and meeting people. We need to move ahead with campaign literature, signs, and everything else. We'll get your name out there."

"I can't afford all that. I don't have a huge campaign budget. This isn't like I'm running for president or something." He was starting to feel a little overwhelmed and didn't want to talk about it right now. Randall's words hung over his head, and he wasn't sure how to banish them. He knew that he had to let it run off his back and just ignore it. If he was going to run for office, people would say nasty things said about him.

"Just remember why you want to do this," Sterling whispered. "This isn't about you but what's best for the community. Randall has spent the past twenty years using the mayor's office for self-aggrandizement. People know that. You want to be mayor to help the community. So we'll make sure that's our message."

Connor swallowed really hard at the *our*. Connor had never really been part of an *our* before. "Why would you do this? Why would you put yourself through this? People are going to be looking at you too, and who knows what they'll decide to say about you." Maybe this entire idea was crazy.

Sterling seemed taken aback. "Why wouldn't I?"

Chapter 15

After dinner, Sterling cleaned up while Connor sat watching television. He understood how Connor felt, but this was politics, and a local race at that. These things could get ugly and very personal. Connor was just beginning to get a taste of that. Sterling finished up and turned out the lights before joining Connor in the living room.

He seemed to be ignoring the television and staring at the wall. Whatever he was thinking, Sterling figured it wasn't good. At times like this, he tended to brood, and maybe that was something they had in common.

Sterling picked up the remote and turned off the television, then extended his hand. He didn't say anything, but Connor seemed to understand what he wanted.

Sterling turned out the lights as they walked through the house, leading Connor upstairs and into the bedroom, where he sat on the edge of the bed. His attitude really concerned Sterling. How was Connor going to make it through the next few months of the campaign if something like this bothered him so much? It worried Sterling, and he knew he had to snap Connor out of it.

He could try sex, but Lord knows the penis was not a healing magic wand—though in the right hands, it could do miraculous things. "Do you trust me?"

Connor nodded. "I do."

0"More pictures?" Connor asked as soon as Sterling stepped into the bedroom.

Sterling set the camera on the table beside the bed, stalking closer to Connor. "Yes. It's how I capture beauty. Will you allow me to capture you?" He swallowed. Sterling wasn't going to do anything without Connor's permission.

Connor nodded, and Sterling climbed onto the bed, straddling Connor, who stared up at him, mouth open slightly, his lips red, eyes wide and searching. Sterling unbuttoned his shirt as he leaned forward. He parted the fabric as he touched Connor's lips, baring his chest while

Sterling took possession of his sweet, intoxicating mouth. Sterling could kiss Connor forever. Each time there was the flavor, rich and slightly sweet, that was all Connor, but the rest changed each and every time, sometimes spicier and herbal, and it didn't seem to have anything to do with what Connor had eaten. Not that it mattered. Sterling loved all the flavors of Connor and feasted on his lips for quite a while, building heat, but only up to a point. This wasn't about sex as much as it was about intimacy, the two of them together.

He pulled back and felt for his camera while holding Sterling's gaze. "Don't move," he whispered and looked through the lens, taking the picture.

"What are you going to use those for?"

"They aren't for me." He smiled and lowered the camera. "They're for you." He snapped another image and one more, then kissed Connor again before capturing the wildness in his eyes. "These are so you can remember who you are and what you do to me." He slipped Connor out of his shirt and unfastened the kilt so the fabric flowed free around Connor's legs.

"Sterling." Connor smiled and groaned, holding the fabric in place. "I don't want any naked pictures."

Sterling grinned. "I said these pictures were for you. If I took naked ones, those would be for me." He winked and tugged half the kilt open, baring one leg and hip all the way up, and snapped another image. Connor was so enticing, and the camera loved him. Sterling could watch him through the viewfinder for hours. He swallowed hard, his throat dry when Connor sat closer, using his arms to prop himself up.

Sterling took another picture—*snap*—and held his breath. Connor's half-lidded eyes glistened, his lips parted slightly, muscles taut and long. His head leaned slightly to the side as the fabric pooled around his waist. *Snap*. Sterling had trouble keeping his hand steady as Connor drew even closer. *Snap*. He didn't move, just let Connor play out in front of him. Sterling held his breath as Connor leaned his head back—*snap*—raised his leg enticingly—*snap*—

Sterling wanted to put down his camera, but he didn't dare. Connor was going with what he'd asked, enticing him, almost daring him to stop. Yet Sterling was unable to. Connor drew him in, and now that he was here, this close to him, he couldn't look away. *Snap*.

Connor slowly lay back down, his movements unhurried, deliberate. It might have only taken a second, but through his camera, it seemed to take a long time. *Snap.* Sterling didn't want to miss a second, so he continued watching, his finger depressing the shutter button.

He had long ago come to realize that there were some parts of his life that he only experienced through his camera lens. Seeing them was one thing, but capturing them on film or in a digital image was so much better. Not because he could look at them again, but because the camera allowed him to catch something fleeting and search for the perfect. The perfect image, the perfect moment, and maybe, if he was lucky, the perfect human form. Like a Renaissance painter or sculptor, he wanted to use his art to capture the best of humanity. *Snap.* The images of Connor lying on his bed, gazing up at him, might just be as close to an image of passionate perfection as he could ever hope to capture. Not that he would know until he developed the film, but it didn't matter. Just seeing Connor this way was almost too good to be true.

"Sterling," Connor whispered as he settled back on the pillow, the word calling to Sterling's heart. Without thinking, he snapped another image before finally setting down the camera.

Now he felt as though he could breathe. Sterling blinked and let his mind settle in the present. Connor stretched out, and Sterling leaned over him, kissing those incredible lips once again. He had expected heat and passion, but what he got was almost better. Patience, gentleness, and care engulfed Sterling as Connor's arms encircled him, drawing Sterling down to the bedding.

"Is that what you wanted?" he asked breathily.

Sterling nodded.

"Good, because I feel like I need a cigarette and we haven't even actually done anything." He seemed almost as breathless as Sterling. "I'm looking forward to seeing those pictures."

"Me too." Sterling reached for the camera, and Connor drew closer.

"Ummm…." He leaned nearer, and Sterling wondered what was wrong. "Isn't that number supposed to be something other than one?" He pointed to the exposure counter, and Sterling looked, groaning.

"You have to be kidding me. You piece of…." He wanted to shake the damned thing. "It wasn't advancing the film. I must have loaded it wrong. It's been quite a while since I used…." His cheeks heated. He felt like an idiot.

Connor began to laugh, and Sterling glared at him heatedly.

"Damned thing." He wanted to throw it against the wall, but Connor gently stilled his hand.

"Come on. It's funny. You misloaded the film and we did all that sexiness for nothing." Connor rolled to his side and kissed Sterling on the cheek. "Just think about it. I guess you'll have to do the whole thing all over again whenever I need a little cheering up." Connor nestled nearer, his warmth joining with Sterling's. "Only next time, you'll remember to actually load the film right." Before Sterling could protest, Connor's fingers slid along his side, and Sterling squirmed. He did it again. "I'm not going to stop until I get a smile." Connor's fingers went wild, and Sterling laughed and shimmied half off the bed.

"Come on," he grumped, trying not to smile, but Connor's laughter was contagious. Sterling grinned and grabbed Connor's hands to stop his tickling fingers.

"Okay, okay. I give in." He scooted back on the mattress and lay quietly. "I must have loaded the camera a thousand times and…."

"It doesn't matter." Connor settled next to him, the kilt fabric draped over his hip. "I know the pictures and things were just a way to distract me and help me feel better, and it worked." Connor's hand slid over his lower belly and rested there as he drew Sterling to him. "They're just pictures, and you can take more." He yawned, and Sterling knew Connor was right. "We should go to sleep. I have a list of things I need to get done tomorrow, and in the last few hours, it grew immensely. If I want this job, I'm going to need to fight for it. I just need to figure out the weapons I'm going to need."

"Just as long as you fight Randall, and keep your tickling fingers to yourself." Sterling got out of bed and cleaned up. By the time he returned, Connor had shed his clothes and was already asleep.

"That's marvelous," Sterling said. "You need yet another printing?" The calendar was becoming a huge success, and with the local publicity, they had sold out, and Lucille had already arranged for another printing.

"It gets better. Last night, the Philadelphia news station picked up the local story, and now we're getting inquiries from stores there. The printing company said that if we wanted, they would take over orders and distribution for us. It will cost more per calendar sold, but we won't have to coordinate all the details." She was practically giddy, and Sterling was happy for her.

"You know this is causing problems for Connor." Over the past two weeks, his mayoral opponent had wasted no time in trying to make an issue of the fact that Connor had posed for the calendar. He had even apparently managed to bring it up in front of the council, which was legally dubious, but making a huge deal out of it would only highlight the issue. "And I'm worried about him."

"I am too. No good deed goes unpunished," she said gently. "And it sucks, and not in the good way." Sterling stifled a snort. There were times when she said the most unexpected things.

"What are we going to do?" he asked. "Connor is out there almost every day meeting people and shaking hands. He's working hard, and I'm afraid that everything he's tried to do is being undone because of his desire to help." There was no need to put too fine a point on it. He had been trying to help Lucille in agreeing to take part in this project, and Sterling felt guilty as hell because he had convinced him to run. What he should have done was just pull the calendar from the printers and rework it. But no, he had let it go forward because that was the easiest thing to do and he hadn't thought they would sell all that many copies. Now the danged thing was making the statewide news, and who knew where it would go from there? Each step in the upward popularity of the calendar meant a step back for Connor and a decrease in his chances of winning the election.

"Let me think about it."

"Okay, but think fast. The longer these attacks go on, the worse things go for Connor." Connor had such energy when he was out talking to people, and Sterling saw the way that energy evaporated as soon as he was behind closed doors. It worried him, and the last thing he wanted was for Connor to lose. A door closed in the house, which meant that Connor was back. "I need to go. I'm glad things are going well for the club." He ended the call and turned to see a red-faced, fuming Connor, who paced the room with all the stomping grace of a lame elephant.

"That bastard. It's Wednesday, and I was at the farmer's market talking to people like I have for weeks, and Mayor Dip-twaddle started making trouble. He made a pass through the crowd, and I heard him talking to someone, saying that what the town needed was someone with a good moral compass and inherent decency. That if his opponent could 'corrupt the garden club,' who knows what he would do as mayor. Or some such crap." Connor seethed. "We have to find something to fight back with. If we don't, then—"

"No," Sterling told him. "You need to be above this." Sterling held Connor's hand. "Getting down into the mud with him isn't going to help you at all. You need to be out there, and if someone asks you to sign their calendar, you do it gladly and with a jovial grin. Make light of it, like it was fun and that you did it to help raise money for a worthy cause. Don't get rattled and let that blowhard bother you." God, he wanted to be able to help him. Connor's upset was like his own.

He was coming to care deeply for Connor, but Alexander still loomed like a dark shadow over his heart, no matter how much he tried not to think about it. And the fact was, he was falling for Connor a little more each and every time he lay eyes on him. It thrilled him and frightened him. Not that he worried that Connor was like Alexander. It was more his own judgment he was worried about. "Please. If I sounded like I was lecturing, I'm sorry."

"No. I think you're right. I let him get to me, and as a consequence, he pushed me away from what I was doing, which is probably exactly what he wanted." The heat in Connor's eyes was enticing, even if it was tinged with anger. "Historically, the best politicians are the ones who take adversity and turn it into an advantage."

"Exactly." Sterling wished he could do more to help. He checked the clock and stood. "I'm sorry, but I have an appointment in a few minutes. Do you want to stay and have dinner with me? I can make something after I'm done."

"That would be nice." Connor stroked Sterling's cheek, and a zing of excitement raced through him. After knowing this man for months, he still felt like he did the very first time Connor did that. Sterling took his hand, held it to his cheek, and then brought it to his lips.

"I'll be back as soon as I can. Can I suggest that you call your great-aunt or my father? I'm not good at political matters, but I know that they are." He gave Connor a kiss and then left through the door to the studio, turning on the lights and getting everything ready for his appointment.

HE HAD little trouble concentrating, which was a relief. His client was a man in his forties who had asked for intimate pictures for his husband as a birthday present. Sterling guided him through the process, and they had a good session, with the sitter becoming more and more comfortable as the session went on. After an hour, he put down his camera, very pleased with the pictures they'd gotten. He arranged an appointment to review the pictures and then saw his client off. When he got inside, he found the house empty and Connor gone… and he smiled.

Chapter 16

As soon as Sterling left for his appointment, Connor checked the clock and left the house, striding back down the block in his best kilt, toward the square where the market was held. He'd be damned if he'd let Phillip Randall control his actions.

"Good evening," he said as he approached a woman waiting to cross at the corner. "I'm Connor Hillyard, and I'm running for mayor."

The woman, who appeared in her late forties, lifted her gaze at him. "Are you the calendar boy the other man was referring to?" she asked seriously.

Connor steeled his insides. "Yes, ma'am. I posed for the garden club calendar in order to support their programs. And the man I posed with is my boyfriend." He smiled and held his head high.

She put her bags down at her feet. "Then it's nice to meet you." She grinned and pulled out a calendar.

"Would you like me to sign it as Mr. April?" he quipped, and her smile shifted to a grin.

"Please do. That man always gave me the creeps, so when he was talking about what you did and all that decency that man tries to wrap himself in, I bought a copy just to wave in his face."

Connor signed it for her and handed it back. "I thank you. The garden club is a worthy organization, and they do a lot for this community, as I hope to if elected." He flashed his best smile, and she patted his shoulder.

"You hang in there."

She put the calendar back in her bag, and when the light changed, she hurried across the street.

Connor crossed after her and joined the groups of people at the market, introducing himself as he always did.

"I see you're back. Got more guts than I thought you would to show your face again," Mayor Randall said.

"Please." He grinned. "You've seen my face, as well as pictures of the rest of me. I have nothing that needs hiding." He looked Randall over. "You, on the other hand, should be the one hiding." A few people snickered from behind him. "What I did was for a community service organization," he said more loudly. "You only serve yourself." He turned away and shook hands with one of the men standing behind him, as well as some of the others, introducing himself and asking what sort of improvements the borough needed to make.

"What about the parks?" one lady asked.

"Which park, and what can we do?" he asked while pulling a small notebook and pen out of his sporran and making notes.

"Do you really think the people of this borough are ready for a gay calendar boy as mayor? You probably have fluff between your ears… and other places," Mayor Randall stage-whispered.

Connor didn't rise to the bait. "You were saying, before we were interrupted?" He kept his attention on the woman and heard her complaint. "I'll add it to my list of items and go out to look at it myself." If what she said was true, it meant the entire play structure at one of the main parks was unstable. "Thank you so much." He smiled, and she thanked him and continued on her way.

"And how do you intend to pay for everything these people want?" Mayor Randall asked more quietly.

"Maybe in reduced liability insurance premiums once it's proven the equipment is properly maintained." He moved away.

"You know that beauty is only skin deep," Mayor Randall said, loudly enough for others to hear.

"True. But ugly goes clear through to the bone." He strode away to a chorus of snickers, and it seemed Mayor Randall had had enough for the day. Connor suppressed a snicker of his own and wandered through the market, speaking to the vendors and looking through the goods offered for sale.

"I thought I'd find you here," Sterling said as soon as he crossed the street. "Where is the mayor?"

"I took your advice and returned, and while I was meeting with people, he was terrible, but I took the high road, and apparently the pressure was too much for him." Connor did not snicker or even break into a smile. "My campaign will be about what's good for Carlisle and the people who live here. I have a list of places I need to visit because I want to see if what I'm told is true. There are things here that are being neglected." He motioned, and Sterling joined him as he took another pass through the market.

Connor and Sterling left the market as the vendors were packing up. "You seem much happier."

"It's the people here. They don't care about calendars and things. All they want is their government to help them and make things better. The current mayor doesn't care about anyone but himself. I did my best to listen."

"Sometimes that's all you can do." They waited at the corner to cross the street. "Oh, and I think you need to call your great-aunt. Apparently your phone is off and she has some things to speak to you about."

Connor pulled out his phone. "Danged battery. I really need to get a new one." He shoved it back into his pocket and walked with Sterling back to his house, where he plugged in the phone to call his great-aunt while Sterling made dinner.

"Sorry I missed your calls."

"I was talking to Grant, and I think you should attend all the borough council meetings up until the election. Sit right in front and make sure people see you. You can't campaign on borough property, but you need to be there."

Connor swallowed hard. "What are you up to?"

"Just be there." His great-aunt said goodbye, leaving Connor puzzled.

He set down his phone and joined Sterling. "I'm starting to think that Aunt Lucille is beginning to lose it. Either that or she likes treating me like a child." He sat in one of the kitchen chairs. "Apparently I'm supposed to go to the next council meeting, which I intended to do anyway. After all, if I hope to be mayor, I should not only see how things run but be familiar with the current issues. Because many of the ones up before the council will still be there next year in one form or another." He sighed and watched Sterling work and sway a little to the music he had playing.

It didn't take Connor long to forget about his great-aunt and stand up, sliding his arms around Sterling's waist and moving along with him. Sterling had this thing when he danced with moving his backside in these circles. It made him look like one of those bobble-waisted hula dancers people used to put on their dashboards. "Sometimes you dance like you have spiders in your drawers."

Sterling stilled. "I'm sorry."

"It's sweet, and I love that you're so free around me. But relax and move your butt a little less. Let the music flow through all of you." He tightened his grip, setting the pace and guiding Sterling through the movement with his hips pressed to Sterling's firm butt. "That's it." He pressed closer, and Sterling groaned.

"You know, we aren't going to get any dinner if you keep that up." Sterling pressed back against him, and Connor was about to tell Sterling to forget the food and go upstairs when Sterling's phone rang. He stepped back and let Sterling get it. Sometimes he wished Alexander Graham Bell had gone on to be a farmer.

Connor sat back down and waited as Sterling set up an appointment. Then he finished dinner, and they sat down to what he hoped would be a quiet meal for two. "What has you so distracted?"

"It feels like there are half a million balls in the air and it's my job to keep them there. This race is more complicated than I thought it would be. The journal loved my article and wants another, and I am supposed to put together my package for tenure. Because I knew that was coming, I've always kept my accomplishments documented, with copies of articles and all the things I've published so that I would have it. But it just seems that nothing is going the way I thought it would."

"Okay." Sterling set down his fork. "Would you change anything if you could?"

Connor shrugged and thought for a few seconds. "Probably not. I love all the things I'm doing, and my life is pretty good right about now. I have a great job and a chance to do good for a lot of people. I have someone special in my life, and I'm happy." He squeezed Sterling's hand.

"It's right about then that the wheels fall off," Sterling said softly, and Connor had to agree with him.

"But it's the bad stuff that happened that got me here. Sure, my parents aren't accepting, caring people. Growing up, they were distant, and they only got more so when they learned I didn't fit into their molds. I think my dad wanted a carbon copy of himself, and my mother would have loved it if I had been a girl. I suppose I was an equal-opportunity disappointer." He tried to make light of it.

"They're the ones who let you down, not the other way around." Sterling placed his hand on top of Connor's, and he turned it over, lacing their fingers together.

"Sometimes I used to wonder if I was ever going to have someone who would be able to put up with me. My parents certainly didn't. The only person I had who truly cares is Aunt Lucille."

"And me," Sterling whispered.

Connor put his napkin on the table and leaned forward, tightening his hold on Sterling's fingers. "Do you really? Not that I doubt you or think you're lying, but I've never really been able to tell when someone really liked me or was just using me. I mean… sometimes guys really suck… and not in that eyes-rolling-to-the-back-of-your-head kind of way. But I can tell with you. At least I hope so."

Sterling chuckled lightly. "I do, honey." He pulled Connor closer. "Look, I was never the kind of guy to go around talking about my feelings. With you, it's easy. I know what I want and I'm not afraid to say it." He paused, and Connor half held his breath, wondering what he was about to say. "Look, I have a terrible record at looking into the future. If I'm honest, I've spent the last few years trying to build a life here while at the same time hoping that my old life would somehow call me back. There, I said it, and it's the truth. I did good work, and I miss my old life. I don't miss Alexander, but he still casts this shadow that I can't seem to get away from."

Connor tensed. "What is it you're trying to say?" He had this feeling that Sterling was about to say goodbye. This was how things started with the guys in college. They always started with nice things before they dropped the bomb and were out the door before he even had a chance to say anything. Connor swallowed hard, and his heart pounded in his ears. "On second thought, you don't need to tell me anything. I get it." He pulled his hand away.

"Connor, I'm saying that you've become part of me. The time we're together goes so fast, and when we're apart, I'm looking forward to seeing you again." He tugged Connor's hand to his lips. "I love the time we're together, and this isn't just about sex. I mean, being with you that way is incredible, but I like waking up next to you and seeing you when I go to sleep. I look forward to going on walks with you and making dinner with you."

Connor ran through what Sterling had said just to make sure there wasn't something he should be worried about. "Sterling, I…."

"But…." There was always a *but*, and Connor stiffened as he waited for the disappointment. "I still have this crap with Alexander that I can't seem to let go of. I loved him, and I thought he loved me, but he didn't."

"I would never treat you that way."

"I know that, and sometimes it takes someone wonderful before you realize that what you had wasn't all that great."

Connor nodded. "But that shadow you talked about is still there anyway." Just like his own past cast a shadow, though less and less each day. Maybe it was the fact that he had found someone like Sterling who engaged his heart. That had to be it. This whole shadow business was because Connor wasn't good enough or didn't cast enough light to banish it.

"It gets less and less dark," Sterling said. "But I don't know how to make it go away completely."

"It doesn't have to. You are the man you are because of what happened to you." He squeezed Sterling's hand. "Are you the same person you were when you came back here and started your business? Heck, are you the same person who used to photograph models all day long and was celebrated in the fashion world?"

Sterling shook his head. "No. I doubt you would have liked that person very much."

"Really?" That seemed a little pat.

"No. You wouldn't. When I was with Alexander, I was jumpy and nervous. He was always surrounded by beautiful people, and there were times when I was jealous. I got over it and figured if I became a success in my own field and had a life separate from his, everything would be great. He'd be successful, I'd be successful… together we'd be unstoppable. But…."

"It sounds like a marriage of careers," he snarked. "Can you imagine the ceremony?" Connor motioned broadly with his hands. "Picture it on a beach in Saint Croix. Do you, fashion photographer, take thee, fashion model, to be your lawfully wedded career choice? And do you, Sterling, the photographer, promise not to take pictures of other guys… and do you, Alexander, vapid fashion model, promise to only pose in your skivvies for Sterling?" He batted his eyes, and Sterling shook his head, mouth hanging open. "I now pronounce you a power couple. You may take a selfie, post it to Instagram, and will from this day forward be known as Sterlander."

Sterling gaped for a few seconds, his mouth hanging open. "Damn, I…." Connor hoped he hadn't gone too far. "You have a quick wit."

"I try." He smiled and waited for Sterling's reaction. Finally he tossed his head back and laughed.

"You know, I think we've talked about all this too much." Sterling gently rubbed the back of his hand. "There are times when talking about things gets you nowhere. Maybe we could switch to more pleasant topics."

"I have a colonoscopy scheduled for next month…," Connor quipped, and Sterling rolled his eyes.

"Leave it to you to switch the conversation to poop jokes." Sterling chuckled.

"Well, from what I understand, with that procedure, it's the lack of said poop that is the goal…."

Sterling groaned. "Fine. Then you pick the subject." He cocked his eyebrows.

"How about you and I go upstairs, go to bed, and talk about what comes up." Now it was Connor's turn to groan.

Chapter 17

Sterling dressed nicely and waited for Connor to arrive. He breezed inside with sandwiches, and Sterling got a couple of sodas and took them to the table. "You remembered I like egg salad." He smiled at the plate Connor had placed in front of him.

"It's not homemade. I got it at the deli downtown." Connor checked his watch and ate quickly. "I'm sorry I'm so late. My meeting ran late at work, and I had to get home to change and—"

Sterling placed his hand on Connor's knee. "Just relax. You have nothing to be worried about."

"Other than whatever my great-aunt has cooked up." Connor wiped his lips with his napkin and finished the sandwich and the soda. "She told me I had to be there, which can only mean that somehow she has decided to interfere. I love Aunt Lucille dearly, but there are times when she scares me. And that's when she's trying to help."

Sterling groaned. "I know. Lord help us all if she gets angry with us. I somehow doubt that either of us would survive the onslaught." He meant the comment to be humorous, but he had no doubt that she could be as formidable as a mother tiger. He finished his sandwich and took care of the dishes. "Ready to head into the breach… as it were."

Connor nodded. "Let's get this over with." They left by the back and went out the gate and just down the alley before using the side entrance to Borough Hall. The council members milled around in the chamber, and Connor excused himself to talk with them. Sterling, meanwhile, found seats down front and picked up the agenda for the evening. It seemed like a rather ordinary meeting. Connor joined him as others filled in the seats.

"Are you Mr. Hillyard?" a man asked, and Connor nodded as they made introductions. They spoke quietly until the meeting was called to order.

The beginning formalities were completed, and the community issues portion of the meeting where individual citizens could bring issues before the council began.

"I reviewed the minutes of the last council meeting, and I believe they demonstrate illegal campaign activities," Aunt Lucille said as she stood from her chair.

"Excuse me," the mayor said from the center of the council dais. "I believe—"

"The attorney should be consulted, but from the minutes, it seems the mayor has used his official platform—and a borough board meeting—to campaign. I refer to the council notes, page four, paragraphs two, three, and four." Aunt Lucille turned to the attorney. "I have copies for you if you need them." She stepped forward and handed them over. "These paragraphs demonstrate our mayor campaigning and impugning his opponent during an official council meeting." She put her hands on her hips, glaring at the mayor. "This cannot be done, as it is official time."

The attorney leafed through the pages. "I have to agree."

"Therefore," Aunt Lucille continued without hesitation, "it is my proposal that the council take up a resolution to reprimand the mayor for his behavior to ensure it doesn't happen again."

Sterling swallowed. Joan of Arc had nothing on Lucille Hillyard when her back was up. The way she stood there, all of heaven and hell would be scared to death of her.

"He has broken the law, and that cannot be ignored. It is up to the people of Carlisle to determine whether they wish to remove him from office for such a breach, but I believe the council should not and cannot let this blatant disregard for the law slide by." Aunt Lucille slowly sat down, and the council and chambers hummed with whispered discussion. The mayor looked either apoplectic or about ready to give birth to a hippo. It was hard to tell which.

"Should I say something?" Connor asked.

"I'd let Lucille fight this battle and stay out of it. This has nothing to do with you, and you shouldn't react. Just sit and watch. Keep your expression bland," Sterling whispered. This must not appear to be something Connor had anything to do with, and Sterling hoped Connor would take his advice.

"Is it not true that you are the great-aunt of my opponent?" the mayor questioned, leaning forward slightly in accusation.

Aunt Lucille got to her feet and walked to the speaker's lectern. She moved slowly, as though she were in pain, and damned if she didn't appear sympathetic as hell. The Royal Shakespeare Company had nothing on her performance. "The law has been violated, and the proof is in the council minutes. It matters not who I am. Anyone could bring this matter to the council's attention." She swayed a little but held herself upright. "This isn't a question of politics but of breaking the rules… and getting caught." She held the sides of the lectern, holding the gaze of the council, not a hint of smugness in sight.

"Ma'am," the deputy mayor said, "I believe that you have a valid point. I propose that the council get a full opinion from our lawyer before we continue and table this point until the next meeting, when we will take up whatever disciplinary action should be taken." There was agreement, and the council voted and prepared to move on.

The mayor appeared as sour as a lemon and faltered, seemingly unable to get back to the business at hand. Sterling might have felt sorry for him if the guy hadn't brought this on himself. And if not for the fact that after nearly twenty years in office, he should have known better.

"Thank you. I'd also like to propose that all candidates for the mayor's office be invited to an open forum where the people of Carlisle can meet the candidates. After all, this is the highest office in our town. We should be able to speak and get to know the candidates better."

The deputy mayor turned to the legal expert, who leaned forward. "The borough council cannot be directly involved in a political campaign. However, I see nothing wrong with holding a forum as long as all candidates are welcome to attend. I do suggest that the candidates meet to discuss a date and time. This council chamber could be used for the event." He leaned back, and it now seemed the mayor could barely function.

"Very good," the deputy mayor said. "Now I suggest we return to the items on our official agenda."

The mayor seemed to find himself and called for the next item on the agenda, and the council moved on. Sterling shared a smile with Connor, but they said nothing more. Connor paid attention to the proceedings. Sterling spent much of the meeting watching Connor and the way his focus didn't waver for more than a few seconds, even when they seemed to talk in circles. Few items were dispensed with quickly, and most took a great deal of discussion, which bored Sterling to tears. If he hadn't been near Connor, watching him, occasionally catching a waft of his scent in the ever-more-stifling room in which fewer and fewer people stayed as the business went on, he would never have stayed until the end.

Finally the meeting was adjourned, and the council members stood and prepared to leave. Connor smartly stayed where he was, and a few members came over to talk to him.

"I'm glad you came but said nothing," Brent Woodridge said. The only reason that Sterling knew his name was because of the name plate that he'd sat behind for hours.

"It seems my great-aunt is able to do plenty of talking on her own," Connor said gently.

"Did you know what she was going to do?" Brent asked.

Connor shook his head. "No. Because I'm a candidate for office, I decided to attend all meetings until the election so I could become familiar with the business before the council. She didn't share with me what she was going to say."

"I find that hard to believe," the mayor snipingly interjected as he pressed into the group. "I'm willing to bet this was all planned to—"

"What?" Brent asked as he turned. "Discredit you? Bring to light your illegal behavior? You made the council appear foolish with your outburst last month, and you were cautioned. Now it's become an issue for the entire council, and we're not going to have much choice in our course of action." He glared, and the mayor actually took a step back.

"I will not withdraw. This town needs decency and morality, not calendar boys." He turned on his heel and strode out of the room.

Sterling bit his lower lip to keep from saying something Connor might regret.

"He plays dirty," Brent said very quietly. "If there is anything in your past for him to find, he'll dig it up. And if he can't find anything, he'll put two and three together, come up with ten, and present it as fact. He's done it in the past."

"And a snake will strike when it's cornered," Connor added with surprising ease. "I'm aware of his past and that it is likely to repeat itself. The thing is, I don't have all that interesting a past, and that has to frustrate him. The most interesting thing I've ever done was pose for that calendar with Sterling." His smile sent heat through Sterling, and he wished they were home rather than in the back of the borough council chamber.

"Still, be careful," Brent cautioned and said goodbye.

Sterling and Connor followed him out of the building and walked around the side toward the alley, then down to the back gate of Sterling's house.

"I should go on home," Connor told him once they were inside and the gate was closed behind them. "I have a lot of work to do, it's late, and I'm sure you have appointments in the morning." He leaned closer. "I want to stay, more than anything."

"Then do."

Connor paused. "I can't…." He pulled away. "Something Brent said has me wondering. If the mayor can't find something on me, he may come after you. We haven't hidden that we're involved, and he may try to hurt you to get to me. It's pretty obvious that he has no scruples."

Sterling had thought of that. "Don't worry about me. I can take care of myself, and if he wants to dig in my past, we know what he's going to find… and so do you." He suppressed a shiver. He *did* know what was going to be found, and that old video that had made the rounds of the internet a few years ago was likely to find the light of day once again. "I'm more worried about you being hurt."

Connor moved right into his arms. "What a pair we make, each worried about the other." He rested his head on Sterling's shoulder, then tilted it up for a kiss. "I really have to go or else I won't get to bed, and I have an early meeting in the morning." He stepped away. "I'll see you Friday evening?"

"Yes, definitely." Sterling watched as Connor left by the back gate and then turned toward his own home, heading inside.

STERLING SET down the Thursday paper with a sigh. It certainly hadn't taken the mayor long to decide on his course of action, though Sterling wasn't sure how effective the story was. Apparently the mayor had published, through his personal Facebook account, a doctored image from the calendar with unflattering comment bubbles. The post had already been taken down by the company because the images were copyrighted and the mayor didn't have permission to use them, but the local paper had picked up on the story without pictures. Still, it was hurtful and petty.

Sterling picked up the phone and called the newspaper to inform them of the issues around the mayor's campaign materials and remind them that it was just another example of the mayor breaking the law in order to further his campaign.

He had barely hung up when Connor called, out of breath and angry. "What is wrong with this man?"

"He's dirty. But it's catching up with him." Sterling informed Connor of the actions he'd taken.

"Yeah, but to call us sodomites and to infer that I got paid for what I did. Like I'd…." Connor sputtered, and Sterling understood exactly how he felt. Connor was an honorable man with integrity. Sterling was so angry he wanted to wring the mayor's neck. Connor didn't deserve this; no one did. "At least it was taken down."

"It was removed because it was reported. The mayor didn't suddenly have a change of heart."

"What am I going to do?" Connor asked. "How can I keep fighting against a stream of lies and innuendo? It comes out of the woodwork and fades away again. It doesn't matter if it's true, because all people remember is the sensationalist crap he's putting out. I mean, where does he get this stuff? Apparently I'm now his 'opponent in a skirt.'" At least Connor chuckled over that one.

"He's only showing how ridiculous he is." Sterling had to try to soothe him, but he felt like he didn't have the words to do his feelings justice. "And we need to show him up for what he is."

"I agree, but how? My boss at the college asked me about what was being said. I spent an hour explaining what was happening and how I was being treated. He was outraged. But I can't do that with everyone in town." Connor was getting more stressed by the second.

"Come to the house. I'll be here, and I'm going to call my dad and your great-aunt. I think it's time for a council of war. If we're going to put an end to this, it needs to be spectacular and capture people's attention."

"Okay. I'll be there as soon as I finish here in the office," Connor agreed, and Sterling got busy making calls before his next appointment arrived.

"DAD, WHAT do you think? You're the one with more experience at this than the rest of us," Sterling said.

"First thing, you shouldn't stop what you're doing because of the mayor. Meet people. They seem to love you, and you come across well. I have contacted both the Carlisle and the Harrisburg papers about an endorsement. That is some free publicity and helps get our message out."

Aunt Lucille spoke next. "I have been in touch with the mayor's campaign manager, his wife, and have set up the town hall meeting for next month. School will be back in session and summer will be over, so September will be a wonderful time to get this into full swing." She smiled. "It's also a chance to remind people that the mayor himself is under review for improper campaign activities. As long as that issue is outstanding, it casts doubt. However"—she turned to Connor—"you shouldn't mention it. Let the rest of us do it. You stick to your message and the positive things you hope to accomplish. And I think that Sterling needs to be with you sometimes."

"I'm not sure that's a good idea," Sterling said. "It's only going to remind them of the calendar. I'm pictured with him. This is Connor's fight and will be his accomplishment, not mine. I'll help him every way I can, but I won't cause him any additional trouble."

"If that's how you feel," his dad said. "But Connor being in a stable, caring relationship can only be an asset."

"Is that not what you want?" Connor asked. Sterling looked to the others, and his father stood and took Aunt Lucille's arm, leading her from the room. "Sterling, if I'm not the person you want or if you don't want to be part of this, then all you have to do is say so. There's no need for you to pretend that you want me or are interested in a relationship just because I'm running for mayor. I had hoped...." His voice faltered.

"Of course I want this... I want you," Sterling said forcefully. "Why would you think I didn't? I just don't want to hold you back. This is too important to you, and I don't want to cause any issues that would hurt you." He swallowed hard around the lump in his throat, his heart racing. "I want you in my life, and I hope that when we know each other better and… that…." His words failed completely. Was it too soon to say what was in his heart? Would he scare Connor away if he told him how deeply he had taken root inside? The thought of Connor hurting was enough for him to head into battle with just a teaspoon as a weapon if he had to. "I'm falling in love with you." The words tumbled out before he could stop them.

Connor inhaled sharply and blinked but didn't say anything. Sterling was damned sure that he had gone too far too fast and that Connor was ready to bolt.

"Look, I know it's too soon, and if I freaked you out, I didn't mean to. The words just came out, and while I won't take them back, I will understand if you don't feel the same way. The last person I used the 'L' word with ended up throwing everything I thought I had in my face. Things haven't worked out for you either, so…." God, he was prattling on like a damned teenager at their first dance. He needed to shut the hell up.

Connor snorted. "The 'L' word. Are there only so many times you're allowed the say the word *love* before your head explodes? Or maybe you think if you say it too much your heart will shrink and you'll turn green and end up as the Grinch in a Dr. Seuss movie."

"I…." What the hell did he say to that?

"I've been falling for you for a long time. But affairs of the heart don't work out well for me either." Connor squeezed his fingers. "Yeah, you can make fun of me because I sound like something out of a Jane Austen novel." He rolled his eyes. "But Jane knew all about the heart and its trials and tribulations."

"You've read her work?" Sterling asked, and Connor nodded. "What's your favorite?"

"*Persuasion*," Connor answered immediately. "I love the 'second chance at love' idea. That they used to be in love and the embers were still there. That they needed to speak to one another and not just talk, but really communicate from the heart."

"That's the hardest thing to do. You either get what you want most or your heart stomped into tiny pieces. It's an all-or-nothing kind of proposition. And Jane Austen does that so very well. But it always takes them so long before they get there."

Connor tugged him closer. "That's the beauty of it. The journey is the satisfying part. The ending is just a way to say that the journey is over. Everyone today wants instant gratification. Jane knew how to make the anticipation last and build until it becomes this burst of adrenaline for the characters and the reader." He sighed. "I never would have pegged you as a Jane Austen kind of guy."

"I read them I college. *Sense and Sensibility* was for a class I took, but most of the others I read simply because she transported me to another time and place, and I needed that about then." Sterling tugged Connor closer. "Sort of like you. When you're here, like this...." He stroked his hands down Connor's back until they rested on his butt. "I'm transported."

"To Hornytown?"

"There are worse places." Sterling smiled and squeezed. "I think this is the best feel in the house."

A soft shuffle from the other room caught their attention. Connor stiffened, and Sterling stilled before leaning close. "I wonder what they're up to." He didn't want to step away, but his curiosity got the better of him.

They both turned toward the door. Connor peered into the other room. Sterling followed and then stepped back, putting his hand over his mouth. The two of them went into the back room before the chuckles got the better of them. "Your father kissing Aunt Lucille. I think that's an image I could spend the rest of my life and not have seen."

Sterling grinned. "I thought it was beautiful. Your great-aunt certainly seemed to like it, and can you imagine finding romantic happiness at their age? It's hard enough to find someone at ours, let alone at theirs."

"Yeah, but your father and my great-aunt sucking face?" He broke down into a fit of laughter.

"I believe they were doing more than that. Did you see where his hands were?" Sterling clarified, and Connor stopped laughing. "I mean it. I've seen them together, and they definitely have that look. I think we should leave them alone."

"We need dinner," Connor said. "Come on."

They started cooking. The scent drew the other two back into the room. "Can we help?"

"The pasta is in the water, and the sauce is warming. I have the garlic bread in the oven, and Connor has the table set. So all you need to do is take a seat." Sterling stirred the sauce and turned away from them to keep from chuckling.

"What is with you two?" Aunt Lucille asked, her hands on her hips. "Yes, your father and I have been seeing one another, and there will be times when the two of us will show affection. You young people are not the only ones who need affection." The edges of her lips curved upward. "And you all seem to think you invented sex. Well, you didn't, and I'll have you know that people of our age could teach you young people a thing or two."

Connor had grown pale, and Sterling's father was grinning like an idiot. "Your great-aunt and I are figuring out if there's something between us. Do the two of you think it funny?"

"No," Sterling answered quickly. "I want you to be happy, Dad, the same thing you always wanted for me." The mirth in the entire situation vanished in an instant.

"I'm thrilled for both of you," Connor added. "And I agree with Sterling. If the two of you are happy and wish to pursue a relationship, whatever form you decide that will take, I'm happy for you." He kissed his great-aunt on the cheek. "Now stop glaring at both of us." He smiled and gave her a hug. "You have our blessing if that's what you want." He drew himself up with the bearing of an earl from two hundred years ago. He was stunning, and for a second, Sterling could see him like that.

"Your blessing?" Aunt Lucille barked. "We don't want your blessing. You are my great-nephew and I love you to pieces, but I don't need your blessing for anything. I have been choosing my own men since before your father became a shot in the dark. And I have great taste, if I do say so." She smiled at Grant and winked. "Why do you think I never married any of them?" She grinned wickedly and then took Grant's hand. "Now let's eat and drop this unwelcome intrusion into my personal life." She pulled out a chair, and the two of them sat down. "Instead we can delve into yours. Sterling, what are your intentions regarding my great-nephew?"

Sterling felt all words slip from his lips. "My intentions?" he finally managed to ask.

Connor thankfully came to his rescue. "Aunt Lucille—"

"Goose and gander, my boy." She grinned, and Sterling figured it was best to say no more and bring dinner to the table. Things with Connor felt just right at the moment, and he didn't want to try to explain or talk about what the two of them had said. His gaze locked on Connor, and they shared a soft smile and entwined fingers under the table for a few seconds, warmth spreading from the touch to the rest of him. Suddenly his ravenous hunger for food was gone, replaced by something different entirely, and each gaze from Connor only heightened his appetite.

GRANT AND Lucille departed quickly after dinner. Sterling had barely tasted a bite, his attention focused on Connor and the more carnal appetites. It was a miracle he'd been able to keep his fork on the path to his mouth. Each time Connor's lips closed around a morsel, he wished those lips were being put to a very different use.

"Did you really mean what you said before?" Connor asked once they were alone in the house.

Sterling sat on the sofa in his family room with Connor next to him. "Of course I did. I'd never make something like that up."

Connor drew closer. "I didn't think you would. I was only looking for reassurance." He lifted his gaze, and it met Sterling's. Connor blinked, his blue eyes glistening. "Man, that made me sound really needy." There were times when Connor could be so strong and it seemed like he could stand up to anything. Yet with Sterling, he was vulnerable, and that was both attractive and frightening. Sterling realized that if he wasn't careful, he could hurt Connor just as deeply as Alexander had him. Then it hit him, a notion he had never thought of before. It was something that would never have occurred to him with his ex—that he had a responsibility. That if Connor had indeed given him his heart and was falling in love with him, then Sterling had a responsibility to care for it… to treat it gently and nurture it. And Connor was the same. No wonder things with Alexander had gone to hell.

"You sound like someone putting his heart on the line," Sterling whispered and slowly closed the distance between them. He understood the dangers of taking a chance with your heart, the ache when it was given and trampled on, and the joy of getting it back so it could be given again.

Connor nodded. "What's wrong?" he asked, and Sterling realized he had stopped partway to Connor. He had intended to kiss him, but instead he'd stilled, with his thoughts once again traveling to his past.

Sterling hardened his resolve and pushed the Alexander-tainted mist that threatened to loom over him back as far as he could. Connor was light and happiness; Alexander was a fog that loomed around the horizon, ready to take over should the light falter. Sterling couldn't let that happen and closed the distance to Connor's lips, holding on to him with all he had to keep the darkness at bay. He craved the light and hoped he could keep it shining on him for as long as possible.

Connor tasted of sunshine and summer as he kissed him, sliding his tongue between his firm lips. Connor held him close, pressing against him, energy radiating from him as he vibrated. Sterling could feel Connor wanting more, much more. His desire couldn't be hidden, pressing to Sterling's thigh. They should probably head upstairs, but that would mean letting Connor go, and Sterling had no intention of doing that, not even for the two minutes required to get to the bedroom.

He pulled at Connor's shirt, baring his chest before sliding his hands under his kilt. Damn, he loved the easy access and the impressive heat and passion he found there. "What was that for?"

"Because I never really gave much thought to the wonders of a kilt until right now." He patted Connor's boxer-briefed butt before peeling away the fabric. "The access is amazing." He rubbed the smooth skin, sliding his hand down Connor's leg.

Connor chuckled, and with a deft motion, the kilt fell away and onto the floor. "See, even more wonders to behold."

Sterling moaned. "Sweetheart, the wonders have always been the *man* in the kilt." He paused his explorations and brought his hands to cup Connor's cheeks. "You were always a wonder to behold. I'm sorry it took me so long to tell you just how amazing you are and how you set my heart alight. You make me want to shout my happiness from the rooftops. But I won't. With my balance, I'd fall and break my neck, and that would be really unsexy."

Connor rolled his eyes. "You're a real sweet talker, you know that?" Sterling loved the way he smiled and the mischief in those glorious eyes.

"I love you in kilts. I have to say that I never thought of how sexy they were until you walked into your great-aunt's in only yours and those boots." Sterling settled his hands on Connor's chest. "Now I can't think of you any other way. You have inspired me… and my heart." He closed the distance between then, taking Connor's lips in a deep kiss.

Connor held him tight and then climbed off the sofa, slipping his shirt off his shoulders until he stood naked in all his muscular glory. Sterling swallowed hard, taking in the sight in front of him. "I could put the kilt back on if you like."

Sterling shook his head. "That would be a shame. The first time I saw you, my imagination ran wild, but now I see that it was not as good as I always thought." He smiled and tugged Connor closer.

"Should we go up to bed?"

Sterling nodded, his throat too dry to speak anymore. He managed to get up on wobbly legs, talking Connor by the hand and leading his naked Apollo to the bedroom.

CONNOR LAY next to him in the dark. Sterling knew by his breathing he wasn't asleep. Though Sterling was worn out and happy, he didn't want to sleep, because this moment was too good to waste. "What are you thinking about?"

"Your work in the studio. The art you're creating and making your own. I thought…."

Sterling rolled over. "The interest in that seems to have drifted away. I can recreate all the pieces that someone else did, but it isn't original. It's just imitating someone else, and I want to do more. Maybe a book."

Connor inhaled. "Like a coffee-table book?"

"Yes. Something that inspires me. Like you in a kilt." He rolled onto his side, and Connor chuckled into the darkness. "What?"

"Nothing," he answered quickly.

"Come on," Sterling coaxed, and Connor slid closer, his head resting on Sterling's shoulder. "What bit of mischief has crept into that mind of yours?" He could almost feel the mirth grabbing hold of Connor, and Sterling loved it. There were few sights more breathtaking than when Connor smiled.

"Okay, so I went to a conference in Milwaukee, and believe it or not, there is still a gay bookstore there." He snickered. "They had a copy of *The Big Penis Book*. That got me thinking that you should do something like that. Only since you love kilts, maybe you could publish *The Big Book of Sporrans: What Goes Up Must Be Held Down*."

Sterling snorted and then lost control of his laughter. "Where the hell do you come up with these things?"

"You know a dirty mind is a terrible thing to waste. I have one, so I'm going to use it. Maybe you should try it." He shifted and stroked Sterling's cheek. "You don't need to do a book of dicks or anything, but the reason the calendar is doing so well is because the images are sensual and loving. They evoke emotion. Do that—take pictures of people showing love. If you make people feel something strong and real, then they'll believe in it."

"But…." Sterling hesitated. He had done that for years. It was what he was good at and what he had hoped to get the chance to do again. In a small way he had—with the calendar. "I have my life and my business." The thing was that they rarely intersected. There was no passion in what he was doing.

"You can do both, if that's what you want to do." Connor patted his chest and settled closer. "You have all the talent in the world. I've seen it. Just find a way to let it loose." He yawned and nestled in tight. "I hate being cold, and you're always like a furnace."

"And you're an air conditioner," Sterling replied gently. He knew Connor was right. The thing was, he had undertaken so many different types of projects to try to bring out his more artistic nature, but up until now, he hadn't found anything that fit. Maybe Connor was right and he had already stumbled across it. Or maybe he could simply do a book of pictures of Connor. Now *that* was a project worth being passionate about on so many levels.

Chapter 18

"WHAT IS it, Dad?" Sterling asked into the phone.

Connor lifted his head off the pillow, peering at the clock next to the bed. Sterling must have gotten up already. He pushed back the covers and swung his feet to the floor. He needed to shower, dress, and get to the college. The list of things he needed to accomplish today was quite lengthy, and he had to get his mind cleared and ready for the mayoral town hall. Because of scheduling conflicts and a stonewalling opponent, the town hall meeting had been rescheduled twice, and each time Connor grew a little more nervous.

"Did he try to get out of it once more?" Connor asked.

Sterling came back into the room wearing a pair of ice-cream-print boxers that said Lick Me on them. The first time Connor had seen them, he had taken those words as a command. "No. It's worse. The mayor is apparently stacking the room. His supporters, such as they are, have gotten together and are bringing people in so that he has a favorable audience." Sterling put his hands on his hips, eyes burning with anger. "That man is a piece of work. Like a stunt like that is really going to help him."

"True, but now my message will fall on deaf ears and I'll get nothing out of them, while his people can get energized. And the reports will be all about how well he does and how the audience was unenthused about my message." Connor was tired of this kind of dirty dealing. "What do I do?"

"You don't do anything. You need to get ready for the town hall. Practice what you want to say for your opening remarks and tailor them to the current mayor's base, without mentioning him at all. Tell them what you want to do, and as for the rest, leave it to Dad. He said he was already working on it." Sterling sat on the side of the bed next to him.

"What would I do without you?"

Sterling took his hand. "The same as I would without you—try to figure out how to make it day to day." He smiled. "You make getting up each and every morning special. If you win or lose, it doesn't matter to me. It isn't going to change a thing with me or for you. There will be another election, and you're young. Mayor Randall decided to put off his retirement plans to run, so one way or another, he's going to be out eventually."

That was true, but another term of the current mayor was not what the borough needed. Under his leadership, things had been put off and weren't changing to keep up with changing demands. It was stagnating, and that was not going to make the problems go away. They'd only get bigger. "I know. But…."

"Don't get me wrong. I want you to win." He squeezed his fingers. "Let's go shower, and you can get to work. I have an appointment in an hour and calls to make." Sterling grinned. "Remember that what's good for the goose is good for the gander. If he's going to try to pack the room, we'll see if we can outflank him." He stood and tugged Connor to his feet, and he followed Sterling to the bathroom. It had become a habit to take their morning showers together. Sterling's old house wasn't the most conducive, but it was important and an intimate way to start the day.

CONNOR'S DAY was nonstop from the moment he got to his office. His colleagues all wished him luck, and some said they planned to come to the town hall meeting. At least he knew he would have some friends in the audience. His department head as well as the academic dean stopped in to wish him luck as well. It seemed they were both ecstatic about the possibility of having the mayor on faculty. Those two ate and drank prestige for lunch.

As he was readying to leave, he called Sterling, who asked him to come to the house. "Lucille already got some fresh clothes for you and brought them over. I swear the woman can move heaven and earth when she wants to."

"I know. I told her what to get. I'll be there in ten, and then I can eat, change, and get this bloodbath over with."

As the day went on, Connor had become more and more convinced that what had started out as a great idea was going to turn into the death of his campaign.

CONNOR KNEW it was early, but he wanted to get a feel for the setup, so they walked over and went inside. The council chamber had been adjusted slightly, with two podiums placed at the front of the dais so he and Randall each had a place to stand and could be seen. Chairs had been put out for the attendees. The mayor sat in his place in the center, looking like he was working, but Connor saw it as a way to try to control the room. Still, he went to his podium and looked out over the chamber as people began filing in.

The mayor looked up and stood, walked around the side, and began greeting people and shaking hands. Connor put his things down on the podium and did the same, pasting on a smile. He received frosty but polite replies as the attendees filled in the front rows. Damn, Connor had known about Randall's plan, but it was disheartening to see.

Grant entered and motioned him off to the side. "The mayor's relatives and friends," he explained.

"What are we going to do?" Connor could imagine the disaster this was going to be, with the room packed with Mayor Randall's supporters. The questions, the reactions. It was certain that the local paper would be there, and the reporting would be abysmal. No one was going to care about a word he said, and every thought he had would be torn apart and thrown back in his face. Connor had no intention of giving up, but he could feel his chances of winning slipping through his fingers. Maybe it had been a pipe dream to think that he would be able to get elected to anything.

"Don't worry." Grant snickered. "The cavalry is on the way." He stepped to the side, and Connor tried to figure out what the hell that meant while he continued to circulate as more people arrived. The best he figured he could do was ensure the night wasn't a complete disaster.

He caught Sterling's gaze more than once, and it buoyed his heart. Sterling was in his corner, and if this completely fell apart, he knew Sterling would still be there. That was what mattered. There would be other elections if he chose to run. Politics was a game of highs and lows, and he needed to remember that. He'd get through this, and at the end of the night, he'd go home with Sterling and he'd hold him.

Connor smiled. To hell with it. Maybe he could get Sterling to go home now, and they could get to the consoling and just skip the certain nuclear-level disaster that his fledgling political aspirations had become.

"Excuse me," said a lady walking with a cane. She made her way to the front and spoke to a few people, and danged if they didn't get up. Another lady with a cane joined her, and they sat down. Other ladies arrived, and they all headed to the front few rows. Slowly, people rearranged themselves, and some found new seats.

"Aunt Lucille," Connor said as she entered from the back. "Thank you for being here. It's good to see a friendly face."

She patted his cheek. "There are lots of friendly faces here. I brought nearly the entire garden club." His great-aunt leaned closer. "Who would deny a seat to an old lady? So I've packed the room with them. The mayor is going to look out and find his people farther back than he thought they would be and now separated because others were already seated." She nodded, and Connor reminded himself never, ever to get on the bad side of the little old ladies—they were fierce.

"Is everything okay?" Sterling asked as more people filed in until all the seats were taken. Citizens stood toward the back, and additional chairs were brought in and placed around the sides of the room. It was definitely a full house.

Connor nodded. He was as good as possible.

"Who gets this started?"

Connor turned as his great-aunt walked down the aisle and stood up front. "I'm Lucille Hillyard, and Connor is my great-nephew. I was the one who proposed this little get-together, so I'm going to ask that we get started. We'll flip a coin—loser speaks first. Mayor Randall, please call it."

"Heads."

She flipped the coin and showed it to the mayor. "Tails. You speak first. And good luck to both candidates." She sat down, and Connor took his place behind his podium, waiting for the mayor.

"Good evening, fellow citizens. Most of you know me. I'm Mayor Phillip Randall, and I'm running for reelection. Originally I had decided to retire, but Carlisle deserves a better choice than what was offered. This town has a history going back over two hundred fifty years, and in all that time, our town has stood for decency, family values, and hard work. It should not be used to try to further the agenda of a certain section of our town." He turned to Connor, who did his best to appear calm, even while gripping the podium hard enough he was lucky he didn't rip it apart. "You all know what I stand for. I've been doing this job for the past twenty years—"

"Is that why our parks aren't being cared for and play structures are in bad repair? Even dangerous?" one of the ladies from the front row asked forcefully.

"And what about the roads that shake you apart to drive on them? East Street is a minefield," someone else asked. It clearly broke the mayor's train of thought, because he hesitated.

"That's exactly right. We need a mayor who is concerned with what's best for the town. Our parks are beautiful but woefully cared for. That needs to change. Our streets and the trees that line them need attention. Our schools must have our support, as well as the fire and police departments," Connor interjected and then motioned to the mayor. "I'm sorry. It's still your time." Damn, that felt good.

The mayor cleared his throat. "I have a plan to fix all that, but what can't be fixed are the moral implications of someone like my opponent in the mayor's office. We don't need someone using the office to further the national gay agenda." He leaned forward. "We all know what he's done. My opponent and his friend have corrupted the garden club into producing a gay-themed calendar. I'm not sure, but it's my impression that the only one making money on that calendar is him."

There was the baseless, nebulous accusation that Connor had been expecting from him. Tout something false until people started to believe it.

A murmur went through the crowd, but Connor kept himself calm even though he wanted to rip the lying snake's lips off.

"Is this the kind of leadership we want here? Is this the kind of example we want for our children?" He almost sounded like a preacher working up his sermon. "I don't think so."

Connor took a deep breath. "Good evening. I'm Connor Hillyard, and I have never held political office before. Currently I am an assistant professor of history at Dickinson College—and no, there will not be a quiz at the end of the evening." A titter of laughter went through the crowd. "But there will be a test… and that test will show the character of the people of Carlisle. The results will be available on election night." He took a deep breath. "I am running because I want to do what's best for the people of Carlisle. I have a history of community service, as demonstrated by a number of factors, including the garden club calendar. All images and time spent producing the calendar were donated. No one in the calendar is getting anything other than a calendar for their time or the images—

whatever the mayor might *think*." He figured no more need be said. "It was strictly a service to a group who does a great deal for our community."

"But the pictures are disgusting," someone called.

Connor didn't let it rattle him. "That's your opinion, and as a citizen of this community, you are entitled to that, as we all are. But I have to ask, have you looked at the calendar? From what I understand, nearly ten thousand people have. At least that's the number of orders that have been placed. And the proceeds from that will fund scholarships and the flower baskets that hang downtown, will help beautify our parks, and will light up the square at Christmas—things all of us will enjoy." He stepped down from behind the podium to get closer to people.

"But you have no experience. You said so yourself," a man commented from the center of the room.

"True. But I'm a student of history, and that means I'm an expert at studying what has been done right and wrong so we can learn from it." He continued on to detail his plans for the town and what his priorities were. Connor loved the interaction and answered question after question.

"What about the mayor's moral accusations?" a gray-haired gentleman asked. He had come in with the mayor's group of folks, and his gaze was intense.

"Morals are about right and wrong. Let me put it to you. Was I wrong to do the calendar and help my great-aunt and keep her ninety-year-old garden club from folding? Was it wrong to support scholarship programs and the rest of their work? If not, then what's the morality issue? Other than the mayor doesn't like it. He's entitled to his opinion, just like everyone else, but when he guides the town by those opinions, it shuts some people out and marginalizes others. That isn't what we should be doing. This town needs everyone. If we want to make it better, then we have to work together, not tear each other apart." He glared at the mayor for a moment and then turned his gaze back to the room.

"There had to be other ways. There was no need for you to corrupt the old people of the garden club," the mayor spat.

"Now you see here," Judy from the garden club said. "I'm a garden club member, and I thought Lucille had lost her mind when she proposed this. I honestly did. I didn't *think* this sort of thing was good for the club, and I wondered if it was even proper. But…." She wagged her finger at the mayor. "How dare you insinuate that we can't think for ourselves and can be 'corrupted'?" She made air quotes, and her tone rang with disdain. "I am more than capable of making my own decisions, and so is everyone else in the club." Twenty ladies, mostly from the front, stood up. "As I said, I thought we were crazy. But I was wrong. Those images are beautiful. They are expressions of love and gorgeous flowers, period." She was a small, frail woman, but in that moment, she might as well have been a knight in shining armor. "Now let's get back to what's really important—the business of figuring out who our next mayor is going to be." She picked up her cane and began moving back through the room, stepping slowly toward the door.

"Judy…," Connor said.

She stopped and turned around. "I don't need to stay any longer. I know who will do his best for our community and who I'll vote for." She turned and left the room, the door closing behind her.

Connor blinked, and it took a few seconds for him to get his thoughts together. "I don't think I can follow that," he commented. A snicker went through the room, and he glanced at the mayor and then turned back to the assembled group to answer more of their questions.

"You were amazing," Sterling said as soon as they left the town hall. "I don't think the mayor knew what hit him."

Connor nodded. "I have to agree. He came prepared with his argument and positions, and we turned them back at him. Once that happened, he had nothing else left and looked like an intolerant fool. I still have some work to do in a number of areas. I can speak to people, but I need to determine the budgetary impact of what I want to do and figure out how that can be accomplished. I know that what I want is possible, but I'm not going to promise something I can't deliver. There are things that are critical to handle right away."

"Connor," the deputy mayor called as he hurried up behind them. "You spoke about the critical defects at some of the play areas. Do you have a list? The council members want to make sure those repairs are made immediately." He stopped.

"Of course. I'll email you the list as soon as I get home." Connor introduced Weston and Sterling.

"You slayed it," Weston said. "Maybe now we can get some real leadership." He thanked him and turned back toward Borough Hall, and Sterling and Connor continued on their way home. It was still a while before the election, and there was a lot to do, but it seemed he was already having an impact.

"You're doing great already." Sterling took his hand. "The calendar is a success, and you're well on your way to being elected mayor. It seems the things we set out to do are coming to fruition."

"Yes." Connor didn't mention that Sterling needed to find another project that he was excited about. Sterling went to work each day, but Connor didn't see any of the spark, the creative energy that he'd had when they had been shooting the calendar. He smiled and seemed content, even happy when they were together, but Connor sensed there was something missing, and he didn't know what to do. Connor wanted Sterling to have the success that he was enjoying right now. But he knew that had to come from Sterling. As much as he wanted to, Connor couldn't do it for him. "It does seem that way."

Sterling tugged him closer, and they walked together to the back gate and into the yard. "We'll go through the studio. I need to check on something before I go in for the night." He unlocked the door, and Connor followed Sterling inside.

Connor wandered the space while Sterling did what he needed to do.

"I thought you decided that this wasn't working for you." He looked down at a table and water pitcher near a window. He picked up the jug. The setup looked like one of Vermeer's paintings. None of this had been there the last time he'd been in the studio.

"I decided to give it another try." Sterling seemed more resigned than excited. "I've gotten some interest based on others I've done." He stood beside him, and Connor set the pitcher exactly where it had been.

Connor didn't say anything, but the lack of enthusiasm in Sterling's voice was telling. "Are you all set?"

"Yes." Sterling led them through the studio to the house. They got a snack and something to drink before heading to bed. Maybe Connor was looking for trouble, but he couldn't get past the idea that Sterling needed something exciting to do. Either that or excitement was going to find him.

Chapter 19

"THAT'S GREAT," Sterling told his football-player sitter. He had wanted to pose in his jersey, but both Sterling and his mother had convinced him otherwise. Sometimes it felt like he had the same conversation three or four times a day. Maybe he needed to put together an informational email regarding the types of things that made a good picture. It might help, though somehow Sterling doubted it. "Very good. Now smile a little and keep your eyes right where they are." He snapped the final pictures of the session, and his subject went to change.

Connor was waiting in the reception area along with the boy's mother. Sterling handled the business end of things and spoke with her until her son was ready and they could leave.

"What brings you here?" He smiled at Connor, thankful that had been his final client of the day. The routine was beginning to get to him. "Not that you need an excuse. Did something happen?" Connor usually didn't just come to the studio. The past few weeks had been quiet on the election front, but Sterling always expected some dirty trick out of the mayor, especially as the time ticked down and the election got closer.

"No. I'm getting a ton of support, and I may actually win. It seems the mayor isn't as popular as he'd like to think he is, and what people really want is someone who will help them." He came closer. "As I was approaching the house from the front, I saw someone familiar. He was knocking on the door, so I let him in the backyard."

"Who?" Sterling asked.

"It's your ex, Alexander." Connor shifted his weight between his feet. "I...." He swallowed. "Holy hell, I see why he was able to turn your head. The man is gorgeous." He took a step back. "Do you want me to leave so you can talk to him?" Connor seemed like he wanted to disappear.

Alexander had that effect on people. Sterling had seen it before. Sometimes when Alexander arrived, he seemed to suck all of the air out of the room, overpowering it in such a way that there was nothing left for anyone else.

"No. If anyone is going to be leaving, it's him." He locked the studio door and turned out the lights.

Sterling tried not to let his hands shake as anxiety like he hadn't felt in years slammed into him. Sterling didn't want to see Alexander and was tempted to ask Connor to just tell him to go, but that was the coward's way out. He'd hear why Alexander had come all this way, and then send him packing. Still, he found his hand resting on the doorknob without moving.

"Get it over with?" Connor asked, and Sterling nodded, pulling open the door and going into the yard.

Alexander's expensive citrussy cologne reached his nose before he saw him. For a second, Sterling inhaled. He had loved that scent and came to associate it with warmth and love. "Alexander, what are you doing here?" he asked before he even saw him.

Alexander stood near the outdoor table, looking at the flowers nearby. "Baby, it's good to see you." He turned slowly, his smile as wide and bright as ever. For a second, Sterling's mind skipped a beat. "I missed you." He strode closer and hugged Sterling in his powerful arms, then kissed him as though he were trying to take possession of him.

It wasn't until he took a deep breath that he could speak. Inside, something snapped like a cog falling into place. "Stop!" He pushed Alexander back. "You don't get to do that any longer. Remember Cannes, Monaco, and that woman you decided you wanted? The articles, you ripping me apart?" He glared at his ex.

"That was a mistake. Those other people never held a candle to you. I realize that now." He put on those puppy-dog eyes, parting his lips just so, giving Sterling the look that sold, well, *everything* by the millions.

A throat cleared, and Sterling remembered his manners. "This is Connor, my boyfriend."

Alexander extended his hand, and Connor took it, at the same time sending Sterling some of his strength. The world seemed to spin, and Sterling knew he was being dramatic. Alexander was just a man like any other. His package was superb, but that's all there was. Sterling looked into Alexander's eyes, realizing that, like the pictures, there was so very little there.

"Yes. I understand he's running for mayor of this quaint little town." The way he said it made Carlisle sound like a dump. "That must be so *interesting* for you."

"What did you come for?" Sterling pressed, the scales falling from his eyes. "You want something, and all the airs and sweet talking aren't going to get you anywhere. So just spit it out and say what it is you want. That way I can tell you no and send you on your way."

Alexander's smile didn't fade a single watt. "I knew you'd be like this. But I had to come." He looked around the yard as though deciding where he wanted to sit, but Sterling made no invitation. "When I saw the little calendar you did in a bookstore in Philadelphia, I took it upon myself to show your work to a few people, and they sent me here to talk to you. I still care for you, Sterling. I always have, no matter what happened."

"Don't feed him your lines of manure to try to get him to do what you want. It isn't going to work, and it makes you seem stupid." Connor came closer.

"This doesn't concern you, kilt boy," Alexander retorted.

Connor snickered. "Is that the best you can do? That's like me saying you're a box of rocks. It's too damned easy. How about…?" Connor turned to Sterling. "Maybe 'you should drop your pants to let your brain breathe'? Or 'beautiful house, empty windows.'" He grinned. "What do you think, Sterling?"

"I think you're right. Alexander needs to drop the crap." He squared his shoulders. "I'm not going to come back to you or let you into my life. And I'm not interested in whatever you're peddling." Sterling took a step closer, examining the fine lines around Alexander's eyes and the way his right index finger kept moving slightly. "What is it you've gotten yourself into?"

"Excuse me?" Alexander asked.

Sterling turned to Connor. "When he's nervous, Alexander always gets a twitchy finger. His model training taught him how to move and control his entire body, but that one finger never learned the lesson, and when he's nervous or upset, it twitches." He grinned and tugged Connor closer. "What is it you want? Who asked you to come here?" He had a growing suspicion that after two years, Alexander wasn't going to just show up unless there was something in it for him, and it had nothing to do with wanting Sterling back. "Someone asked you to come?"

"Endrea asked me to speak with you," he finally admitted.

Connor's breath hitched. "Even I've heard of her." Endrea Monteros had burst onto the fashion scene less than a decade earlier and had taken the entire industry in a tsunami of praise and publicity. She was featured in high-end department stores but also had a line of clothing that every man or woman could afford. She brought fashion and style and made it available to everyone. Couture customers loved her too, because of her ability to create something special for them each and every time. Endrea was stunningly talented and kept each of her brands distinct, which kept all the lines fresh. In short, she was a fashion genius.

"Well, congratulations," Alexander sniped.

"That's enough. You're here, uninvited. You will be pleasant to my boyfriend." Sterling turned to Connor. "Would you please give me a few minutes with Alexander? It seems he can't be civil." Sterling kissed Connor hard, wrapping his arms around him and drawing Connor close. He knew he was putting on a show, but his body didn't know the difference, and Connor responded with gusto. Sterling wanted to push Alexander out the garden door and caveman Connor into bed. Damn, he wanted that badly. But he had old business to finish up, and this was his chance. "I'll find you as soon as we're through."

Connor's eyes shone, and Sterling pulled strength and love from them. Nothing he'd had with Alexander was anything like what Connor offered. With Connor, it was better, free, and without strings or conditions.

Connor nodded and left the yard, turning back before disappearing into the rear of the house. "Just call if you need me to put anything out to the curb."

Sterling reveled in the support… and Connor's jealousy. Not that Connor had anything to be worried about, but maybe a little jealousy could do the heart good. Then he whirled back on Alexander. "You and I are over, and I will never come back to you or work with you. Quit your games. You ripped my heart out two years ago, and I *loved* you. But to you I was just a step up the ladder, and when I didn't rise fast enough, you tossed me aside." He put his hands on his hips. "And as for seeing the calendar and thinking of me, I call bullshit. You said you were in a bookstore. Please… when did Alexander ever set foot in a bookstore? That would mean you'd need to read." He rolled his eyes. "I found someone a hell of a lot better than you, and I love him."

Alexander swallowed, and his broad shoulders slumped slightly. "I saw your pictures with him, and they—"

"Made you realize what you'd lost? Too little too late. Now that the horse manure portion of this conversation is over, what does Endrea want? Or more importantly, what is it you want from her?" Sterling knew how Alexander's mind worked. He wouldn't be here if there wasn't something in it for him.

"Endrea saw your calendar and apparently went back through your catalog and was impressed. I'm told she read the reports about us and approached my agent, who has been courting her for months on my behalf. She wants you to meet with her, and I want to work with her." Alexander's eyes actually lit up for the first time during the visit.

"And you got this idea that if you could get me to meet with her— say by the two of us walking in arm and arm or some such fantasy— that she might hire you." If Endrea were to agree to use Alexander, then he'd catapult to male supermodeldom. The rarest breed in the entire profession.

"It's your chance to come back from this backwater. You wouldn't need to take senior pictures any longer. The fashion world would welcome you back with open arms, and you and I could work together. It would be just like old times."

"No, it wouldn't, because I'm not doing it. If Endrea is interested in working with me, then she can get in touch with me easily enough. All it takes is a phone call." Sterling wasn't convinced that Alexander was telling him the whole story or that there was much truth in any of this. "As for us, there is no us. Not any longer. There's me and Connor."

"A history professor?" Alexander questioned.

Sterling stood and guided Alexander toward the door. "Yeah. And it's something you should learn about." He opened the door and pressed Alexander out onto the sidewalk. "Because you're history." Then he closed the garden door with a bang.

"Is he gone?" Connor asked a few minutes later. Sterling hadn't moved, and Connor's arms slipped around his waist, chest and hips pressing to his back. "What did he want?"

Sterling was still trying to process the possibilities. "He was trying to pull me back to him."

"He's realized he loves you?" Connor asked. "Of course he did—how could he not?" Connor said it like it was a plain-as-day fact. "What did you do?"

Sterling turned slowly. "First thing, I threw him out. And it felt goooood." He nuzzled right close to Connor's neck. "But no. He doesn't love me, no matter what he says. There's something else going on, but all I got from him was a bunch of supposed facts that may or may not be true." Sterling held Connor tighter. "One thing is true, I think. It's possible that Endrea saw the calendar and realized it was my work. She might be interested in me, and Alexander thinks he could use that to worm his way into her fashion house."

Connor stilled. "I see."

Sterling chuckled. "I'm glad you do, because I don't. Something is going on, but I don't know what exactly. Maybe something will come of this and maybe it won't." He wasn't going to get his hopes up. People got notions and ideas every day, and they changed their minds or something else got priority and nothing came of it.

"But he came all this way to see you. Would he do that if there wasn't something for him?" It seemed Connor understood Sterling's ex pretty well.

"I doubt it, but getting the facts out of Alexander when everything is filtered through his own wants and agenda is like pulling teeth." He sighed and decided he wasn't going to worry about it. "If something happens, then it does." He smiled. "What I'm most proud of is I sent him packing. He told me he was interested in getting back together, and I told him to pound sand. He got pissy and then found himself out on the sidewalk." Damn, that had felt amazing, and when he looked at Connor, the shadows that always seemed to encroach around his heart weren't there anymore. Damn, that had been too easy… and predictable.

"Feel better?"

"Yeah. I probably should have looked him up and had it out with him months ago."

Connor shook his head. "Wouldn't have worked. The only reason you feel better is because he came to you." Connor hugged him. "You're a badass, you know that? You threw your ex to the floor and stomped on what he wanted."

"When you say it that way, it makes me sound mean and awful," Sterling said.

Connor grinned and ran his fingers through Sterling's hair, making little tingles that started in his scalp and continued through him. "Maybe. But didn't it feel good? Welcome to the kick-your-ex-to-the-curb club." Connor chuckled and kissed him. In a matter of seconds, they were heading toward the bedroom.

"How much of what we said did you hear?" Sterling asked, pausing their progress.

"Not much… enough…." Their gazes locked, and Sterling wondered for a few seconds just what was enough. He swallowed but didn't turn away. Sterling couldn't for a second, not with the way those incredible blue eyes glistened. "Okay, almost all of it." He smiled and closed the distance between them. "For the record, I love you too, and I'm glad you kicked his ass out and chose me."

Connor kissed him again, and Sterling hefted Connor off his feet. Connor wrapped his legs around Sterling's waist, and he slid his hands down those strong legs and groaned when he realized that under that kilt was more and more luscious skin all the way to….

Connor nipped at his lower lip, and Sterling headed to the bedroom with as much haste as he dared. Damn, he loved his man in a kilt, with a kilt up around his waist, and most definitely with a kilt in a pile somewhere nearby.

"Alexander couldn't hold a candle to you—not in a million years." Connor was handsome, yes, but he was also beautiful all the way to his heart, and maybe that had been what Sterling had been missing all this time.

THUNDER SHOOK the house, waking Sterling from a sound sleep. He tugged Connor closer, holding him as the storm raged outside. But Sterling was content, peaceful inside with Connor next to him, his butt pressed to Sterling's hips.

"I hate these, you know," Connor whispered as the next clap of thunder rumbled deeply, vibrating the entire building. He rolled over and pressed Sterling back onto the mattress.

Sterling guided their lips together, wrapping his legs around Connor's waist. "Forget the storm and make love to me again," Sterling whispered and pressed a foil packet into Connor's hands.

Connor whimpered and shifted, the thunder becoming louder, sound waves crashing over the house, eventually eclipsed by the passion that flowed out from Connor, pushing away everything until the crashes in Sterling's mind overruled everything and all that mattered was him and Connor, their movement together, his heart reaching out and finding Connor's in the dark.

A crack split the night, so close he could feel the electric jolt race through him as their bodies joined. Another flash illuminated Connor's eyes, just for a second, but they were as deep and dark as the bottom of the sea. Sterling arched his back, and the next flash silhouetted Connor against the window, muscles straining, a god in stop motion. There was no way Alexander could ever compete with this man, and even in the dark, the shadow of Sterling's past had lifted and his heart was light, shining the way to Connor.

Chapter 20

"Don't forget that the subjects for your term papers are due by next Friday," Connor said to his final class of the day late in September. He tried to think where the months had gone.

"Have a good weekend," a few of his students said as they filed out in a hurry, probably making plans for their weekends. Connor's was planned already, with talks with two community groups, and tomorrow afternoon, the campaign had gotten a booth at the Harvest Festival in town, so he'd be there all day.

Connor gathered his materials and closed down the room before heading to his office, where he filed his notes and checked email before heading out.

"See you tomorrow. I'm volunteering at your booth," Gary said as he passed his door. "I think it's cool that you're running for mayor. Maybe now we aren't going to be forgotten." He smiled. "Oh, and I know you said you wouldn't sign calendars at school, so I'm bringing mine tomorrow, Professor April." He laughed as he hurried away, and Connor rolled his eyes.

So far, everything had indeed worked out. Sterling had been right. The calendar issue had largely died away, especially when it became known that the garden club had sold tens of thousands of copies after the state news outlets all picked it up. His campaign was in high gear, and his ideas for the town were gaining traction.

Connor picked up his messenger bag, locked his office door, and left the building. He stopped at home to get his things for the weekend before heading to Sterling's, passing along the cars that had parked up the street, then letting himself inside. He checked his messages and found one from Sterling telling him to come on back to the studio.

When he opened the door, he heard Sterling on the phone. "Are you serious?" he heard Sterling ask. "Okay, I guess you are. That's what Alexander told me last month, but I wasn't sure how much of it was true. … I see…." Sterling smiled when he saw him and motioned to the phone. Connor was curious, but he didn't want to listen in on Sterling's phone call. He sat down anyway when Sterling patted the nearest chair and put the phone on speaker, turning down the volume.

"You are probably aware that we are interested in using Alexander. He's assured us that won't be a problem."

Connor's eyes widened.

Sterling shook his head while the woman finished speaking. "I want to be clear. I won't work with him. That part of my career is over. I'm not going to rehash what happened, but if you want him, then find another photographer." He leaned back in his chair, and Connor got up and stood behind Sterling, placing his hand on his shoulders.

"We feel that he would be wonderful as the face for our brand, and your images and the sensuality you've captured would be perfect," she said.

"I'm sorry, it's either him or me, and I'll understand if he's your choice." Sterling patted one of Connor's hands. "My mental health is worth more than that."

"But Alexander is intense, and his look is unique. He's also—"

Sterling cut in. "Demanding, conniving, self-serving, hard to work with, a complete diva, a backstabbing pain in the ass, and more trouble than he's worth. If you want my opinion, you're better off finding a fresh face that you can build the style and look of your brand around from the ground up."

Connor's mouth fell open. He rubbed the building tension out of Sterling's shoulders.

"I see."

Sterling leaned forward, and Connor moved with him. "Endrea, in the end you have to do what's right for your new line and be true to your vision. Think about what it is you want and then let me know. I will tell you this. You cannot have both of us. It's just not possible."

"You know I'm very used to getting what I want," Endrea said.

"That may be. But in this case, you can't have it. I know I'm only the photographer and Alexander is a known factor, but that's the way it is." He turned and held Connor's hand tightly. "You decide what you want and let me know."

Endrea's rich laugh came through the line. "Okay. Then I choose you."

Connor could hardly believe it, and he silently jumped for joy that Sterling was going to be able to return to the world that he loved.

"We'll send over the details of the offer, and then we'll schedule a call to review it before it's finalized." She sighed. "You know, I've seen your work many times before, but it was that calendar you did that clinched it for me. Those pictures were stunning, and when I learned none of the men were professionals—that you used local men and got images like that—I knew you were the man for what I needed and for our future."

"Well, thank you. It was an exceptional project." He turned to Connor, his eyes shining. "It was rewarding, and it brought me a great deal of happiness."

"Let's see if we can add to that. Look for more information soon." She ended the call, and Sterling got to his feet, pulling Connor into a hug.

"I can't believe it," Sterling said. "I'm trying not to get too excited because until I get the offer, she could still change her mind."

Still Connor was thrilled. "We need to celebrate."

"Perfect. I'll have food delivered, you go pop open a couple beers, and we'll celebrate." He picked up the phone and placed an order while Connor went into the kitchen and pulled a couple bottles from the refrigerator. By the time he returned, Sterling had locked the studio doors and closed the blinds, and he immediately started opening the buttons of Connor's shirt. "Let's make a few moments Kodak will never forget."

STERLING WASN'T kidding. Thank God the delivery guy didn't come to the back door.

"Don't move," Sterling said forcefully as he leapt away. Connor glanced around, wondering why there was whipped cream in the studio refrigerator and how long it was going to take before it melted completely and his buttcheeks got glued together.

"Sterling…," he called and reached for a towel just as Sterling came in carrying a pizza box and two beers. "I know you thought this might be sexy, but the mess sure as hell isn't." He managed to sop up the last of the whipped cream and reached for his clothes. In the heat of passion, some things seemed like a really great idea, while others were just messy. "My asscheeks are going to be stuck together for days."

Sterling set down the box and the beer. "You'll just be all that much sweeter when it's time for dessert." He wagged his eyebrows, and Connor couldn't contain himself any longer.

"I don't think so." He wiped himself off once again and wrapped his kilt around his waist, and they sat on the floor with the pizza box in front of them. Sterling gave him the stink eye for a second, and Connor stifled a sated yawn. "I'm going to need food and a little time to recover… stud." Sterling preened and actually flashed a bicep, which only made Connor laugh a little harder. "Come on, Arnold, let's eat."

"I look good."

"Sweetheart, you're sexy and I love you." It felt wonderful to say those words.

"I feel a *but* coming on." Sterling opened the pizza box and handed Connor a slice.

"We already did that," Connor quipped with a wink. "And I think mine needs a rest. But I like that you like my butt, *but*… don't do that muscle thing again. It's not attractive." He held his serious expression as long as he could while Sterling pouted before grinning. "But I am glad you like my butt. It's my best ass-et."

"Very punny," Sterling teased. "I think that's enough. If we keep this up, we'll devolve to dick jokes and potty humor. Lord knows no one wants that." He rolled his eyes, and Connor chuckled, leaning in as he set down his pizza. They shared a spicy kiss before scooting a little closer together.

"You know, who would have guessed how things would work out? The calendar is a huge success, and Aunt Lucille is thrilled… and it seems has a boyfriend. Your dad is happy, and you just got a chance to return to fashion, all from a project we both thought was doomed at one point."

"You could be the next mayor." Sterling sighed, finishing his slice of pizza. "And we both found something special that we weren't looking for." He put his arm around Connor's shoulders, drawing him closer.

Connor slipped his arms around Sterling's waist, and they rolled back onto the floor, dinner quickly forgotten.

"CONNOR." STERLING came into the bedroom, and he pulled the covers over his head.

"It's Saturday," he groaned and yawned, nestling deeper under the covers as Sterling's weight settled near him on the edge of the bed. "I should be able to sleep in." He lowered the bedding, blinking as he slowly sat up. "Do you have appointments today?"

"The first one is in an hour," Sterling told him without cracking a smile.

He pushed the covers lower and hoisted himself into a fully seated position. "What's going on?" Connor wiped his eyes. "Why so serious? Did you get the offer from Endrea? Was it really bad?" He hoped Sterling hadn't gotten his hopes up only to have them dashed. That would suck.

"It's a great offer. They want to pay me a huge amount of money, and I'll be at Paris Fashion week, Milan, all the big shows. They want me to shoot for them exclusively, and Endrea says that she wants me to work with her to find the model that will be the new face of her brand for men. She wants images that will be as iconic as the Mark Wahlberg Calvin Klein underwear campaign."

Connor was confused. "Then why aren't you excited? You can do this, I know you can." Sterling should be bouncing with excitement.

"It isn't that. I already have some ideas. There are great models with amazing looks that I know of who haven't made it big. They're great to work with, talented, but haven't caught the industry's attention yet. Finding the model isn't the issue, and once I see the clothes, I'll know how to showcase them. That part is a piece of cake."

"Then what?" Connor asked.

Sterling got up off the bed. "Endrea works out of Paris. That's where she lives. Yes, there would be a lot of travel. But the contract has a relocation allowance." He paused at the door. "I'd have to move to Europe."

And just like that, the carefree joy bubble they had created last night popped. Even though the sun was shining through the bedroom windows, the room began to darken.

"I see." Connor pushed the covers away. "Then there's only one thing you can do."

"Yeah, I have to turn down the job."

Connor shook his head. "You'll do no such thing. You have to take it and see where this leads." His heart skipped a beat, and he felt the disappointment begin to build. Connor should have known something like this was a possibility. When Sterling had been working in fashion, he had traveled all over the world. Any job he got would require him to rejoin that life. It came with the territory, and Connor knew that no matter what Sterling might say, it was his dream, what he had been holding out for the entire time he'd been back here in town. There was no way in hell that Connor was going to stand in his way.

"Connor…," Sterling said softly.

"No." He grabbed what little of his clothes were in the bedroom and headed for the door. "This is what you have to do." He swallowed hard around the basketball that seemed to have decided to bounce in his throat.

"*I'll* decide what I want to do."

Connor crossed his arms over his chest. "Fine. You decide what you want to do—just as long as you agree with me and do what I say." He glared at Sterling. "Let's look at this rationally. You got this great offer from a world-famous designer who loves your work and is making you the offer of a lifetime. You turn it down and you'll regret it forever. And eventually you'll get angry at me because you decided not to take this amazing job, one that someone else will take, and then you'll see their ads everywhere. Each time you do, you'll see my face in every model, and eventually you'll want to rip their heads off, which is easy because they're paper and it's just an ad. But you'll still get angry, and sooner or later, that anger will be directed at me because you gave up this job you've always dreamed of for me."

Sterling opened his mouth.

"Shhhh… I'm not done."

"Oh goody," Sterling snarked, but Connor was on a roll.

"Five years from now, you and I will be trying to decide where to go on vacation. You'll say Yellowstone and I'll say I want to go to Paris. Then you'll say, 'I could have worked and lived in Paris, but I didn't because I fell in love with you.' Then you'll stick your tongue out, and we'll go to Yellowstone, have a terrible time, which you'll blame me for because I wanted to go Paris but you didn't, and you could have worked there if you had taken this amazing job, but didn't because of me."

"Are you done? Good God, that was weird." Sterling sighed.

"Yes, I'm weird, and you'll say worse things to me, all because I stood in the way of the job of a lifetime and your big chance."

Sterling shook his head. "What does a vacation in five years have to do with this? And man, your mind can go in more circles than a hamster."

"I know. But am I wrong?" Connor lowered his arms, and Sterling didn't answer. He simply sighed, which was all the answer Connor needed. "I'm going to get dressed and go on to the festival. I need to be at the booth in an hour."

"Do you want me to come?" Sterling asked quietly.

"Of course," Connor told him with forced brightness. The world beneath his feet had been rocked by a mega earthquake, and he did his best to keep it from showing, though everything had changed in just a few minutes.

"I'll get dressed when you're done." He left, and a few seconds later, Sterling's trudging steps on the stairs grew softer.

"Sounds good." Connor used the bathroom to clean up and then returned to the bedroom to dress. He put on his best kilt and a pressed white shirt. Over that he wore his sash and brooch. Then he added the sporran and put on his socks and shoes and checked himself in the mirror.

"You look every bit the highlander," Sterling said as he slipped his arms around him from behind.

"Thanks," Connor answered softly. "What are we going to do?" he asked. "I know you'd give up the job for me, and I think that's amazingly sweet of you." He turned slowly. "I'd love you for that alone. But you can't, and you know it."

"Get rid of all that resentment stuff, okay?" Sterling whispered.

"Fine. Let's put that aside." He caressed Sterling's smooth-shaved cheek. "How could I live with myself knowing I was the cause of you not getting what you've always wanted? The studio here is great, but it wasn't your dream. Endrea is offering that to you, and if I stood in your way, I'd never be able to forgive myself." He swallowed hard. "She said on the call that she wanted you to review the offer. Did she say when… and is there any indication of when she wanted you to start?"

Sterling sighed softly. "She asked to talk on Wednesday. She said she'd be in New York and is apparently making arrangements to come here to meet with me." Even Connor knew that was huge.

"I have a meeting, and the guys in the department have been asking me to go out with them. They have this 'middle of the week' thing, so I'll go, and you can have the time you need with Endrea." He would have to get used to doing things on his own.

"You know I'm not going to stop seeing you. I'll come back. My dad is here, your great-aunt is here, you're here. This is still going to be my home."

"Yes, but it's not going to be the same. You'll be gone for months at a time, surrounded by beautiful people." He tried not to get maudlin. "I know you'd never cheat on me, but we've known each other five months, and you'll be gone for that long." He really didn't see how this would work. There would be so many demands on Sterling's time. "I know we would mean well and we'd talk to each other every day to start with, but then you'd get busy, we'd have less and less to talk about, and pretty soon…."

"So you wouldn't want to try?" Sterling asked.

"Of course I would, but we can't deny reality." God, how could things go from perfect to purgatory in the matter of an hour? He rested his head on Sterling's shoulder. "I guess I always knew that you were too good and too talented for this town. The world is calling, and you need to answer. I promise I'll be here." But how long would Sterling be willing to come back?

CONNOR'S BOOTH at the festival had been placed next to the one for the garden club. He hadn't requested it, but apparently his great-aunt had. Sterling had taken charge of designing it, using blown-up images of Connor from around town with his slogan, "Using Our History to Build Our Future." He had fliers, and Sterling had made a cutout of him in the kilt for pictures. He thought it was a little over-the-top, but Sterling had insisted that it would be fun. Who was he to argue?

The ladies had their booth filled with flowers, informational packets, and of course the calendars for sale. "We have the model couples coming in throughout the day to sign them," Aunt Lucille said as she and Judy set up their beefcake display.

"We're all set," Sterling pronounced as he looked over the booth. "It's dynamic, and it looks fun and community-minded."

"Thank you." People were already strolling the street, so Connor stood out in front of the booth, wishing people a good morning and talking with those who stopped. Volunteers arrived, and they talked with people as well. Connor did his best to put the morning's news out of his head and concentrate on the task at hand. He liked this sort of thing. The meet and greet, listening to people—those were his forte, and he didn't stand under the tent, just glaring at people as they walked past, the way his opponent did across the way and four booths down. Though maybe he was just glaring at Connor. Didn't matter—Connor projected energy and excitement, even if he didn't feel them at the moment.

A volunteer brought him some water, and he thanked her and drank between talking to still more people and signing calendars. So far the day was split between folks who wanted to speak with him and those who wanted their calendars signed.

"Sterling," Connor called, and he reluctantly approached and signed a few pictures.

"You two are adorable. Are you really together?" a woman asked.

"Yes," Sterling answered. "He's my boyfriend, and I'll let you in on a secret. The calendar brought us together."

"That's so sweet." She held her signed calendar and hurried out of the booth, only to return twenty minutes later with five other people, who all bought calendars and had them signed.

"You know all that is disgusting," a male voice called. Connor knew it was Mayor Randall, and he ignored it.

"So help me," Aunt Lucille said as she stepped into the booth, "one of these days I'm going to beat that man with my purse of death." She held up a huge bag that must have weighed ten pounds. "I have to have extra supplies for days like this, and I swear I'll accidentally slip a brick in it and just happen to hit him in the head." An image of his great-aunt swinging her purse over her head like David taking on Goliath flashed through his mind.

"There's no need for violence, accidental or otherwise. He only makes himself look small." Connor had had enough of the guy and figured it was best to ignore him. He turned and waved, and in return he got a glare that basically kept everyone away from Randall's booth.

"How are you holding up?" Aunt Lucille asked more quietly. "Something is bothering you. I know you have the energetic thing going on, but something isn't right." She gave him that look like he better not try to prevaricate. "Trouble in paradise?"

"Just life being a donkey and giving us a kick in the ass." He shrugged and turned away, smiling. There was nothing he could do about it.

"Then kick it back," Aunt Lucille said, and Connor wished it were just that simple.

Chapter 21

STERLING WAS helping in Connor's booth, but he sat down in back out of the way when he realized he really wasn't needed. Connor was doing great on his own. At noon, he got Connor something to eat, and they sat behind the back wall of the booth and hid for fifteen minutes. "Drink a little more so your voice doesn't wear out."

Connor took the bottle and drank before finishing his salad and chicken wrap.

"I know this is bothering you," Sterling said.

"I'm trying not to let it. There's nothing I can do about it, and I need to be at my best." The small lines around Connor's eyes told Sterling a lot more than his words. "It will be okay. I don't know how, but somehow I know it will." He brushed his hand over Sterling's shoulder. "You'll do amazing things, and your images will appear forty feet tall all over the country. I have school breaks, and I'll go where you are, and you said you'd come back here when you can. Maybe we can have spring in Paris." Connor was trying to put a brave face on things, but Sterling saw the darkness in his eyes. Connor always seemed so positive, and his eyes always radiated intense heat and excitement, almost no matter what he was doing. The public wouldn't notice it, but Sterling saw that was missing. Connor could put on his smile and talk to people all day, listening to what they wanted to say. But only Sterling could see past the façade to know he was hurting. His eyes, with their intense blue that drew him in each and every time, had lost their sparkle, and Sterling hated beyond words that he had been responsible for that.

"Are you done?" Sterling asked, gathering the trash. "Drink a little more water and take the bottle out with you. I'll take care of this." He wished he could take Connor in his arms, kiss away the hurt, and tell him that nothing was going to keep them apart, no matter what. But he couldn't make promises—not like that. This required action, not words.

"I EXPECT HER in an hour," Sterling told Connor when he called for the fourth time. Apparently he was as nervous about this meeting as Sterling was. They had spent much of the past few days together, but Sterling felt like things were different. During the day, everything seemed normal. Connor went to work, and Sterling had his appointments. But the evenings were strained. An elephant had suddenly sprung up from the ground and stood right between them. There was no need to talk about the offer and what it meant, because they already had, but it was there nonetheless. Connor thought he was hiding his worried expressions, but Sterling saw them when Connor didn't think he was looking. "I have everything cleaned up and the appetizers you made ready to go." Sterling could not believe that Connor had insisted on making something to serve.

"Do you want me to come over when I'm done with work? I can stay away if you want the time alone."

Sterling was well aware that Connor wanted to come over, and he figured Connor needed it. Maybe if he met Endrea then she wouldn't be this bogeyman-type person who was trying to break up his relationship with her employment contract and job offer. "Come over about six. That will give me about an hour to review things with her. We planned to have dinner, and then she's apparently going on to Pittsburgh." Though Sterling had no idea why.

"Okay. I'll see you then." He paused. "I hope everything goes well and you get what you want."

For the past few days, Connor had been vocally supportive every chance he got, and it was starting to drive Sterling crazy. He knew that Connor was saying what Sterling wanted to hear, and sometimes he wanted to scream. What Sterling really wanted to know was exactly how Connor felt in his own words—he didn't want to read between the lines to try to determine what Connor was actually saying.

"Things are going to be fine. Just relax and have a good class. I'll see you in a few hours." He ended the call and put away the last of the cleaning supplies. Then he got the food ready to serve before peering out the window as a limousine pulled up right in front. Sterling went to the door and opened it as Endrea regally got out from the back and joined him at the stoop. "It's good to see you again," he said, extending his hand.

She took his hand and smiled. "It's been since Paris a few years ago." She released his hand. "This is a beautiful town. Parts of it feel like home," she said with a flowing French accent that made her sound exotic.

"Please come in." He motioned, and she floated past him like one of her runway models. "I have us in here." He motioned toward the living room. "Would you like something to drink? I have some nice wine or, if you prefer, a cocktail."

"I would love a martini, please, dry," she said, and Sterling went to the kitchen. He was aware of what Endrea liked, so he had the fixings ready. After mixing the drinks, he brought them in along with the hummus Connor had made and set everything out on the coffee table. She sipped from the glass, smiled, and then set it back on the table. "I thought we would get our business completed before we went to dinner."

"I agree." He picked up his tablet, where he had the agreement loaded. She pulled a paper copy out of her bag. "I've reviewed the document in detail, and there are parts that are fine. The pay is acceptable, as is the travel. I'm aware of what this kind of job entails."

"Yes. You will be my right-hand man when it comes to visuals for this line. I will need you close."

Sterling wasn't surprised at her response. He reached to the table beside him and handed a copy of the calendar to her.

"Yes. I have seen this. It's why I am here."

"Of course. I'm aware. Open it, please, and tell me what your favorite images were." He sat back and tried to look comfortable even as his heart raced.

"I love this one. It's very evocative." She showed him the picture of Red and Terry.

"He's an Olympic gold medalist, and the other man is a police officer here in town. They're a couple." He leaned forward. "The lighting is because Red has scars from an accident, and we used it to minimize them. If you look closely, you can see them, but you wouldn't if you didn't know they were there. But… see that look, it's all them. All I did was capture their feelings for one another." He smiled, and she flipped a few pages.

"This one with the firefighters. They're too big for models, and yet they seem softer and kind of gentle, like guys I'd like to meet and have to dinner with, one on either side of me."

Sterling liked her more and more, especially her smile.

"They're also a couple. They met on the job. I wanted them to look like firemen without the usual accessories, so we used the hose. But those eyes and that look, it's also a reflection of how they feel. The only fire in that picture is the one they light in each other." Sterling waited as Endrea began to nod.

"I see that." She thumbed through the pictures. "And this one is you." She paused at April. "And this man…." She smiled and nodded. "Your Scotsman?"

"Yes. His name is Connor, and he's a history professor. And yes, that's how he dresses most days. Connor is very proud of his heritage."

She continued looking at the image. "What does he think of this job offer?" she asked without looking up.

"He told me that I had to take it. That he wouldn't allow me to give up the chance of a lifetime." Sterling figured it was best to be honest with her. "That's the kind of guy he is. Connor is unselfish, and he would never put himself first. He's running for mayor right now so he can make the town better."

Endrea set the calendar beside her. "What is it you're saying? That you don't want this job?"

Sterling rubbed his hands together. "I want to do this so much I can taste it. I have ideas on various models who would be amazing to represent you and your brand. I can't wait to see the designs so we can develop a campaign that will take the world by storm."

"Wonderful. I need you in Paris next week, and while you're there, you can look for a place to live and—"

Sterling put his hand up. "But I need Connor more than any job. I can't do this without him. I've already done the globetrotting thing, being away from the person I'm with, and you know how that worked out. The entire world apparently got a ringside seat. I can be in Paris next week if you want, but I won't move there. This is my home, and it's where Connor is. I won't relocate, and I'm not going to spend my entire life on planes going back and forth. I know you're based in Paris, but if you want me, then I'll be based here. I can be in New York by train in under four hours. I will travel to Paris, Milan, Morocco, Rome, wherever you need me, but at the end of the day, I come back home to Connor." He leaned forward, picked up the calendar, and opened it to April. "I can't give him up because this was as much him as it was me." He pointed. "This image was his idea. He made this happen, and as you can guess, I wasn't even behind the camera. Connor is my inspiration. He makes me better. I can't give him up, and I know you're aware that long-distance relationships don't last." Look at him and Alexander—a prime example. "But people in happy, stable relationships make the best business associates because they're happy."

She picked up her glass, sipped, and didn't answer right away, her intense brown eyes unreadable. "This was not what I was expecting." She held the glass, swirling the liquid as she watched it. "I like to keep my people close to me. This is a creative business."

"Yes. But it's a business." He leaned forward. "How many times a year do you travel to New York? A dozen? More?"

"Not as much as I used to. I Skype, or we have internet conferences, and…." She sipped from the glass and smiled. "You made your point."

"And let's not forget that fashion is a business. Travel is expensive, and so is relocating people to live in Paris only to have them travel around the globe." He had her attention at least. That was good. "Let me ask you something. Do you see your men's brand as international or more American-based, as far as the look?"

She didn't hesitate. "American. Without a doubt. It needs to be clothes that men will want to wear every day, and yet they need to have style and a great cut." She brought out some boards and handed them to Sterling. "This is confidential."

"Of course." He looked them over. They were amazing, and he could see himself in them. "I bet these would work for guys no matter the size."

"That was the idea. I wanted something real men could wear, not just models or teenagers." Sterling handed the boards back, and she slipped them into her bag.

"Will you take a walk with me?" Sterling asked.

They set their glasses aside, and Sterling quickly took care of the food before guiding Endrea out of the house and leading her toward the main street. "This isn't your everyday American town. It's vibrant and understands its history." He led her to the courthouse. She stepped around front and stopped at the fluted red stone columns that soared up almost forty feet.

"I see what you mean." Sterling could almost see her mind going to work. "That's too new over there. But this—it's like Rome meets America, old world meets new."

"Just like your clothes," Sterling said as his phone vibrated in his pocket. He pulled it out and answered Connor's brief message, telling him where they were. "I'm thinking that instead of trying to make New York or Paris or Milan the background for your clothes, we make it places like this—American places, coast to coast, and that includes New York, Philadelphia, Los Angeles, Chicago, but also New Orleans, Natchez, Savannah, Albuquerque. Iconic places backing up looks that we want to be just as iconic."

Endrea put her hand up. "Okay. I'm convinced." She smiled, her eyes filling with excitement. "I do want you in Paris next week so we can start laying out the plan for the entire campaign. I have samples of all the clothes, and we'll start our model search." She held out her hand, and Sterling shook it.

"I see you came to an agreement," Connor said quietly as he approached.

Sterling couldn't help smiling as he turned.

"This gorgeous man must be Connor," Endrea said, shaking his hand. "Yes. We have agreed to many things." Her gaze traveled over Connor, and Sterling felt a growl welling in his throat. There was no way he wanted anyone looking at Connor like that. "If you were a model, I'd have you in one of my Paris shows in two seconds."

"I'm not. I only appear in pictures for Sterling, and that's just how I like it. Now… if you decide to design a line of kilts, then I'd certainly be your man." Connor smiled, but it didn't go all the way to his eyes.

"Do you always dress this way?" Endrea asked.

"Yes, he does. Connor is Scottish, and these are his clan colors." Sterling slid an arm around Connor's waist and turned to Connor, letting his smile shine through.

"When do you leave for Paris?"

"I need him there next week."

"I see," Connor said, tensing.

"It's only a business trip for a few weeks. Endrea and I have agreed that my home will be here. There will be travel and a lot of work, but much of it will be over Skype and videoconferencing."

Endrea actually patted his shoulder. "Sterling, I'm going to walk back to your house."

"We won't be long," Sterling told her, and she nodded and smiled, heading back the way they had come. "Look, honey, I know what you're thinking, but you're wrong. I took the job with Endrea and I'm going to Paris next week, but I'm coming back, because this is my home. *You* are my home. Yeah, I jumped at the opportunity, but I'm not moving. It will mean travel, but I know that you'll be waiting at the end of each trip."

"But… she could have said no."

Sterling shrugged. "Yes, she could have. But Endrea is creative, smart, and a businessperson. She also wants amazing images for her campaign, and she wants the feel of what I've been doing."

Connor lightly smacked his shoulder. "You could have blown your entire chance, and I told you not to because…." He groaned. "I would have felt awful if you had lost your dream job because of me."

"But I didn't. I got the job *and* I got you." Sterling tugged Connor closer. "That will be the best of both worlds. Now… I think you and I better go to my place, because my new boss is walking there, and I don't think it's a great idea to leave her waiting on the sidewalk. She might change her mind, or worse." He smiled and took Connor's hand, and they walked back toward the house.

"Worse…? What does that mean?" Connor paused as though trying to figure out the nuclear option.

"Yeah. She might try to turn you into the face for her brand." Sterling shivered at the thought and continued walking with Connor. He'd seen the way Endrea had practically devoured Connor. "I think one model boyfriend is enough for a lifetime."

"Maybe I'd like being the face of a brand and being in front of the camera." Connor stepped back, legs apart, hands on his hips, chest out, the breeze blowing his shirt and the hem of his kilt. Connor presented quite a sight as squealing brakes sounded from behind them. Yeah, he was definitely enough to stop traffic. A semi passed, swirling the air, and Connor's kilt took on a life of its own.

"Come on, Marilyn. No flashing the town." Sterling pulled Connor into his arms, where he belonged. "Besides, if you want to be in front of a camera, that can be arranged whenever you want, no modeling—or clothes—required." He held him tight. "I love you, Connor," he said, barely loud enough to be heard over the traffic.

"And I love you," Sterling read on Connor's lips, which he then kissed hard and deep, right there on the street.

"Get a room, Professor!"

Sterling backed away, and they both chuckled. Then he took Connor's hand and headed for home.

Epilogue

STERLING'S PHONE beeped a dozen times in rapid succession as soon as he turned it on, once the plane had landed. All of them were from Marcel, Endrea's assistant. While the plane taxied, Sterling checked the pictures and smiled. Her preliminary designs for the following fall looked incredible, and he sent his praising response.

Sterling deplaned when his turn came, got through passport control, picked his luggage off the carousel, and had just breezed through customs with a smile, when his phone rang. "Don't you ever stop working?" he asked Endrea. It was after eleven her time.

"I wanted to talk to you. You got the updates, and you're going to need to change your concepts to fit."

"Take a look at what I sent you before I left. Your designs will work even better with what we reviewed. You saw what I presented, and I updated your designs to fit." Endrea was a perfectionist, but she had probably been up two days by this point to get everything finished. He continued through the Philadelphia airport, pulling his bags and talking to her.

"You're right," Endrea told him. "They're perfect, and everything goes together. I just need to finish the jewelry and accessories."

"Get some rest and you can figure it all out. There are amazing jewelry manufacturers you can partner with. Marcel and I were talking about a few just the other day, and he has their information."

"What would I do without you?" He could almost see her smile. "I'll talk to you later. Give my best to Connor." She ended the call, and he placed one to the limousine service he'd arranged for before he left. They said his driver was on the way and told him where to wait. Sterling arrived at the meeting spot just as his driver did, and he climbed in back, stretched out, and breathed a little sigh. "Get me home as soon as you possibly can."

"Traffic is murder on the Schuylkill," the driver said.

"Then go around it if you can. Just get me home as fast as possible." He sat back as the driver pulled away. Fortunately, the driver did know a better route, and they got to the turnpike sooner than expected. Sterling called Connor and ended up leaving a message.

Outside Reading, it began to snow, and by Harrisburg it was coming down heavier. Sterling checked the time and called Connor once again, but he still didn't get an answer. The driver continued through to the Carlisle exchange, where finally the snow let up. Sterling tried Connor once more, his worry increasing as they made the turn toward town.

"Where is he?" Sterling asked as he checked the time for the fourth time in five minutes. "Just take me to the house." He waited until the car stopped and got out, and the driver retrieved his luggage. There were lights on inside, and he hurried in to find Aunt Lucille, his father, and Connor all in the living room.

"We were waiting for you," his dad said. "Why didn't you call?"

Connor wore his best kilt, looking stunning with his sash, brooch, and all the accessories.

"I did. But you didn't answer."

"Oh crap. The phone is upstairs." Connor raced to get it, and Sterling met him at the bottom of the stairs, where Connor stepped right into his arms. "We need to go."

"Everyone in the limousine," Sterling said without letting Connor go.

His dad patted his shoulder on the way past. "Don't take too long, son." He and Connor's great-aunt left the house, leaving them alone.

"I was starting to think you weren't going to make it, with the snow and everything." Connor rested his head on his shoulder, holding tightly like he could hardly believe Sterling was here.

"Of course I would. It just took me begging the captain to get him to fly faster, coaxing all the passengers to flap their arms through the entire flight, and finding a limo driver who used to race for NASCAR, but I'm here, and I wouldn't have missed this for the world."

Connor drew him into a kiss, and Sterling wrapped his arms around Connor's neck, tasting the man he'd been away from for two weeks and was so glad to have come home to. "I brought you something, sweetheart." He backed away and slowly went down on one knee, handing Connor the small box that had been in his pocket for almost twelve hours. Endrea had designed the engagement and wedding rings for them, and a friend of hers in Paris had made her design into reality. "Connor, my Mr. April, will you marry me?" He showed Connor the ring, which was white gold with a vine motif in an endless circle on the entire band.

Connor nodded. "Yes," he barely choked out, and Sterling slipped the ring on his finger.

Sterling stood and kissed Connor once again, then held his hand as they headed toward the door. "Let's go get you inaugurated as mayor, and when we get home, we can go to the bedroom and see about your first official… act."

Keep reading for an excerpt from
Hello Goodbye Amore
by Andrew Grey!

Chapter 1

Two minutes—that was all Chase Anderson had left before the morning meeting when the elevator doors slid open and he strode breathlessly to his office, past the department admin's desk.

Loretta lifted her gaze from her computer and smiled. "Dewey canceled the meeting this morning," she told him gently. "But he wants to see you in his office at eight fifteen."

Breathing heavily, Chase gaped at her and thought about banging his head on her desk, but with the way things were going, he'd end up with a concussion. "Thanks." Chase shook his head as he looked skyward, not daring to slip off his jacket until he reached his office and closed the door. Then he hung up his jacket, sat at his desk, and quickly went through his email. His inbox had been clear when he left last night, so he answered what he needed to and then slipped his jacket back on for his meeting with Dewey. After all, the world would scream to a halt if he showed up without it.

The company had officially gone to an office-casual dress code. But his VP, Dewey van der Veer, had other ideas, and while he never said anything outright, it was made clear—by his attitude and his expensive Italian suits—that he expected everyone who worked for him to continue to dress the way they always had, which meant jacket and tie, even when it was ninety degrees outside. It would be okay if the guy weren't such a complete douchenozzle. Chase had been in his position for barely a year and had already sent out a few inquiries about positions in other departments of Smithson Biomedical, if only to help him keep his sanity.

Chase knocked on the frame of Dewey's door and took a seat when he motioned him in. Dewey was on the phone and building up a head of steam. "I don't really care. You need to bring this in on the cost we talked about and on schedule. We have three teams waiting on it, and you don't get to tell me a week before it's due that you need two more weeks. I'm paying you to deliver."

Chase had heard that sort of talk to suppliers a number of times. It was Dewey's standard reaction to anything that didn't go his way. Dewey was every cliché of a bad boss, right down to his "do what I say, not what I do" mentality. Others who had worked for him for years had told Chase he'd get used to it. Chase wasn't so sure.

With a final threat, Dewey tossed his cell phone on his desk, and it slid to the edge but didn't dare fall to the floor. Then he leaned back in his chair as though he had all the time in the world. Maybe yelling at suppliers gave the guy a thrill. Hell, he looked like he wanted a cigarette. Everything in the office was designed to keep everyone hopping and on their toes while Dewey relaxed and looked like he was ready to put his feet up.

"You've done an amazing job on the design of the adjustable breathing implant, and we got word yesterday that the initial trials were a success and have been approved to move on to large-scale testing in a few months." As usual, Dewey dove right in and actually smiled like this was all his success, his perfect teeth—probably all crowns—actually shining. Not that Chase doubted he was taking credit for whatever he could, whenever he could. That was his usual method of operation. "The biggest stumbling block is the coupler that makes up the center of the design. The requirements for that piece are so exacting, we've had difficulties finding a company to produce them."

Chase wanted to ask how hard Dewey had looked, but he bit his lip instead. "I see." Chase wondered exactly what Dewey was up to. "I made a list of firms that should have been able to meet our specifications."

He nodded. "And you did great, but the FDA approval process tightened the specifications further and ruled most of them out. However, one firm has agreed to supply what we need." Dewey leaned forward, his hands on his desk, and looked at Chase as though he were a rabbit and Dewey a fox. They had gone through this active listening training a year before, and this was Dewey's attempt to comply with that. Instead of appearing engaged and attentive, he looked more like a constipated predator trying to pass his last meal. "We need someone to work with this firm to make sure that they can and will meet our specifications."

Chase knew the list he'd made by heart. "Which firm is it?"

"Glorioso Metallurgy out of Italy."

Of course. It had to be them. That firm had most certainly *not* been on his list for a number of reasons, not least of which was that they were overseas, and he had been told to concentrate on American suppliers. But just the name brought up unpleasant memories that hit Chase right in the gut. Hell, a punch would be more pleasant than the twisting agony of old pain he tried to push back into its box. But he couldn't let any of that show on his face in front of Dewey. It wouldn't be professional, and it wasn't like Dewey gave a damn about the things that had happened to Chase years ago and changed his life forever. No, that man cared about nothing but himself and what affected his image as the perfect supervisor.

"Do you want me to have someone contact them?" Chase asked. He wasn't sure where Dewey was heading.

"No." That gaze of his didn't shift, but he smiled, like everything was no wonderful. "I need you to go to Florence and work with them to make sure they truly can deliver what we need. Oversee quality and production schedules as well as arrange shipping and be the liaison back to the office and staff here. The project is important enough to the company that we thought we should have someone on-site there." He sounded so reasonable, but Chase was praying for the floor beneath him to open up so the earth could swallow him whole. That would be preferable to what Dewey had just proposed.

"But I'm not the project lead. That's Dave." He swallowed. Yes, Chase had done a lot of the design work, but Dave was the lead engineer and the one who had spearheaded this project. Normally he should be the one to take on this role.

"Dave isn't able to go. His daughter and son are in high school, and his wife isn't able to manage it all on her own." Dewey sounded almost sympathetic, which was something Chase had thought impossible. Dewey leaned closer. "You should be able to handle this for us. It will only be for about five months." The tone was the same as if he had asked Chase to get him can of soda from the machine in the break room.

Chase could just imagine how all this had come about. Dewey would have spoken to Dave first, and between Dave pleading hardship and the fact that he had his lips and nose buried so far up Dewey's ass that when Dewey opened his mouth you half expected to hear Dave's voice, Dave was off the hook. So now Chase was expected to uproot his life and Ricky's.

Chase's insides felt like they had just been put through a wash cycle and tumble dried. Yet none of that could show on his face, not for a second. He already knew that any expression of fear or dissatisfaction would be used against him. "I have a son in school." Just the thought of Ricky being involved in this was enough to make him break out in a cold sweat. Ricky was settled in his school and was a happy child, and that was one of Chase's proudest accomplishments. After all the upheaval in his early years, the last thing he needed was to be uprooted, and the very last thing on earth that Chase wanted was for Ricky to be anywhere near Florence, or the Glorioso family. The thought was enough to make him regret the breakfast he'd eaten with Ricky just an hour ago. But Chase was like a damned duck, calm on the surface while paddling like crazy under the water, even if in his case it got him nowhere. If he wasn't cool, Dewey would pick up on it and then expect an explanation Chase was not willing to give.

"A lot of the time will be in the summer, and Dave's son is going into his senior year." Clearly the family argument would work for Dave, since he was one of Dewey's cronies, but wouldn't fly for Chase.

Chase tried to think of some sort of argument he could use, but came up with nothing—s not that bulldozer Dewey gave him a chance to say anything.

"This is something I'm asking you to do for us. In the next year, if this project goes well, there will be directorial positions opening, and I won't forget this." He sat back once again.

And there it was. The big, shining, gold-plated carrot, glinting in the sun, dangling right in front of him. And fuck him six ways from Sunday if it wasn't too much to pass up.

"This is a very important project for the company, and there will be a lot of eyes on it. Upper management will be watching all of us, so this will be an excellent chance for you to show what you can do. If this turns out well, and I have every confidence that it will, then there will be plenty of rewards to go around." He smiled, and all Chase saw was the damned fox again, only this time he knew was caught… and not in a good way.

Of course Dewey had to extend the carrot of a possible promotion—one that Chase had been hoping for. Before Dewey had moved into his position, James Sweet had been the VP, and he had been grooming Chase for a promotion. James was a good man and had been a great boss who believed in building up and developing his people rather than lording it over them from on high. "Can I think about it?" Chase asked.

"Yes, definitely." That predatory grin told Chase that Dewey already thought he had what he wanted. "Give me an answer tomorrow and let me know."

Dewey's phone rang, and he snatched it up off his desk and answered it as though Chase wasn't there. Using it as a chance to escape, Chase left the huge office to return to his own, letting Dewey talk at someone else for a while.

"How did it go?" Loretta asked as he passed her area. She was always friendly, but Chase was wary of anything he said to her, not knowing if she was one of Dewey's pipelines of information. Loretta had been James's admin before Dewey was promoted, and Chase had always liked her, but with Dewey's management style, he couldn't take any chances.

"Pretty well, I guess," he lied, and got a look over the top of her glasses, just like she'd done in the old days. "I have a decision to make, that's all." He tapped the counter and then returned to his office.

As soon as he closed the door, Chase collapsed into his desk chair, head in his hands, wondering how in the hell he managed to get into these messes. All he wanted to do was make a living so he could provide for Ricky. His mother, Elaine, was Chase's twin sister and his best friend in the whole world. Chase would have done anything for her, and in the end, after her death in an automobile accident, he had stepped in to raise her son—now *his* son, Ricky.

This was not the life he had envisioned. When Elaine first told him of her pregnancy, Chase had pictured himself as the world's best guncle, taking his future niece or nephew to Disney, giving them drum sets, teaching them about good food, and showing them some of the best parts of life. And once he had spoiled them rotten, he could take them home to mother. It was supposed to have been perfect.

What little Elaine had, she'd left to Ricky for his care, but to Chase, in addition to Ricky, she had left her secrets and their shared hurt. That was something Chase had hoped he would never have to face again. And now it looked like his work and his and Elaine's past were destined to come crashing back into Chase's life. He could only hope that he didn't end up as emotional roadkill.

A knock pulled him out of his thoughts.

"I hear you're going to go to Florence," Dave said as he came in and closed the door. Chase wanted to smack the suppressed smugness off the brown-noser's face. "I want you to know that…." He looked around. "Look, I really appreciate you doing this." He shifted his weight slightly and wrung his hands. Chase wasn't sure if he was even aware he was doing it. "They asked me to go, as I'm sure Dewey told you, and I pled the family." He grew more agitated. "Things at home aren't good right now. My youngest is having a very difficult time, and we are trying to get him the help he needs, but I can't do that if I'm over there or if I take the entire family along with me." He paled and his breathing grew more rapid. This was a side of Dave that Chase had never seen.

"I get it." He understood family difficulties and drama. Elaine had had plenty of that when their very Catholic parents had learned she was expecting a baby, and when she told them that she wasn't going to marry her boyfriend at the time, Rodrigo, their mother had practically started sewing scarlet *A*'s for her clothes. Mom was definitely all about the drama. "Your wife and kids have to come first." Just as Chase would do anything in his power for Ricky.

"Just so you know, I was the one who suggested that they send you instead. You've done good work on this, really solid out-of-the-box thinking, and that's why we've made the progress we have." Dave's praise seemed genuine.

"I haven't agreed to go yet," Chase told him.

Dave sat down in one of the office chairs. "You know that once you say no, they stop asking. I'm aware that by turning this down I've gotten a black mark with Dewey and some others no matter what happens. But I can't be away from my family for all those months. My oldest will be a senior, and pulling him out of school like that…." He shook his head. Chase would almost feel sorry for him if he weren't so sure that the entire time Chase was gone, Dave would be cornering the market for butt polish. "He plays football, and he's very good. Colleges are looking at him, and that would end if I took them away." His leg bounced as he sat, nerves getting the most of him. "You'll be doing the company, me, Dewey, and quite frankly, yourself a favor by going and making this a success."

Chase didn't agree to anything. Fear warred with the chance to give Ricky more of the special things in life. "I really have to think about it," he said. He knew the only thing holding him back was fear over Ricky… and the chance of seeing Antonello again.

Antonello Glorioso had been the third side in a close friendship triangle. Elaine, Antonello, and Chase had been inseparable through four years of college. He and Elaine met Antonello first in freshman English and then chemistry. Since there were an odd number of students in the class, the three of them ended up as lab partners, and their friendship grew from there. The last two years of college, all three of them had shared an apartment. It was like Antonello had joined their twin fraternity, until hormones and God knows what else got in the way. Chase developed feelings for Antonello, with his dark eyes, long wavy hair, and body worth sculpting in stone. Hell, there were times when he thought a breeze would blow up every time Antonello stepped outside, just to fluff that hair.

At one point, Chase thought Antonello might reciprocate those feelings, but Antonello and Elaine had started dating, and the chance was just too great to take. Chase kept his feelings to himself because his sister seemed happy—deliriously so—and Chase didn't want to get in the way. The three of them had talked about starting their own business and moving to a larger place to start building their lives. A makeshift family of sorts. Then, right after graduation, Antonello announced that he was returning to the Glorioso family business in Florence, and that was the last either of them heard from him. Elaine was angry and hurt. Chase had offered to hunt Antonello down and fill his perfect ass full of grapeshot for lying to them and killing their dreams. "He won't be able to sit down for a month at least. I promise."

She had laughed, thanked him, and then hugged him tightly. After that, they never mentioned Antonello again, except in the context of a curse or as an insult. And now it looked like he was being thrust back into his path.

"Don't take too long." Dave leaned forward. "This is a real opportunity, and you know as well as I do that they don't last very long or come around that often. Take it. Spend the summer with your son in one of the world's grandest cities. It won't be all work all the time. You can go to Rome or Venice for a weekend. And if I may offer you some advice, make sure they pay for you being over there. You'll need a house close to the center of town where you'll be working, and care for your son. If you decide to do it, make sure you get everything you want and get it in writing." Clearly this was a man who knew Dewey well. Chase had thought the same thing, but it was good that Dave agreed.

"School is out in a few weeks," Chase said, and realized that as much as he feared going, he was already thinking he didn't have much choice. And maybe Dave was right—he should make the best of it. Chase was no longer a college student, and just because he would be working with Antonello's family's firm didn't mean he would ever come in contact with any of the family. Hell, maybe he could kick Antonello's butt halfway across the Arno River just for old times' sake. With all that hair, he might even look like a drowned Afghan hound. "I suppose that as long as they are willing to wait until school is out for Ricky…."

Dave nodded slowly. "Just do what's right for you and your son. Five months is a relatively short period of time, and the benefits of this kind of assignment could last much longer than that for you and your family." He stood and opened the door, stepping out.

Chase sighed and shook his head. All fear and worry about the past aside, the real ordeal was going to be keeping the past where it belonged.

SCAN THE QR CODE
BELOW TO PREORDER!

Andrew Grey is the author of more than two hundred works of Contemporary Gay Romantic fiction, including an Amazon Editors Best Romance of 2023. After twenty-seven years in corporate America, he has now settled down in Central Pennsylvania with his husband of more than twenty-five years, Dominic, and his laptop. An interesting ménage. Andrew grew up in western Michigan with a father who loved to tell stories and a mother who loved to read them. Since then he has lived throughout the country and traveled throughout the world. He is a recipient of the RWA Centennial Award, has a master's degree from the University of Wisconsin–Milwaukee, and now writes full-time. Andrew's hobbies include collecting antiques, gardening, and leaving his dirty dishes anywhere but in the sink (particularly when writing). He considers himself blessed with an accepting family, fantastic friends, and the world's most supportive and loving partner. Andrew currently lives in beautiful, historic Carlisle, Pennsylvania.

Email: andrewgrey@comcast.net
Website: www.andrewgreybooks.com

Follow me on BookBub

STEAL MY *Heart*

ANDREW GREY

Hilliard Bauman's life and his law practice are in Ohio, so when he inherits a home in California, his first instinct is to sell. Then again, his law partner is also his ex-partner, so maybe starting over wouldn't be so bad. Either way, he needs someone to fix up the house first. That's where Brian Mayer comes in.

Brian Mayer will do whatever work he can get, whether that means dog walking or painting fences. But in a small town where everyone knows everything about everyone, finding jobs can be difficult—especially if you've been wrongly convicted of theft. When Hilliard hires him to fix up his great-aunt's place, it's a relief on Brian's strained bank account… but tests Brian's heart to its limits.

As Hilliard digs into Brian's case and the botched investigation of the original crime, things really start heating up—both between him and Brian and in what should've been a cold case. This time when cops try to lay the blame at Brian's feet, he has Hilliard in his corner. Can they solve the mystery, put Brian's past to rest, and find a new beginning together?

Scan the QR Code
Below to Order!

ANDREW GREY

PAINT BY NUMBER • BOOK ONE

PAINT BY NUMBER

Can the Northern Lights and a second-chance romance return inspiration to a struggling artist?

When New York painter Devon Starr gives up his vices, his muses depart along with them. Devon needs a change, but when his father's stroke brings him home to Alaska, the small town where he grew up isn't what he remembers.

Enrique Salazar remembers Devon well, and he makes it his personal mission to open Devon's eyes to the rugged beauty and possibilities all around them. The two men grow closer, and just as Devon begins to see what's always been there for him, they're called to stand against a mining company that threatens the very pristine nature that's helping them fall in love. The fight only strengthens their bond, but as the desire to pick up a paintbrush returns, Devon also feels the pull of the city.

A man trapped between two worlds, Devon can only follow where his heart leads him.

SCAN THE QR CODE
BELOW TO ORDER!

ANDREW GREY

THE NORTHERN LIGHTS IN HIS EYES

When Garvin Haverton lost his husband, he lost himself. Unable to bear the reminders of their love, he left his friends in Los Angeles for the remote Alaskan wilderness, cut ties with his old life, and started over.

Model William Moreau has let Garvin hide for long enough. He misses his friendship, and he has to know if the spark he felt between them could ignite the love of a lifetime. So he packs a bag, books a flight, rents a car… and almost gets himself killed in a blizzard.

When William shows up half-frozen, Garvin is furious. Unlike William, he doesn't need to be rescued. He has a life in Alaska: new friends, a dog, a job. But he can't kick William out into the cold, and it doesn't take many long, cold Alaskan nights before he realizes that he may have a life, but he hasn't moved on. He could do that with William. The chemistry between them could heat his little cabin all on its own. But William's life is in LA, and Garvin can't go back. Is their unlooked-for romance doomed from the start?

Scan the QR Code
Below to Order!

ANDREW GREY

HEARTWARD

He doesn't know that home is where his heart will be….

Firefighter Tyler Banik has seen his share of adventure while working disaster relief with the Red Cross. But now that he's adopted Abey, he's ready to leave the danger behind and put down roots. That means returning to his hometown—where the last thing he anticipates is falling for his high school nemesis.

Alan Pettaprin isn't the boy he used to be. As a business owner and council member, he's working hard to improve life in Scottville for everyone. Nobody is more surprised than Alan when Tyler returns, but he's glad. For him, it's a chance to set things right. Little does he guess he and Tyler will find the missing pieces of themselves in each other. Old rivalries are left in the ashes, passion burns bright, and the possibility for a future together stretches in front of them….

But not everyone in town is glad to see Tyler return….

SCAN THE QR CODE BELOW TO ORDER!

ANDREW GREY

HOMEWARD

Second chances only happen in the movies… right?

For the past several years, Matthew's life has been one challenge after another. Keeping his sister's four orphaned kids fed, clothed, housed, and entertained has him run ragged. Now he's losing the kids' mentor and maybe his job, if the plant where he works as an electrician shuts down like the rumors say. When his car won't start outside the hospital, it's the last thing he needs. Matthew could use a hero… so of course that's when Lucas Reardon shows up again.

A-list actor Lucas Reardon returned to his Michigan hometown to say goodbye to his father. The last person he expects to see is Matthew Wilson, the one who got away. Lucas helps Matthew out with the car, the kids, whatever he needs. But really, *he's* the one who needs saving. Years of the fast-paced Hollywood life have worn him down to nothing, and a deranged stalker is making his life hell. Matthew becomes his refuge. But relationships need time to grow and bloom. With the paparazzi breathing down their necks and a deadline on Lucas's return to LA, can they build a life worthy of the big screen?

SCAN THE QR CODE
BELOW TO ORDER!